THE FACE OF EVIL

George Marrus De 'Ath

THE FACE OF EVIL

George Morris De'Ath

An Aria Book

This edition first published in the United Kingdom in 2021 by Aria,
an imprint of Head of Zeus Ltd

A CIP catalogue record for this book is available
from the British Library.

ISBN (E): 9781800245846
ISBN (PB): 9781800246010

Cover design © Lisa Brewster

Typeset by Siliconchips Services Ltd UK

Aria
c/o Head of Zeus
First Floor East
5–8 Hardwick Street
London EC1R 4RG

www.ariafiction.com

Printed and bound by CPI Group (UK) Ltd, Croydon, CR0 4YY

One

Darkness on the Edge of Town

Grim arctic clouds hang heavy in the night sky above Decanten City. The streets below are a blanket of white, except where spindly limbs of giant, dead-looking trees encroach upon them like arachnid legs creeping from the darkness, shivering in the icy wind. Perched upon these sinister branches, great flocks of ravens swivel their beady eyes, scanning the pristine ground for fresh prey.

Ravens are smart creatures; tactical, strategic, coordinated and, most of all at this moment, impatient. One of the horde spreads its inky wings and swoops low to drop the remnants of a previous meal near a battered aluminium trash can that has tipped onto its side. The chunk of flesh lands softly, staining the snow around it a deep crimson, and right on cue a set of curious whiskers peek from within the metal shelter.

The critter is cautious, but sees only the quiet of the street. The shadowy monsters teeter on the edge now, their blood burning, hearts screaming for the kill. Yet still they must be patient. Claws tighten upon branches as the sacrifice scuttles greedily towards the bait. Immediately another breaks cover, unwilling to miss out on the feast. Three, four, five, a flood of tiny bodies all bound together now at the centre of the trap. There will be no escape for any of them. Nightmarish wings swish and glide like merciless angels of death, snatching up the helpless prey that wriggles in their scythe-like talons, shrill cries of victory fill the air. The massacre is over.

A soft growl fills the night sky. At first the ravens don't hear it, devoted as they are to their meal, but then the growl becomes a roar and suddenly the whole gory scene is bathed in blinding light. The birds flee in confusion, the sky momentarily littered with black-feathered fears as a rogue red sports car speeds by. The driver watches the creatures scatter. To her eyes, they seem more bat than bird. As they vanish back into the darkness, her attention reverts to the road ahead.

Slender fingers with perfectly manicured crimson nails flex atop the leather steering wheel, and a fine silver ring inlaid with a single flawless ruby, flashes beneath staccato streetlights. The hands release their grip on the wheel to sweep thick, expertly-bleached blonde hair from smoky eyes. It has been a long trip, but she is used to spending time alone with only her thoughts for company.

As the countryside eases gradually into residential territory, the black and white tapestry either side of the road is punctuated by twinkling coloured lights strung clumsily from windows and the odd tree, Santa or snowman bathed in their disco glow. They elicit revulsion, a full-body sickness that makes her physically tremble.

Her hand slips down to finger a delicate gold necklace that disappears into a white silk shirt beneath an intricately woven black jacket. It lingers for just a moment before being called sharply to action. A high-heeled shoe stabs the brake pedal as the woman catches sight of a well-weathered sign by the roadside. "Mortem Asylum" it reads, in broken letters. An adventurous smirk creeps across her glossy lips, rendering her pretty face momentarily childlike, impish. *Mortem Asylum for the Criminally Insane*, she repeats its full title in her head. The stuff of legends. And of nightmares.

The trees with their leering arms reach over the car as it turns down another deserted road, long and straight, ending in gates of speared bars flanked by stone angels. Caring maidens, she presumes, by intent. Guardians of the unfortunates within. Though now worn and filthy, their presence speaks more to abandonment. She shivers, without knowing why.

As gravel crunches beneath tyres, she passes a stone fountain overlooked by forlorn cherubs. It looks like it hasn't worked in decades. She parks the car and checks herself in the mirror. First impressions are important, she knows, particularly when the people you meet have such high expectations. She reaches for a black leather bag on the passenger seat and retrieves a small, golden cylinder from within. With a practised movement she pops it open, twists the glistening lipstick into view and applies a fresh coat as she reviews the checklist in her head. Satisfied, she steps out, locks up, and makes her way towards the entrance. Even by night, the building's sheer stature is intimidating. Its grand, gothic architecture exudes history from cracks in vine-covered walls like sweat from pores. Darkness, too. It has a malignant nature.

Some of the history she knows already. That this was the ancestral home of the Mortem family, and that part of the reason for its dilapidated condition is years of neglect due to their dwindling finances. But there is more here, much more, and she is determined that she will be the one to discover it, to lay it bare in black and white as only the great Lydia Tune knows how. The public expects nothing less from one of the world's most famous authors. The latest and, perhaps, the last, as Lydia intends this to be her crowning achievement. The final act of her own story, wherein she will at last unmask the Face Of Evil. Whatever horrors lie inside this cursed place, she will be a match for them.

A distant howl triggers a shiver that travels from the base of her spine all the way up the back of her slender neck before settling back uneasily in her chest. Slowly her head tilts to look, not into the surrounding woods, but up towards the building's highest windows. In her mind, the image of a man she has never met. Long, dark hair framing a handsome face set with sly, wolfish eyes. His shadow seems to loom out of the night sky over the building, a great and terrible presence. It is the owner of this shadow that she is here to see. Jason Devere. The Krimson Killer.

What little she knows about him she has read in the newspapers; descriptions of horrific deeds, the sickening stories of his victims. A young waitress found dead in a booth at the restaurant where she worked, her heart expertly removed and served on a plate in front of her. The Dimitroff twins, whose skin was flayed and switched one with the other. Millionaire property developer Randall Hunt, half buried in the foundations of a new apartment complex, his stomach full to bursting with pennies. And those, Lydia strongly suspects, were the lucky ones. The full extent of Devere's bloody legacy is known to only himself, a situation that Lydia intends to remedy.

She leans into the heavy wooden door beneath an arched crown of thorns, the Mortem family crest. A blast of warmth hits her, not pleasantly, but as though stepping from an air-conditioned building on an unbearably hot day. Nothing is quite right here. Nothing is in equilibrium. Ancient light fittings bathe the foyer in a glow that is too intrusive to be intimate, yet too gloomy to be comforting. The interior is at once grand and beautiful and suffocating. The floor bleeds. The walls ooze. The ceiling drips. Everything feels oddly alive. Ancient family portraits follow her with cloudy eyes as she approaches the desk.

"Lydia Tune," she states confidently to the woman behind it, who takes a moment to finish her scribbling before acknowledging the greeting. Her name tag says 'Charlotte', and everything about her seems washed out, from her mousy brown hair to her grey, almost translucent skin. Even the heaviness with which she finally lifts her head and the glassiness of her eyes. "I'm here to see Doctor Engel."

"Ah, yes," the woman replies. "Take a seat. I'll let her know you're here."

"Thank you."

Settling in one of the hideous orange chairs in the reception area, Lydia's mind begins to drift, picking apart all the little details she noted about the receptionist and using them to compile a profile. Early thirties, but looks closer to forty-five. Married, but probably not for much longer. Few relationships can withstand the emotional toll of a miserable job. She hates her job, but long ago lost the will to imagine herself doing anything else. Lydia checks herself. This isn't a useful exercise. Charlotte, whoever she is, is not who Lydia is here to see. She needs to stay focused, keep a clear head. At times like this, having such investigative instincts feels like a blessing and a curse. She wonders if this is how it is for all gifted people, that their minds never allow them to fully rest.

Minutes pass, slow fans spinning high above causing shadows to dance in the corner of her vision. Focusing on them allows her to keep other thoughts at bay, at least temporarily, like a dam holding back a stormy river. But the dam is broken by the sound of footsteps clacking on the hard floor. Two sensible black shoes appear in her field of vision.

"Lydia Tune?"

Lydia looks up to find a woman with striking red hair, like flowing fire, framing the same tired expression as Charlotte, half-hidden behind thick, black-rimmed spectacles. Intelligent, practical, kind. World-weary yet still a touch naïve, with the kind of fragility that emanates from the soul. The figure slim, but hanging awkwardly from her bones. If she were a pair of shoes, she might be described as well worn-in.

"Yes?"

"I'm Doctor Gretchen Engel, head of patient care here at Mortem. It's nice to finally meet you." She reaches out a pale hand and Lydia accepts it, pleased that this time her analysis will not be in vain. Doctor Engel is an important figure here, and the poor woman's obvious fatigue may make her sloppy. This is knowledge that Lydia can use to her advantage.

"It's nice to meet you too, Doctor Engel."

"Please, call me Gretchen." The words are accompanied by a smile, but not a convincing one. "If you'd like to come with me."

Lydia stands, smoothing the creases in her jacket, and follows Gretchen across the foyer to an antiquated metal elevator that appears to hang in place like a birdcage. The doctor pushes a large, round button and the skyward arrow upon it illuminates. "Have you travelled far?" she asks automatically.

"From New York," Lydia replies. There is no follow up. The elevator rattles to a halt and Gretchen heaves aside an accordion-like grate so that they can enter. She pushes an identical button to the one outside, but this one does not illuminate. Lydia wonders how long ago the bulb died, and whether anyone ever thought to replace it. "Have you worked here long?"

"Um," Gretchen replies as the elevator begins to rise. "About… eight years?" Her brow furrows as she wrestles with what should have been a simple enquiry. "Yes, eight. Nine in February." She seems somewhat taken aback by her own answer. Lydia is not surprised. *Life gets away from so many of us*, she thinks. A few seconds pass. "Have you visited a facility like ours before?" Gretchen asks, finally.

"Not… quite like yours, no."

Gretchen raises an eyebrow.

"I mean," Lydia hesitates. Flattery is a risky business. "Mortem is quite famous, as I'm sure you know." She sees Gretchen's lips thin. "For its standard of care, I mean," she adds quickly.

"Amongst other things," Gretchen mutters, eyeing Lydia. *She knows why I'm here*, Lydia thinks. *Best just be honest.*

"You do have some… colourful inmates. I mean patients." She laughs, surprised at her own clumsiness.

"It's okay, Miss Tune."

"Lydia, please."

"Lydia. I'm fully aware of Mortem's reputation. But those days are behind us. This is a professional institution now."

As the elevator slows, a piercing chime makes Lydia jump. "Goodness!" she exclaims. "Does it have to be so loud?"

"I guess not." Gretchen shrugs. "It just is."

Nothing in equilibrium, Lydia thinks again. *Nothing here is quite right.* She follows Gretchen down a narrow, dimly-lit corridor lined with abstract frescoes that hint at human shapes lurking like ghosts within the walls. They reach a door with Doctor Engel's name stencilled in black on opaque glass that reminds Lydia powerfully of the front door of her grandparents' house when she was a little girl. Gretchen fishes a small bunch of keys from the pocket of her white coat. "I have to tell you," she says, weary fingers fumbling to fit the key into the lock, "we all felt a little honoured when we received your call."

"Really?" Lydia is surprised. It isn't an unusual thing for

8

her to hear, but Gretchen doesn't seem like the type who is easily impressed.

"Oh yes," Gretchen says, finally fitting key to lock and opening the door with a click. "I've read all of your books." Her red hair contrasts so sharply with the washed-out nature of their surroundings that it reminds Lydia of a cartoon. "I think *The Masks We Wear* was my favourite. It was so interesting and the descriptions were so vivid. I felt as though I could see everything so clearly, as if I were there myself, you know?"

"Thank you." Lydia blushes. This is the part of fame she enjoys.

They step inside a cramped office with papers strewn haphazardly over every surface. The walls are stained brown, and the windows are covered by blinds that Lydia thinks must be quite thick enough to keep out any natural light when the sun is out.

"Please, have a seat." Gretchen gestures to a well-worn leather chair. It is surprisingly comfortable. "Is there anything I can get you? Coffee?"

"No, thank you." Lydia's eyes roam hungrily around the room, over the stacked papers and heavy steel filing cabinets, imagining the files within spilling their macabre tales like blood over the crisp, white pages of her book. Gretchen tosses the keys wearily on top of a stack of papers on her desk and half-falls into a threadbare office chair behind it as Lydia's gaze settles on one drawer in particular. While all of the others are labelled with letters (A – F, G – K), this one bears no designation other than a small, red, circular sticker.

"To remind me not to use that one," says Gretchen, reading Lydia's mind. "The lock's broken." For the first time, Lydia thinks she sees something approaching a twinkle in Gretchen's eyes. Maybe there is more to this woman than she supposed.

"Oh," Lydia replies, a carefully weighted mixture of surprise and disinterest. She doesn't want to come on too strong.

"Please," says Gretchen, gesturing to a vacant chair across the desk. Lydia settles herself in it and clasps her hands over her bag, her ruby ring glinting strangely under the eerie, artificial lights.

"So," Lydia begins, business like, "as I said on the phone—"

"Yes," Gretchen interrupts, "I should be upfront with you, I don't think this is a very good idea."

"Oh?"

"I understand why you're interested in Jason—"

"*Professionally* interested."

Gretchen gives Lydia a cold look, and Lydia knows why. For all Gretchen's fulsome praise of her books, only one of them wears the unmistakable white coat of a professional. *I'm just a tourist to her.*

"He won't tell you what you want to know," Gretchen says, an edge to her voice now, "and he'll make you suffer while you try."

Lydia's blood boils with fury at this blatant, casual disrespect, but she masters herself in a split second and meets Gretchen's icy front with a defiant smile. "You're probably right," she replies lightly. "You know him much better than I do of course, but I wouldn't forgive myself if I didn't at least try."

"Alright then," Gretchen shrugs lightly, "I've said my piece and I won't stand in your way. The powers that be have asked me to give you whatever you need," she sees Lydia's eyes light up, "within reason, of course. We still have to be aware of patient confidentiality, so obviously I can't go into detail about his treatment, but you can see him. Tomorrow."

"Tomorrow? But I thought—"

"Yes, unfortunately we had to give him a sedative this afternoon. He'll be out cold until the morning, so you can see him after lunch if you like."

"Thank you," Lydia says, hiding her disappointment. "That would be great."

"But since you're here now, if you like, I can give you a quick t—"

A shrill bell sounds, like a curdled scream from within the bowels of the building, reverberating through the corridors and making the walls themselves scream.

"Oh hell," Gretchen mutters, already out of her chair and halfway to the door. "I'm sorry, I have to..." she gestures helplessly. "I'll be back as soon as I can."

Lydia's hand is inside her bag even before the tails of the doctor's white coat have whipped out of sight, and in an instant, she is on her knees before the stickered filing cabinet, sliding a pair of stiff wires into the lock and adjusting them with her slender fingers just so. The alarm stops ringing, and in the heightened silence that follows, the soft click of the lock opening sounds like a pistol being cocked right beside Lydia's ear. She glances anxiously over her shoulder and listens for footsteps, but there are none. She slides the drawer open and finds, to her surprise, only a few files within. Lydia flicks through them, counting in her head; *one, two, three, four, five*. Jason Devere's is the last. She knows she hasn't much time, but an impulse she trusts is telling her to lift them all out, and so she does. You can learn much about a person by the company they keep, she knows, and these four patients are in rare company indeed. With another quick look at the door, she opens the topmost file and scans its contents:

PATIENT NOTES: PRIVATE... CASE FILE: HENRY NASHTON... FULL NAME: HENRY ALBERT NASHTON... OCCUPATION: THERAPIST... 5 FT 10 IN... 183 LBS... SUMMARY: ... wife diagnosed with terminal brain cancer... decided to end her suffering, but the attempt was unsuccessful... she died a short time later, in hospital... driven mad with grief, Nashton killed nine patients with poison... claimed to have been 'putting them out of their misery'... delusional and extremely dangerous.

Lydia has already assessed Henry Nashton before she finishes reading the summary. Though monstrous, his is too simple a case. To be driven mad by grief is a tragedy, but not an uncommon one, as serial killers go. *It's been done, darling*, Lydia can hear her agent saying. She drops the file back into the drawer and flips open the next one:

CASE FILE: HILLARY BROWN... FULL NAME: HILLARY ELIZABETH BROWN... OCCUPATION: MOTHER AND HOUSEWIFE... 5 FT 6 IN... 135 LBS... SUMMARY: ... divorced mother of two... as a child often assaulted by her alcoholic father... found out that her husband was having an affair... stabbed him and his lover violently and repeatedly in the head with such frenzy that dental records were needed to identify the bodies... since being institutionalised, has taken to viewing herself as the mother of the other inmates... has a healthy loving maternal relationship with her own children... has convinced herself that her husband is still alive, most likely as a coping mechanism.

Lydia hesitates briefly. Hillary Brown seems like another fairly straightforward case, but the tingle at the back of Lydia's brain is telling her there's something more here, probably more than Gretchen realises. The greatest evils are often hidden behind a deception we all want to believe: the illusion of love. And no love is stronger than that of a mother for her children. The idea of Hillary Brown makes Lydia shudder. But this is not what she is here for. She drops the file into the drawer and moves on:

CASE FILE: HOLLY ADDAMS... FULL NAME: HOLLY MICHELLE ADDAMS... OCCUPATION: HEIRESS... 5 FT 8 IN... 123 LBS... SUMMARY: ... despite inheriting a fortune from her wealthy parents, Holly's desire to accumulate ever more wealth led her to marry several times... each of her husbands meeting their demise under suspicious circumstances... she resembles somewhat of a black widow... deeply sociopathic and antisocial... narcissistic... hyper-sexuality... manipulation of men in order to get them to do her bidding... seems frustrated to have a female doctor.

Lydia is intrigued. Though one-dimensional for a serial killer, sex is always a good seller. But she feels that this case is too much of tired cliché, as well as missing that extra something. The pure, chaotic darkness, perhaps, that the most dangerous human beings possess, that makes their minds impenetrable to most people. She makes a mental note of the name to look up later, returns Holly's file to the drawer and reaches for the fourth:

CASE FILE: WAYLON WARRINGTON... FULL NAME: WAYLON EDWARD WARRINGTON... OCCUPATION: STOCK BROKER... 6 FT 2 IN... 205 LBS... SUMMARY: ... once a successful stockbroker... hiding a passion for cannibalism... suffered bullying and abuse from his mother as a child... developed a sadistic streak... extremely uncooperative... displays a complete lack of empathy for his victims, primarily young men... could point to repressed sexual appetite as a contributing factor.

Waylon Warrington is compelling and mysterious, it's true. The cannibalism is appropriately taboo and the possible sexual component intriguing. This would make for a good case, Lydia thinks. Maybe the best of the bunch, but still something is missing. Hands trembling, she slides Waylon's file back into the drawer and pulls the last one towards her, opening it with an almost religious reverence:

CASE FILE: JASON DEVERE... FULL NAME: JASON THOMAS DEVERE... OCCUPATION: NONE... 6 FT 0 IN... 195 LBS... SUMMARY: ... extremely uncooperative in our sessions. I have hardly gained any knowledge from him in our time together... outwardly, he seems quite normal, if somewhat detached... enjoys playing games... only period of his life he will willingly talk about is his childhood... speaks fondly of 8th grade teacher in particular, one Mrs Eagle... severe bipolar disorder with frequent suicidal thoughts... the multiple murders to which he has himself confessed reveal him to be a cruel psychopath with an unparalleled and frankly horrifying appetite for torture... has a br—

Quick footsteps outside in the hallway set Lydia's heart racing, blood pounding in her ears as she throws the file back into the drawer, sliding it closed with her foot as she rises and turns to see Gretchen Engel appear around the door. For a moment the doctor looks suspicious, but Lydia's mind is quick and before Gretchen can speak, she is raising the phone that she slipped from her bag as she stood.

"Reception," says Lydia, simply, waving the device in the direction of the nearby window. "I thought it might be better over here, but..."

"Oh," Gretchen replies, disarmed. "It's these thick walls. You have to go all the way outside. It's very irritating."

"Ah, no worries." Lydia perches herself on the corner of the desk. "Everything under control?"

"Hmm?"

Lydia nods towards the door.

"Oh!" Gretchen looks around. "Yes. I mean, no. I mean, nothing's ever properly under control here lately. Not since the last round of budget cuts. I *told* them there's a reason we're supposed to have a ratio of staff to patients, but *as usual*—" She catches Lydia's eye. "Anyway, it doesn't matter. But I'm sorry, I won't be able to give you that tour this evening after all."

"Tour?"

"Yes," Gretchen looks confused. "Like I said... didn't I say?"

Lydia shakes her head.

"Oh, well I was going to before... but now I have to get back to this thing, I'm sorry. I'll see you tomorrow afternoon?"

"Sure," Lydia replies. "No problem."

"Do you need me to show you out?"

"I can manage." Lydia smiles, extending her hand. "Thank you."

"Sure."

The doctor's hand feels warm against Lydia's cool skin, and softer than she remembered it being the first time around. There is a look in her emerald green eyes that Lydia cannot quite place. Is it worry? Fear? No, something more complex and interesting than that. Something evasive, illusive. Lydia doesn't know. But it's that haunting look she dwells upon as she makes her way back through the dark corridors of Mortem. She can just hear the muffled strain of something that might be human voices soaking through the walls, lingering in the air like ghosts. Then they fade away, the deep gravel of the car park crunches beneath her feet, and the night's chill stirs a familiar, gnawing hunger.

Two

Driven Desires

Lydia kicks off her red stilettos, and they land with a soft thump on the thick, patterned brown carpet. Soft, warm light from the antiquated fixtures makes the floral-patterned wallpaper look old and dirty, and the desk upon which she now sets her laptop is vandalised with a thousand tiny dents and scratches. *Is this what passes for five-star accommodation, she wonders? Maybe this is what rich people enjoy, the illusion of living a humbler life in a previous era. They're not greedy, just nostalgic and misunderstood.*

A knock at the door heralds the arrival of a waiter in a crisp, dark green waistcoat. He is young, and somewhat awkward, with uneven black hair that looks like his mother still cuts it.

"Manhattan, Miss?" He presents the cocktail to her on his little round tray shakily, like a peasant offering a sacrifice to a cruel queen. Lydia gestures towards the desk, then sinks onto the bed and stretches her legs, wiggling her stockinged toes. It has been an awfully long day. She notices the boy watching her, and he looks away instantly, cheeks flushing red. "Will there be anything else, Miss?"

"Please," she eyes the name badge on his chest, "Daniel, call me Lydia."

"Yes, Miss…" he shifts uncomfortably, "Okay."

Lydia lets the boy marinade in his awkwardness for a few moments. Being in control of people was an addiction, and this was as easy as scores came. An innocent young man in service to a beautiful woman. She could make him do practically anything she wanted. Not that she would. Knowing she had the power was enough.

"No, thank you, Daniel," she says finally. "That will be all."

The boy gives a little bow as he backs out of the room, forcing Lydia to stifle a laugh until the door closes. She knows he will be dreaming about her on that bed for a long time. As she dwells on that satisfying notion, her laptop chimes an alert. Lydia rises with a sigh, makes her way to the desk and taps a key. A chubby, middle-aged woman in heavy makeup and a cobalt blue suit that pops against the stark white background of her office appears on the screen.

"Oh, hi Donna," says Lydia, settling herself in the chair.

"How's it going down there?" Donna's voice is brash New York, but with the unmistakable rattle of a chain smoker. "You managed to locate food and water?"

"I'm in Decanten, it's not the sticks."

"Darling, everywhere outside of New York and LA is the sticks."

Lydia rolls her eyes. Part of her is offended; the young Lydia who grew up in the suburbs of Philadelphia, but it is a part of herself she recognises less every year. She is becoming more like them, more like the Donnas of the world who don't have time for anyone who isn't important and connected. She prickles at the thought.

"Well, don't keep me in suspense," Donna presses her. "What did you find? Something juicy I hope." Lydia remembers Gretchen's teasing. *Oh god, I really am becoming like her.*

"I didn't meet him yet," she replies, reaching for the cocktail. "They had to sedate him before I arrived. I don't know why. I'll find out tomorrow."

"Ooooh!" Donna purrs with delight. "He sounds like a live wire! Do be careful, darling, won't you?"

"You're worried about me?" Lydia smirks, one eyebrow raised.

"Of course I am!" Donna looks comically offended. "You're like a daughter to me."

"You're worried about losing your commission."

"Oh honestly, the way you talk people would think I'm some sort of monster."

"More like a wicked stepmother, really."

"Tough love is still love, darling. So when do you think you'll be finished?"

"Good grief." Lydia almost spills her drink. "I haven't even met the guy yet."

"You don't need to meet him to start writing, do you? You know what he's done; use your imagination for goodness sake. We have to turn out a book a year, Lydia. You're only hot for as long as you're hot."

"I don't even know what that means."

"It means get your backside in gear... and don't look

at me like that, darling. I'm only looking out for your best interests."

"Yeah, and your bank account."

"What was that, darling?" Donna inclines her ear towards the screen. "There was some noise outside."

Lydia purses her lips. She knows Donna heard her just fine. "We've already had this conversation," she says more loudly, "I can't keep doing this."

"But you've got so much talent. Please don't make any rash—"

"Not now," Lydia snaps. "I'm tired, and I just want to go to bed." She sips her drink and looks away from the screen. At moments like this her agent feels like the mother she never had growing up and Lydia hates the feeling of disappointing her.

"Alright," Donna says, somewhat coolly. "You get some sleep, darling, and I'll speak to you in a couple of days."

"Goodnight," says Lydia, closing the laptop before waiting for a response. Reaching for her bag on the floor nearby, she pulls out a ragged bundle of newspaper clippings and carries it, along with her drink, to the bed. Settling herself amongst the half dozen chintzy cushions, she starts to look them over for what feels like the hundredth time. Amongst breathless descriptions of crime scenes and courtroom drama, the photographs of the victims rise up off the paper and embed themselves in the front of Lydia's mind. These people, these real people, men, women, children, their faces calm, happy even, blissfully unaware of the sheer agony and horror that lay ahead of them. What went through their minds in their final moments, she wonders? What would it feel like to die that way?

A sick feeling begins to rise from the pit of her stomach, and she takes a large gulp of her cocktail to suppress it. A question that haunts Lydia in moments like this, dances mockingly around the fringes of her consciousness as she tries to force it away. Is it possible to truly understand evil without either becoming evil, or becoming a victim? She shakes her head firmly to dismiss the thought and turns to another clipping. Krimson Killer Caught screams the headline, and as Lydia's eyes travel down the page, one line in particular stands out:

"It's him," said Detective Gilbey of Decanten PD. "We're sure, but I urge the public to remain vigilant as we're still looking for several missing persons and time is a critical factor."

"Detective Gilbey," she says out loud. She feels like she knows the name from somewhere else. A flicker of a memory she can't quite catch. She thinks for a moment, before setting her drink down on the bedside table and reaching for her cell phone. It rings, and rings. This sound has always made Lydia anxious, and she has no idea why. It seems to her to grow louder with each repetition, like a warning. The line clicks.

"Decanten Police Department," barks a weary female voice.

"Yes, I'm looking for Detective Gilbey."

"Do you have information about a crime?"

"No, well…" Lydia hesitates, "actually I was hoping he could give me some information."

There's a noticeable pause. "Ma'am, this isn't an information service. Do you have a crime to report?"

"No, but listen, please," Lydia says quickly, "I might be able to get some information for him. About a murder."

"What murder?" The woman's tone is sharp now.

"I don't exactly know yet."

"Ma'am, are you aware that false reporting is a crime?"

"I'm not reporting anything!"

"Then why are you wasting my time?"

"Look, can you just give him my number? It's 212-505-6868. Please. It's important."

"I'm sure it is. Have a nice day, ma'am."

Before Lydia can reply, there's a click and a dial tone. She drops the phone onto the bed with a heavy sigh. Why are phone calls always so difficult? But of course, she already knows the answer. Lydia likes to see a person, to hear their tone of voice, and look into their eyes and read their body language and use her own to manipulate them. Without those tools she is disarmed. Weak. Vulnerable. She stretches out the fingers of her right hand and centres her frustration within the gem that she wears upon one of them. Despite the light of the bedside lamp, the ruby looks more black than red.

Lydia closes her eyes. Her body is pleading for sleep, but her mind is wide awake. With a weary sigh, she pulls herself up from the bed and crosses to the desk, opening her laptop and staring at the glowing screen. Of the hundreds of thoughts swirling around her brain, one has momentarily clarified. What she had managed to read of Jason Devere's case file emphasised his childhood. Doctor Engel must think there's something significant to be found there, but she hasn't yet. And there was a teacher. What was her name? Lydia's face tightens, her fingers half-clenched like claws as she tries to remember. Her thoughts are racing now, soaring, as if through a clear, blue sky, searching, scanning...

"Eagle," she says out loud, her fingers darting for the keys. A few carefully-framed queries later, she has her lead. A story from the Decanten Chronicle over a decade ago:

Saint Catherine's bids farewell to much-loved teacher.
Staff and pupils gathered for a special assembly to thank Dorothy Eagle, 66, for almost half a century of service...

With a quick tap, Lydia opens a new window and enters the details to search the electoral roll. There's only one match. A smug smile spreads across Lydia's face. She checks her watch. It's ten-thirty. Too late? She reaches for her phone, but it lights up before she even touches it.

New Voicemail

announces the screen.

Unknown Caller

With some trepidation, Lydia taps the notification to hear the message.

Three

Monster

"**N**ervous?" asks Gretchen, tapping in a security code on a chunky metal keypad beside a heavy steel door.

"A little," Lydia admits. This place is designed to make a person nervous, she believes. The corridors they walked to get here are narrow and claustrophobic, such that the footsteps of two people reverberate around them in a foreboding cacophony. The door in front of them has no window, and when Gretchen finishes punching the numbers and its lock clicks, Lydia's instinctive human fear of the unknown kicks in. She has learned over the years to suppress the fight or flight reflex, but there are limits even to her mastery of the mind. Her heart rate quickens as Gretchen pushes the door open. Lydia closes her eyes, takes a deep breath, and follows the doctor inside.

Everything is a dirty off-white in here; the walls, floors, lights, everything but the man in the orange jumpsuit sitting on the far side of a large, wide window that Lydia recognises immediately as a two-way mirror. He is hunched forward, long, lank strands of dirty brown hair hiding his face, but not out of reserve or shyness. Lydia at once understands that this is for her benefit. A performance, to prolong her anticipation, to feed her fear. And it's working. She feels her heart quicken, and breathes deeply in order to counter it, forcing herself to look at him. Even bound and still, Devere has a powerful aura, the broad shoulders, the wiry frame, strong forearms resting on the table. An animal caged, but not tamed. Subdued, but not broken.

Next to the window is another door, guarded by a middle-aged man in a pale grey uniform. Asylum camouflage, Lydia thinks, making a mental note of the phrase for her book. The man holds out the palm of his large hand and Lydia glances inquiringly at her companion.

"Your bag," says Gretchen. "It's procedure."

Lydia hands over the bag. "Of course," she says airily, but she's resentful of the lack of trust. Or perhaps more pointedly the lack of deference. Don't they know who she is? The thought makes her ashamed, and she tries to banish it. "Hey, can I ask you something?"

"What's that?" Gretchen replies, her flat tone of voice speaking to an exhausted mind.

"Does Jason talk much about his childhood?"

Gretchen peers at her through that thick, red-gold hair, a look half suspicion and half understanding. "Sometimes," she says finally. "Why do you ask?"

"I was just wondering," Lydia replies, casually. "Just because, you know, a lot of the issues with people like him are rooted in childhood experiences. Parents, friends, school…" She watches Gretchen's eyes carefully, and the doctor seems to sense that she's being read because she looks away.

"Why don't you ask him?"

"I will."

"But don't trust the answers." Gretchen turns back to her, that odd duality in her eyes again that Lydia cannot place. The frustration causes her to flex her fingers gently.

"Don't worry," Lydia smiles, "I know when I'm being lied to."

"Do you?" Gretchen's eyebrow lifts ever so slightly.

"I've interviewed plenty of murderers."

"Not like this one, you haven't."

"What do you mean?" Lydia asks sharply, unable to conceal her irritation at this stranger's presumptuousness.

Gretchen looks through the window at the still man. "He's dangerous."

"They're all dangerous, aren't they?" says Lydia, waving a hand as if to gesture at the asylum itself. "I mean why else would they be here?"

"He's different," says Gretchen. She sees the incredulous look on Lydia's face and sighs wearily. "You'll see."

Lydia studies the doctor's face for a moment. She is beautiful, or was at any rate before this place sucked the life out of her. Is she batting away these questions because she's tired or because there's something she doesn't want Lydia to know? "Any advice?" Lydia asks as the guard rifles through her personal property, every click of lipstick, of phone, of keys setting her teeth on edge.

"He might not say very much," Gretchen offers. "He doesn't like these situations. Sessions. Interviews. I think he finds them quite impertinent."

I know that feeling, Lydia thinks, and as if sensing her empathy Jason Devere turns his pale face, surrounded by long, dirty, matted hair, to look at her. And smiles. A shiver runs all the way up Lydia's spine and then washes over her whole body like a frozen, crashing wave. She had compared him to a wild animal, and now she knows what kind of animal he is. The sly eyes, the hungry mouth, the power, the effortless confidence. A motionless swagger. Jason Devere is a wolf, and he can smell blood in the air.

"Can he see us?"

Gretchen glances through the window. "No," she replies, but she too looks slightly unnerved. "I guess he knows we're coming, so…"

"Right," says Lydia. That sounds plausible. Yet she remains unconvinced.

"Okay," grunts the guard, handing back Lydia's bag. There are many men of few words who conceal fascinating personalities, but he, she decides, is not one of them.

"Thank you." She takes the bag and steps forward through the door as he opens it. It creaks. Everything in this place seems to generate its own sounds, as though the building itself is alive. Devere's eyes follow her as she enters the stark room, tracking her like a predator. There is a smirk not just playing about his lips, but deep in his eyes as well that she does not like one little bit. But her gaze passes over the chains around his wrists and ankles that bind him to the ground, then to the guard who has joined her inside the room, and she knows that she is safe. She knows it, even if she doesn't quite feel it. She also notes that Gretchen has not joined her, and Lydia wonders if the doctor is watching them from behind the mirror as she makes her way to a single metal chair some six feet from the bound patient. He hasn't spoken yet. Gretchen had warned her.

"Hello, Jason," she begins, polite and confident. She declines to offer him a smile. That's what he would be expecting, she thinks, from somebody who wants something from him. That they would be friendly. Overly so, perhaps. But Lydia wants to get a feel for her opponent first, to lure him out of his shell and then offer him kindness when she decides it will benefit her the most. "I assume you've been told why I'm here?"

Jason Devere says nothing; his expression barely moves, but his eyes give him away. They are burning with a ferocity that betrays the cool front he wants her to see. He's excited. He wants her to be here. That's good. She can use that.

"We can sit in silence for as long as you like," Lydia says, placing her bag on the ground and her hands in her lap. "Doctor Engel tells me that is your favourite way to pass the time."

Jason Devere shrugs lightly.

"To be honest," says Lydia airily, "I think she's a little hurt that you don't want to be friends."

No response.

"Is there something about her in particular, or is it just people in general to whom you object?" She pauses for effect. "Or maybe just women?"

A flicker of irritation travels over his face. It's a tiny tell that Lydia only sees because she's expecting it, but it's definitely there. Lydia already knows that Jason isn't that kind of monster, but suggesting that he might be scores her two points in a single stroke. It wounds Jason's pride, makes him want to open up and let her know that he isn't what she thinks he is, and it invites him to underestimate her. Just another dime store psychologist. His mistake.

"Well," she presses on, being careful to hide her satisfaction, "what Doctor Engel may not have mentioned is that I'm here to offer you a deal."

Jason sits back in his chair, like a king ready to receive his subjects with easy generosity. He's interested.

"As I'm sure you know I'm a very influential person." Lydia's arrogance comes easily, but in this case it is deliberate. Gloating, she finds, is an exceptionally reliable way to irk those in captivity. "I can make your life here considerably more comfortable than it is now." She lets the idea percolate. Let him imagine the possibilities. "If," she says finally, "you give me what I want."

Jason Devere's mouth begins to open, slowly, as though choosing his words even as they begin to form. "And what would that be?" His voice is low, but confident. Not the growl that she expected, but clear and strong, and packed with indecipherable subtlety. A cold sensation ripples around Lydia's heart. Was it fear she was feeling? Or satisfaction that she had truly found her worthy case study that she had so hoped for?

"To hear your story, of course." Lydia feigns innocence. She knows he will see right through it. Let him believe that he can read her.

"I'm sure you read my story in the newspapers."

"Oh, come now, Jason," Lydia leans forward conspiratorially, "I know better than to believe everything I read in the newspapers."

Jason smirks. He can't help himself. He's flattered by this beautiful woman's interest in him. He enjoys the hint of playfulness in her response. He likes games. Lydia knows as much from reading his patient file. She returns his smirk, acknowledging the connection they've made, giving him the approval he doesn't even realise he wants.

"What do you say, Jason?"

He thinks for a moment. He doesn't want to seem too keen. He wants to be in charge, to dictate the terms. "What sort of things can you do for me in here?" he asks finally, raising his shackled wrists pointedly.

"Well, I'll have to speak to the warden," Lydia replies. This is true of course, but she is at any rate not about to make any cast-iron promises. Not yet. She doesn't need to. The suggestion of reward will be enough to get the ball rolling. "But I'm sure he's prepared to be quite flexible, in exchange for favourable publicity."

"I want books," says Jason quickly. "Paper, pencils, that sort of thing." He's leaning forward now, and the pose accentuates his strong jaw. He's quite handsome, Lydia thinks. Or at least, he used to be.

"That sounds..." Lydia chooses her words carefully, "possible."

Jason throws back his shaggy, matted hair and laughs a deep, rasping laugh. "Possible?" Jason repeats. He's positively beaming now. He's got her all figured out. Just the way she planned. "You're going to have to do better than that. I want it in writing."

"Okay," Lydia replies. Her expression has slipped back to pleasant, neutral. Don't go too hard, too soon. The doctors here could learn a thing or two from her. She glances at the two-way mirror. Had Gretchen been watching this whole time? Had she figured out what Lydia was doing?

"Okay what?" Jason has cooled off a little too. There's a hint of frustration in his voice.

"Okay, I'll put it all in writing and sign it for you when I next visit." Lydia reaches down by her side to pick up her bag.

"When will that be?"

"I'm not sure," Lydia lies. "That depends on Doctor Engel's schedule." She gets to her feet and slings the bag over her shoulder. "It was nice to meet you, Jason." The farewell is intentionally abrupt. She's almost to the door when Jason makes the attempt to extend their brief time together that she is hoping for.

"Why me?" he calls out. Lydia smiles, but checks herself before she turns around.

"You're... different."

"You can say that again." Jason tries to act casual, but the heavy chains that bind him clink and rattle. "You're going to have quite a job figuring me out."

"I like a challenge." Lydia smiles again, inclining her head such that her blonde locks tumble over her eyes. She sweeps them back with those slender fingers and tucks them behind her ear.

"So do I," replies Jason. The feral smirk is back, and for the briefest second Lydia questions herself.

Four

A Difficult Lesson

A shrill scream pierces the late-afternoon sky and Lydia tenses as a pair of children no older than four or five thunder past her through powdery snow, almost trampling her feet in the process, and make for the tyre swings on one side of the large, square playpark. She mutters a curse under her breath, holds up a hand to shield her eyes from the sinking sun, and peers around. At the far side of the park, an elderly woman sits alone on a bench, watching the kids play. She looks so at home that Lydia decides this must be a routine for her, a way of mitigating the loneliness that haunts so many people in their waning years.

Being especially careful to take the widest possible berth around any more children, Lydia crosses the concrete square to join her. "Mrs Eagle?"

"What gave me away?" the old woman replies, without looking at her. Close up, Lydia notes her hooked nose, thick eyebrows and lank, white hair that sticks to her head and neck. *You look like an eagle*, she thinks, but resists the urge to say it out loud.

"You look like a teacher," she offers instead.

"Not that I'm twice as old as anyone else here?"

"Sure, that too."

Mrs Eagle turns her head, with some effort Lydia thinks, and gives her an appraising look. "So, you're a journalist, are you?"

"An author," Lydia replies, sitting down on the bench, crossing her legs and slipping her phone from her bag.

Dorothy Eagle takes Lydia in, from stiletto heels to tumbling blonde locks. "Mills and Boon?"

"Psychology and criminology. Do you mind if I record our conversation?"

"Goodness me, why?" The old woman eyes the phone suspiciously.

"So that I can transcribe it later on."

"Don't you have a life?"

"Not to speak of, no."

"Or perhaps not in daylight hours." Mrs Eagle's eyes linger disapprovingly on Lydia's slender, black-stockinged legs.

Lydia blinks. *Did she just call me a prostitute?*

"Very well," the teacher waves a hand weakly at the phone, "if you must."

"Thank you." Lydia taps the screen and sets the phone down on the bench between them. Dorothy continues to watch it, warily. "So, like I said on the phone, I'd like to talk about—"

"Jason, yes I remember. It was only a few hours ago. My

brains are not mush, I'll have you know." She pulls her coat and scarf tighter around her to protect against the winter chill. "Not yet."

"Right," says Lydia, "because I was talking to his doctor and—"

"Doctor!" Dorothy snorts, huffily. "Is that what they call the maniacs in that place?"

"Mortem?"

"That is where he is, isn't it?" The teacher looks down her crooked nose at Lydia, who is suddenly and powerfully reminded of her own school days, a precocious child feeling condescended to, frustrated and powerless.

"Yes, I saw him there this morning."

"Oh you did?" Dorothy sniffs. "Then what on earth are you talking to me for?"

"Well, as I was saying," Lydia is too tired to bother disguising her impatience, "his doctor told me that he often talks about his childhood, and that he mentioned you in particular." The old woman's dull eyes widen a little, but she says nothing, so Lydia continues. "So I was wondering what you might remember about him."

"Oh, it was so long ago." The teacher lifts a withered hand and flicks it dismissively, "I've taught so many children. After a while they all just sort of blend into each other."

"I'm sure." Lydia eyes a little boy kicking a ball nearby.

"You don't have children, do you?" says Dorothy. It's more a statement than a question, and Lydia glances at her to see that the teacher is reading her expression. Wasn't it supposed to be the other way around?

"No."

"Yes, you don't look the type."

Lydia opens her mouth to enquire just what it is about her that screams 'childless whore', but thinks better of it. *Not the time to open up that particular can of worms.* "Do you?" she asks instead.

"A son," Dorothy replies, "and two grandchildren." Lydia notes that the old woman's face doesn't show any sign of joy when talking about her family.

"How old are they?"

"Oh, they're teenagers now."

"Do you see much of them?"

"No, but I'm not sad about that. They're both fairly ugly and not very bright. I get more stimulation from the weather forecast." Lydia's eyebrows rise slightly. "But you have to love them, don't you?"

"I suppose so."

"Of course you wouldn't know. How could you?"

"Well," Lydia says, "I don't necessarily think you need first-hand experience of something in order to understand it."

Dorothy Eagle looks at her with unmistakable pity. "And you're a psychologist, are you?"

"That's what my degree says," Lydia replies, coolly.

"Did you learn about hubris?" Dorothy cracks a smile for the first time. Lydia can't tell if the emotion behind it is deliberately unkind or not, but either way she doesn't like it. Turning her head away for a moment, she feels a light draft on the back of her neck as a man in a long, grey overcoat passes behind the bench. He's walking a large German Shepherd on a leash, and by the time Lydia's gaze drifts from dog to man, he's ten feet away with his back turned. Her mind idly begins to profile him, but there isn't much to go on and as he reaches the playground gate, she loses interest.

"So, do you remember Jason?" she asks, turning back to Dorothy. "You must have thought about him, you know, when all of this happened?"

"I didn't hear much about it, to be honest."

"Really?" Lydia sounds surprised. "This story was everywhere for months."

"I don't watch the news," the old woman replies, dismissively. "There's so much horror in the world, what good does knowing about it do anybody?"

"But this was someone you knew."

"When he was a little boy, I knew him," Dorothy snaps, "and that little boy wasn't a murderer, was he?"

"What was he like?" Lydia seizes on the thread.

"He was a good boy," the teacher replies, defensively, "far as I remember anyway. Quiet. Not many friends, you know. Apart from that one."

"What one?"

"Funny-looking child." Her old face crinkles further as she tries to remember. "Like a little turtle. Turtle... water... Sprinkler! That's it. Cecil Sprinkler." She slumps back on the bench, as though the effort it took to remember has sapped all of her strength. "Another one with no friends, that's probably what they bonded over."

"Do you remember anything else about him?"

"His mother looked like a turtle too. Met her at parent-teacher night."

Lydia frowns, momentarily confused. "No, *Jason*."

"Oh, not really."

Lydia lets out an exasperated sigh. Why did you agree to meet me if you've nothing to say? "Well, thanks anyway." She picks up her phone, taps the screen and slips it back into her bag.

"Is that what your book is about?" Dorothy asks. "Jason Devere?"

"Depends," Lydia mutters, standing up. "There won't be a book at all if I don't get to the bottom of it."

"The bottom of what?" The old woman's face is placid; she seems either unaware or completely unconcerned about how irritating Lydia finds her.

"Of why Jason did what he did. Of how anyone can bring themselves to do those kinds of things." She swings her bag over her shoulder.

"Be careful." The teacher's voice sounds different somehow, with a wavering quality like a low note from a bass clarinet, and her eyes look suddenly brighter.

"Of what?"

"It's dangerous to go looking for something, when you don't fully understand what it is that you're looking for."

Lydia stares at her. "I will," she says finally.

"No, you won't." Dorothy looks back towards the playing children.

I understand how someone could strangle you, Lydia thinks. But again, she resists the urge to say it out loud. "Well, thanks for your time."

The old woman doesn't respond, so Lydia walks away,

her mind already turning to the only useful piece of information the teacher had given her. The next piece of the puzzle.

Off to catch herself a turtle.

Five

Self-Reflection

Lydia stares at her reflection under the harsh light of the hotel bathroom. Here, away from the carefully constructed sanctuary of home, she is forced to confront her true face. What she sees terrifies her. The woman in the mirror looks older than her thirty-something years. Much older. And weak. Her skin dull, lifeless, soft but not as firm as it used to be.

With a soft click and the swipe of a brush she begins her ritual, cloaking every flaw with a perfect, porcelain finish. It is a form of magic, like witches from days gone by painting their faces with blood to absorb its life-giving power. She lines her eyes and fills her lashes before applying that trademark crimson gloss to her full lips.

Next, the hair, spritzed with tonic, shaken and tossed and thrown until dry straw becomes spun gold. She drapes it over her bare shoulder, exposed by the low-cut black dress that hugs her thin figure, and reaches for a pot of ruby nail polish to touch up those sharp talons like bloody knives.

Fine gold necklaces wind around her neck like serpents, benevolent and loose for now, but threatening to choke with one false movement. On the middle finger of her right hand, that stunning ruby ring. Tonight, it does not glint and sparkle. Rather its black core appears to absorb all light in its vicinity.

Now the final touches. Pale, delicate feet slipped into black high heels. A minimalist black trench coat, belted at the waist. A mystery, but a plain one. Like a box of good, dark chocolates.

Masked and ready to interrogate, Lydia pauses to admire the effect. She is beautiful, there is no denying it. Nature has blessed her with an advantage, and she is not shy to use it. Indulging in her narcissism always gave her a thrill, but this is more than that. When men want her, and women feel intimidated by her, she is in charge of every interaction from the first moment without even having to assert herself. People don't like 'pushy' women, but even the brashest man will eat from the palm of a beautiful, confident woman without even realising that he is. This is what she is counting on tonight. This is her power.

She crosses to the dressing table and taps her phone once, twice. A message begins to play.

Hello, Miss Tune, Detective Gilbey. I just got your message. Can you meet me tomorrow night at the diner on Third and Holloway? Around eight. See you then.

The voice sounds oddly familiar, but she can't place it and anyway, it makes no difference to her. Lydia gazes at her own reflection. *Whoever you are, Detective*, she thinks, the voice in her head practically purring with pleasure, *I am about to own you.*

Six

Reunion

Lydia drives hard, her car alternately roaring and screeching as she toils irritably through the heavy evening traffic. She curses the detective under her breath for making her endure this rush hour misery.

A blaze of light in her rear-view mirror makes her wince and shield her eyes. The car behind her is far too close. She glares at the silhouette of its driver, at this moment in time an anonymous personification of everything she hates about human beings.

Finally, she sees the neon sign of the diner ahead, its letter 'i' flickering in synchrony with the pulsing vein in her forehead. Not the kind of place that she would choose to eat, but she hadn't known the city well enough to make an alternative recommendation. She entertains herself by passing judgement on her blind ignorance for his questionable taste, doubling down when she sees the sign on the door that reads, "Sorry, we're OPEN." She finds this sort of humour desperate. Pitiful. She is expecting the rusty jangle of a bell as she enters, but it still makes her wince.

It's a sixties-style place, soda signs and chrome stools at the bar. Juke box in the corner playing 'Pink Shoelaces'. Anaemic, coloured Christmas lights strung about the place, and a tacky tree in the corner next to the toilets labelled 'guys' and 'dolls'. Lydia glances around at the few diners already here, but none of them is a man by himself. Faces turn as she passes tables, one in particular whose eyes linger long enough to earn him a filthy look from what Lydia assumes must be his girlfriend. They're too young to be married. At least she hopes so, for both of their sakes.

She chooses a booth in the far corner which offers at least a little privacy, slips off her coat and settles into the soft, comfortable, red leather seat. The table is speckled grey, adorned with the usual salt, pepper, napkins, menus and packet sauces.

A waitress in a matte orange uniform approaches, fishing her order pad and pencil from her apron pocket. "Hey, Hun," she says in a warm, homely tone that makes her impossible to dislike, even for Lydia. "What can I getcha?"

"I'm waiting for someone," Lydia replies, feeling a pang of annoyance at the someone in question for being late.

"No problem," says the waitress, lowering her pad. Lydia notes that it is tatty, with only a few pages left. This girl has probably worked here a long time. "Just give me a wave or a holler if you need anything." She smiles and slides off to the next occupied table.

Lydia fishes in her bag for her phone to check her messages, but just then the rusty bell rings out again to herald the arrival of a man in a beige trench coat and a wide-brimmed hat, from under which scruffy sideburns match a bushy moustache. His eyes behind wiry glasses find Lydia right away and he smiles and tips his hat as he approaches her. But then, three tables away, he stops and turns, and seats himself with his back to her. Lydia slumps and exhales in frustration. She looks up at a large, black and white clock on the wall. It is ten past seven. Five more minutes, she decides, then she is gone.

As she begins to compose, in her head, the pointed message she intends to leave on Alex Gilbey's answerphone, a shadow falls over Lydia. She looks up to find a man standing a few feet away, about her age give or take, short dark hair and brown eyes, sporting a brown rugged leather jacket, white shirt and loose necktie. A flicker of recognition sparks in Lydia's brain and cascades across her face.

"Oh!" she says, blindsided.

"Hello, Miss Tune," he says, smiling. "Detective Gilbey. It's good to see you again."

"Alex?" she replies after a second, still in shock. "Oh my God, I didn't even…" She slides out of the booth to embrace him. She knows that he is expecting it with his hands open out ready. Best not to deny the male this sweet embrace she thinks, especially when he is the one she plans to squeeze for information for the rest of the night.

"I knew you hadn't put two and two together," says Alex, smiling even more broadly.

"How? And why didn't you say something on the phone?" She is annoyed with him, but more with herself for appearing so caught off guard.

"We record every call, you know." He slips into the booth opposite her. "I had Renee play it back for me."

"Renee?"

"The woman you spoke to?"

"Oh," says Lydia, "yes. She's very charming."

Alex laughs, and his whole face seems to light up. Lydia suddenly performs a rather girlish laugh. "Anyway, I could tell from that," he says. "You sounded like you were talking about a total stranger."

"Since when did you get so intuitive?"

"Since I decided to do it for a living," he replied. "But hey, look who I'm talking to. The famous Lydia Tune."

"I'm so sorry, Alex." Lydia flushes with subtle embarrassment. "It's been such a long time, and I was very tired when I called."

"It's okay," says Alex, clearly enjoying her discomfort. "At least you recognise me now."

"Just barely," says Lydia, settling back into the booth as her new companion does likewise. "You look so different." She takes in his strong, chiselled features, a far cry from the skinny, awkward boy she remembers. He has kind eyes, big and bright, but a ruthless edge to his voice. Whether that comes from within, or as a result of what he does, Lydia hasn't decided yet. He knows criminals, so he won't be easy to trick. But he's playful, too. Boyish. Her favourite type of prey. Flattery, as she well knows, will often get you anywhere.

"Most people do after seventeen years," Alex replies, looking straight into her eyes. "Not you though. You look just the same." Lydia feels her neck tighten, the dryness in her mouth, the rush of blood in her chest. Was he trying to flatter her too?

"What are you doing here?" she asks quickly, part curious and part buying time to regain her composure.

"You invited me." Alex grins, one eyebrow raised. "Did you forget already?" His eyes scan the table. "Have you been drinking before I got here?"

"No." Lydia smacks him playfully on the arm. Men, she knows, always respond to touch. "I meant... you know what I meant! What are you doing in Decanten City?"

"Workin'," Alex replies with a shrug.

"I'm sure we had police back home," Lydia teases.

"Not many," he replies, "and if you want promoting, you have to wait for them to retire or die. I had to move for the sake of my career."

"Guess I know how that is," says Lydia, meeting his gaze and deliberately, delicately tucking a loose strand of golden hair behind her ear.

"Can I get y'all something to drink?" The waitress has returned. She is very efficient, Lydia thinks. Probably spends most of her waking hours in this place. It would drive Lydia crazy.

"Just water for me," says Lydia. "Sparkling."

"JD and Coke," says Alex. Lydia's internal psychoanalyst gives a small, approving nod. The default move for a man in this situation would be to either order a simple beer or straight spirits. Alex liked what he liked, and didn't care what she thought. Confidence, she is reminded, is a very sexy quality.

"Be right back," says the waitress, already half turned and on her way before the last word is spoken.

"Well, this is a coincidence," says Lydia, resting her clasped hands on the table. "What brings you to this neck of the woods?"

"Probably the same thing took you to New York," Alex replies. "Just wanted to get out of that boring town and see some more of the world."

"How do you know I live in New York?" asks Lydia, slightly more defensively than she intends.

"Are you kidding?" Alex's eyes twinkle mischievously. "You're Lydia Tune, the famous author. I've read about you in magazines. I've seen you on TV, for crying out loud!"

"Of course." Lydia relaxes. "I'm sorry, I didn't mean to… I just, I still can't think of myself as famous, you know?"

"Oh sure." Alex nods. "Yeah, I have the exact same problem." He catches her eye, and they both laugh as the waitress appears again, setting their drinks on the table.

"Y'all ready to order?"

"Oh, sure," says Lydia, snatching a menu and scanning it quickly.

"Ribeye, medium rare," says Alex, "all the fixin's."

"Come here often?" Lydia raises an eyebrow. Alex shrugs playfully. "I'll have the same," she says, replacing the menu.

"A girl after my own heart."

"Let's not get ahead of ourselves."

"Of course." Alex holds his hands up in apology. "I bet you have dozens of suitors, huh?"

"Suitors!" Lydia laughs. "I'm sorry, have we actually travelled back to the sixties?"

"Hey, I was raised to speak like a gentleman."

"In Philly?" Lydia says, incredulously. "You were not."

"I was so," says Alex defensively, "and you're avoiding the question."

"Well," says Lydia, coyly, stirring her drink, "I wouldn't call them suitors so much as—"

"Stalkers?"

"You read about that too, huh?" Lydia is surprised, and a touch unnerved. She isn't comfortable with her companions knowing more about her than she does them. She will have to fix that. "It's true; I have a few... devoted fans, but nothing I can't handle. Well," she corrects herself, "nothing the NYPD can't handle."

"I'm sure," says Alex. "Hey, speaking of crazy, you remember our old French teacher, Miss... um..."

"Hart."

"Hart. Yeah." Alex leans forward on the table, and Lydia catches the scent of his cologne. Flowers on a summer's day. "God, what a bitch."

"No kidding," Lydia agrees, allowing herself to slip into a more relaxed state. "She absolutely hated me. Used to pick on me all the time."

"Don't take it personally. Hart hated everyone. You know she once made me sit by myself for a whole year?"

"Yes, well," says Lydia, a glint in her eye, "that was probably for the best."

"Hey!"

"You know only one person in our year passed that class?" says Lydia, seriously.

"Really? Who?"

"Marty Lawrence."

"Marty..." Alex thinks for a moment. "Oh yeah, Marty. The little kid with the giant rucksack."

"That thing was bigger than he was," says Lydia. "He looked like… what's his name?"

"Dick van Dyke in…"

"*Mary Poppins*," they finish together, then collapse in fits of laughter.

"Gosh, it's so strange how things come flooding back," says Lydia. "The names, the faces…"

"The smells."

"Don't remind me," Lydia warns him. "Geez, what a hellhole that was."

Alex nods in agreement, and they both fill the brief lull in conversation by sipping their drinks.

"So are you still in touch with anyone else from school?" Lydia asks, momentarily.

Alex shakes his head. "I was glad to see the back of them, to be honest." He catches her eye. "Except you, of course."

"Of course."

"So," says Alex, his tone indicating a shift in the conversation, "I assume since you didn't remember who I was, that you didn't invite me here to chew over old times."

"Right," says Lydia, sitting up straight and slipping her phone onto the table to begin recording the conversation.

"Are we on the record?" asks Alex, eyeing it warily.

"Oh no," Lydia reassures him, "this is just for my own recollection."

"Okay… so?"

"Jason Devere," Lydia begins. Alex slumps back in his seat, all traces of laughter gone from his face in an instant.

"I knew it," he mutters.

"I'm doing some research for my new book, and I found—"

"What did you find?" Alex interrupts, irritably. Lydia looks wounded.

"I found out that it was you who captured him," she finishes, cooly. In truth, she is more annoyed by his undermining her attempt to flatter him than the interruption itself.

"It wasn't some kind of Agatha Christie thing, if that's what you're after."

"I'm just trying to find out the truth, Alex," Lydia says, as humbly as she can manage.

"The truth." Alex leans back, one arm draped over the back of the booth, the other hand nursing his drink. "The truth is we hunted that evil bastard for months and never got close to catching him. I was feeling pressure from the bosses, and people were dying. I didn't know what to do."

"But you did catch him?" Lydia prompts, gently.

"We pulled some footage of a guy we thought might be him from the last crime scene," says Alex. "Just half a face really, but I had everyone go through the look books and identify everyone who might fit the profile. Before we could even round them up, Devere turned himself in. Just walked into the station and confessed. Like the motherfucker had enough of playing and wanted to come home for dinner time."

"That's strange," says Lydia, as much to herself as to Alex.

"Strange is kind of a common trait amongst serial killers," says Alex, "but look who I'm telling."

"I'm just a writer," says Lydia, not entirely convincingly. "You're the expert."

"Yeah, well, don't get me wrong, we woulda caught him

eventually. But that was fucking annoying. In my 'expert' opinion." Alex teases before continuing, "I think the creep turned himself in to shame us all, the force I mean. Didn't want to give us the victory of bringing him in ourselves, in handcuffs, so he did it himself. Was frustrating as hell for all of us."

"I can imagine," says Lydia, wondering whether she will get more out of Alex by letting him rant, or if she should rein him in.

"You look around this city; the place is still plastered with missing posters. His victims, I'm sure of it. Not that the bastard will tell us where they are."

"When was the last time you spoke to him?" Lydia asks.

"Months ago. I'd had enough. Never want to see his face again, if I'm honest."

"Would you like me to try?" Lydia asks, cautiously.

"I'd like you to get in your car and drive back to New York," says Alex.

"Without any dinner?" asks Lydia, that twinkle back in her eye. Alex laughs. He can't help himself.

"Listen to me, Lydia," he says, leaning across the table again, "you better not try this with him. You hear me?"

"Try what?" asks Lydia, innocently.

"This, the way you're flirting with me. I don't mind. I mean, I get it."

"Alex…"

"But don't play games with Devere. That's what he enjoys. It's what he lives for."

"So I've heard," says Lydia, quietly. Alex shoots her a curious look. "You know what might help?"

"What's that?"

"If I could get a look at the crime scene reports…"

"No way." Alex straightens up.

"Just a little peek."

"No. Are you crazy? I could lose my job."

"Oh, don't overreact," says Lydia defensively, frowning. "It was just a thought."

"No, it wasn't. It's the whole reason we're here tonight, isn't it?"

"Of course not—"

"Be honest or I'll leave."

Lydia looks at the detective, his chin jutting slightly in a gesture of defiance she finds somewhat childish, and finds herself torn between pity, irritation, and a third emotion she can't quite place. "Fine," she says. "Yes, of course that's the main reason I wanted to meet. But, remember, I didn't know who I was meeting tonight did I? Just came here to know more about exactly what he did, and I'm sure plenty of it didn't make the newspapers."

"You have no idea."

"Exactly."

"So?" He shrugs. "That's not my problem."

"Maybe I could help you," Lydia suggests, lightly.

"Help me with what?" There's an edge to Alex's voice now that's grating on Lydia's nerves. "Devere's already locked up."

"I don't know." Lydia shrugs. "To find those missing people, maybe." She catches Alex's eye. "What?"

"Nothing."

"No, go on. What do you want to say?"

"Okay," he prods his drink to one side and leans forward

onto the table, "look, I've read your books and I know you think you're, like, Miss Marple or whatever…"

"Miss Marple?!" Lydia laughs, but her eyes are hard and cold.

"Or whatever. But this is the real world, and police work isn't a game."

"I never said it was."

"Lots of good people worked on that case – you think you're smarter than all of them?"

"I didn't say that, I just—"

"We don't need your help."

Lydia stares at him for a long moment. "Fine."

"I'm sorry, that sounded harsher than I meant it to."

"Don't worry about it." She sits back and looks over to a table on the far side of the diner, where a young couple are laughing together. Alex follows her gaze and opens his mouth to say something, but seems to decide that giving her a little space to cool off would be the wiser option and takes a drink instead.

"So," he says finally, "what will you do next?"

Lydia shrugs. "I guess I'll just go and talk to him tomorrow, and take it from there."

"Okay," says Alex, brusquely. "But you're wasting your time."

"What makes you so sure?" Lydia snaps.

"We tried a lot of things to get him to talk, Lydia," says Alex. "I mean a lot of things. That place, Mortem, they ain't squeamish. You know what I'm saying?"

"I think I do."

"Don't judge me. I know we have laws for a reason, but

those people deserve to know what happened to their loved ones."

"I would never judge you, Alex," Lydia says with a soft sigh, giving him a beseeching look to keep him sweet. "That's not what I do."

Alex meets her gaze and seems to soften. He nods, and sighs, and sits back again. "So you met him already?"

"Just briefly."

"What do you think?"

"I think…" Lydia considers the question. "I think nobody is born capable of doing what he's done. I think the world made him that way, and I'd like to understand how."

"Yeah?" Alex looks dubious. "That's a real generous appraisal, if you don't mind me saying."

"I don't mind," says Lydia, "but why do you think so?"

"My mother told me if it looks like a duck, walks like a duck, and quacks like a duck, then it's a duck."

"Hard to argue with that," says Lydia, a smirk playing about the corners of her mouth.

"Yeah, laugh it up. But Jason Devere is a monster. And that's the only thing you're gonna find out if you go back there."

"I guess we'll see," says Lydia. The two of them remain silent while the waitress arrives with their food.

"Y'all need a refill?"

"No thanks," says Alex. Lydia shakes her head, smiling, and reaches for a large, crisp onion ring. She takes a bite and chews, thoughtfully, as Alex cuts into his steak.

"That mark from a wedding ring?" Lydia asks casually.

"Huh?" Alex follows her gaze down to his own finger. "Oh, yeah. Divorced. Over a year ago."

"And you still have a mark?" Lydia raises an eyebrow.

"Sometimes I put it on when I'm talking to a suspect or a witness," says Alex, defensively. "Helps them to trust me."

"I see."

"Didn't you say something about not judging me?"

"I'm not," Lydia protests. "I just thought, you know, you might have…"

"Taken it off to meet you?"

"Some men do."

"Well I didn't, okay? I use it to do my job. We all gotta use what we got, right?" He looks Lydia up and down with a feral aspect that reminds her a little of Jason. "You and your dress know all about that, I'm sure."

"What happened to being raised like a gentleman?" Lydia asks, coolly.

"You're right," Alex holds his hands up, "I'm sorry." He turns his attention back to his meal.

"So did you leave her, or…?"

"She left me. Got bored and ran off with a bartender, okay? And I hope they're very happy together."

"No, you don't."

"No, I don't." He pauses, looking up at her with a twitch before continuing, "Listen, I'll save you analysing anything else about me and just tell you that, she… Laura, Laura left me because she felt I got too wrapped up in my work and never made time for her. Which I guess, was true, got no one to blame but myself, I was a shitty husband, but no one can ever say I'm not committed to my job, which, funnily enough, has now taken up even more of my time now," Alex states, taking a long swig of his drink. "Now, can we talk about something else?"

"Why did you become a detective?" asks Lydia, coolly.

"I liked the Saturday morning cartoons," says Alex. "Like Batman, you know, where they figure stuff out and catch the bad guys? I wanted to do that." Lydia nods, smiling broadly. "What?"

"Nothing."

"What?" Alex demands.

"Like Batman?" asks Lydia, with a giggle.

"Sure, laugh it up," says Alex, trying not to smile. "So, tell me, how did Lydia Tune become the world's most famous mistress of the mind, as they say?"

"Well, where to start?" Her fingers rub together as she proceeds to talk. "I started out as a criminal psychologist, then after a few years of private research, writing, and receiving countless rejection emails I finally managed to get my first book deal with *The Masks We Wear*. The book blew up and well, the rest is history."

"I like that, I like hearing the rejection part. You didn't cheat the system. You earned your success."

"Oh believe me, I've more than earned my success," Lydia says rigidly.

"Hmm… so tell me some more about your books? *The Masks We Wear* was your first, right?"

"Yes, it was the first and the best received."

"Oh really?"

"Really. I say that like the other two have received negative reviews, they haven't. *Influencing Hearts And Minds* and *Breaking Down Our Inner Walls* were critical darlings, but that first one, I don't know, people really seemed to love it. It is after all what put me on the map."

Alex tilts his head. "And you feel like the others haven't had the same degree of critical success?"

Lydia's neck twinges as she ponders the question herself, then answers. "Not that, I just felt so... satisfied with that first one. My first victory?"

"Do you feel like you've never been able to make the lightning strike again since?"

"Again, not that, it's just never been the same since *The Masks We Wear*. Maybe because it was all so new to me, the success, I'm not sure."

"Yes, you are." He bluntly chips in, meeting her withdrawn expression. "What was the first one about again?"

"The book was about three different people in society that I analysed. A successful CEO psychopath, a narcissistic housewife and an anxiety-stricken construction worker. Focusing on the social constructs, the personas they had managed to make for themselves in their varying social circles. Families, friends, work lives and such."

"Very interesting."

"Indeed, and it sold well because it was something everyone could get behind and relate to. Everyone could see a part of themselves in the book, how they act. And that scared them."

"And as I'm sure you know, people like to be scared."

"Umm-hmm." She nods in response. "But more so, I think it was a comfort to most, because it highlighted just how numb some of us can be, numb to so many things, behind our masks."

"In what way?"

"The walls, the shields and defences we put up to deal

with pain, after a while they manifest into a way of coping that triggers the brain, trains it to stay in certain states of numbness under certain circumstances. When pressed, dealing with new emotions or scenarios and even, like I said, dealing with pain," Lydia says, looking away.

"Doesn't sound healthy."

"Oh it's not, but I suppose we all find our ways of numbing ourselves don't we?" Lydia concludes, grinning as Alex raises his drink up to chug back more sweet sin. "And I happen to believe there are some things far worse to feel, than simply feeling nothing at all," Lydia states, coldly.

With that, Alex gulped and pondered aloud to her. "Why did you become a writer?"

"Oh, the usual reasons," Lydia replies airily now. "Travelling to glamorous locations," she gestures around the diner, "meeting interesting people." She waves her hand at Alex.

"You're full of shit, Lydia Tune," says Alex, but he's laughing now too. "But what the hell, I'll drink to that." He raises his glass, and Lydia grins as she clinks it with her own.

What a delightful tool he will be, she thinks.

Seven

Evil isn't born it's made

Icy winds buffet Lydia's car as she navigates the frozen streets under a grim, grey winter sky. She doesn't mind the cold or the dark. In some ways they put her at ease, a reflection perhaps of herself. She catches a glimpse of something out of the corner of her eye, however, that causes her pale, slender fingers to clench the wheel tightly and her ruby ring to bite into her flesh. Strung across the window of a house set back from the road, twinkling, multi-coloured Christmas lights. A stark contrast against the otherwise monochrome scene, they are impossible to ignore, though she tries her best until she is past them and out of sight. With a sinking feeling she realises that they are but a harbinger, like the lone swallow to summer, soon they will be everywhere.

Lydia turns a corner, the car's wheels sliding on the frozen asphalt. Now the fierce wind is behind her, urging her on, almost lifting the car up off the road. Perhaps some invisible force is keen for her to reach her destination. In the rear-view mirror, she notices that the car behind her has made the same turn. Most people would dismiss this as a coincidence, but Lydia does not believe in such things. The knot in her stomach tightens as a glowing Santa waves to her from behind a white picket fence. Everything is gnawing at her nerves today. She presses down on the accelerator until she is satisfied that she has left her tail behind, and cruises for another mile or so before the sat nav indicates her destination a few hundred yards on the left.

It is a unique house, tall yet still half-hidden by trees that look to have grown unchecked for many years. She turns into the driveway and crawls up towards the front porch, sturdy wooden beams stained deep brown and a chair that sways and creaks loudly in the wind. What used to be a lawn has been swallowed up by weeds and bushes. Give it a few more years and the whole house will suffer the same fate, she thinks. But Lydia is not surprised, and she does not judge. She has seen many times what happens to places when their inhabitants stop caring. Some people might call it negligence, but she knows better. She knows that you can't hold a person responsible for having been beaten by life. It beats us all in the end.

She picks her way over the rocky path to the front steps, slippery with melted snow and moss. Even the sturdiest hiking boot could fall victim to their treachery. A slender finger reaches out and presses the doorbell. Just an ordinary bell with an ordinary sound, but it reminds her powerfully of the one at her childhood home. She remembers waiting for her father to open the door so that she could run inside and escape the cold, and the echo of that little girl's gratitude makes her feel physically sick. She wishes she could take it back. He didn't deserve it. He never deserved it.

Muffled footsteps on the other side of the door, the heavy scrape of the lock and then a thin, high creak as rusty hinges wake momentarily from their slumber. A large, round pair of spectacles perched upon the small nose of a face at once both old and yet unspoiled by the usual cracks and crevasses that time inflicts. A knitted green cardigan and slippers, both well worn.

"You must be…" his fragile voice trails away. Lydia can't tell if he has forgotten her name, or forgotten that he was speaking. The large, deep, brown eyes behind those jam jar lenses drift out of focus. *This man was at school with Jason?* It doesn't seem possible. Cecil could be his father. "Lydia?" he finishes finally, taking her somewhat by surprise.

"That's right," she smiles her most friendly smile. "And you must be Cecil."

Cecil Sprinkler nods, returning the fake smile with a genuine one, and opens the door all the way. "Come in!" he insists. "Please come in!"

The hallway is lined with closed doors and cardboard boxes, their contents spilling out chaotically over the floor. Lydia remembers a fact she has read somewhere about some three million Americans exhibiting various degrees of hoarding behaviour. Cecil, she decides, is somewhere towards the extreme end of that spectrum. Clothes, newspapers, books, dishes, knick-knacks of all kinds, all over the place.

"I'm afraid you'll have to excuse the mess," he says, as though reading her mind. "I just got out of bed, as you can tell." From the look of the place, Lydia thinks, Cecil Sprinkler hadn't gotten out of bed in years.

"It's no problem," she replies brightly. "I'm just grateful you were able to meet with me."

"Yes, well," Cecil kicks a small yellow pencil on the floor to one side, "there are things that need to be said about Jason."

"Oh really?" Lydia says, trying not to sound too eager. Everyone has an agenda, she reminds herself, and she doesn't yet know what Cecil Sprinkler's is. She doesn't want to let him know just how valuable his information might be to her.

The hallway is long, and claustrophobic, and the air musty. Lydia wishes that Cecil would move a little more quickly. Her breaths deepen and then, as they enter a room, a powerful aroma blasts her nostrils, making her gag. She covers her face with the sleeve of her jacket and looks around for the source of it. Air fresheners, at least three or four of them plugged into seemingly every available electrical socket. The combination of old, sticky perfume and dank, still air is suffocating. Keepsakes and souvenirs sit upon shelves thick with dust. The green floral wallpaper looks yellowish brown in the over-warm orange glow of the only light bulb. Above the hearth, a picture of a couple. The man, she guesses, is Cecil, albeit a different Cecil from a lifetime ago. The woman, his wife? She may ask, once they are better acquainted. Either side of the photograph are propped half a dozen Christmas cards, but they too are faded, yellowed with age, decades most likely. Does he bring them out every year, or just leave them up? Lydia can't decide which would be more tragic.

Cecil presses on through another door and Lydia follows him into a room lined with bookshelves, large potted plants and pieces of animals; a tail that might have belonged to a fox, an ivory horn, a rabbit's foot. The plants, Lydia is surprised to find, seem to be in fine health. They may be the only things in the entire house not blanketed under a decade's worth of dead skin cells. She reaches out and touches the deep emerald leaves of the nearest, a small tree in a colourful Greek vase. It feels cool, soft, hydrated. Alive.

Cecil finally settles himself in one of two antique leather armchairs and gestures Lydia towards the other. Between them, a small table bearing a bowl of green apples. They look like they have been polished. Lydia has an odd vision of Cecil polishing these apples every day and her mind begins to analyse his behaviour before she checks herself. *It's your imagination,* she chides. *Don't get distracted.* A large ceiling fan revolves overhead, keeping the stale air at bay just enough so as to be tolerable.

"Do you like my collection?" asks Cecil as Lydia settles herself in the chair.

"It's very…" Lydia searches for a word that won't offend him. It is not easy. Most of the books seem so worn as to be on the verge of collapse, and the less said about the animal remains the better. Her eyes alight upon a collection of photographs. "Do you travel a lot?" she asks.

"I used to," he replies brightly, rubbing his hands together. "With my wife, Clarice. She…" his voice falters. "She died some years ago." Lydia thinks he hears his own words as if for the first time. She wonders what it must be like to have your mind begin to fail, to have to remember afresh every day the bad things that have happened to you. To have to relive that grief over and over like a recurring nightmare. But she doesn't feel sorry for him. Instead she fears for herself should it ever happen to her.

"Cancer," Cecil says, helplessly. The word interrupts Lydia's thoughts. She has no words of comfort for him. "She was always the one who kept this place together." He reaches out and touches one of the faded photographs gingerly.

"That must have been very hard for you," Lydia offers.

"Yes…" Cecil seems to lose himself for a moment, then his eyes snap back to Lydia suddenly as if remembering she is there. "But enough about me," he says briskly. "You came to hear about Jason."

"Right." Lydia fishes her phone from her bag and taps and swipes her way to the recording app, then pauses as though considering her first question. In reality she has played this conversation out in her head half a dozen times already. "Why don't you tell me when you two first met?" she asks finally.

Cecil's body stiffens. "I was seven years old," he begins. "It was the beginning of the school year and Jason was new, so he didn't know anybody. I told my mother about him, and she said that I should make friends with him because that was the kind thing to do. She said imagine if you didn't know anybody, how lonely you'd be."

"Yes, Mrs Eagle said the two of you spent a lot of time together."

"Oh!" Cecil's face lights up. "You spoke to Mrs Eagle? How is she?"

Lydia hesitates. Be generous. "In good spirits."

"Oh, wonderful," says Cecil, beaming. "She was my favourite teacher. Such a kind woman."

Maybe I caught her on a bad day, Lydia thinks, but she smiles back at him. "So, you and Jason were friends?" She has her notebook out now, resting it on her knee as she scribbles.

"Best friends," says Cecil. Lydia notes that he shows no sign of pleasure, as she might expect a person remembering their best friend to do. "We were always at each other's houses. Our mothers got along very well. She is a lovely woman, his mother. It must have been so difficult for her."

"Why difficult?" asks Lydia quickly, seizing the thread.

"Well," says Cecil, "his father was long gone by then, and his brother died shortly before he started scho—"

"His brother?" Lydia interrupts. She knows she shouldn't; you get more useful details when you let people talk themselves out, but something is pinging the registers in her mind, alerting her that something here is important. Why has nobody mentioned Jason's brother before? Not Gretchen, not Mrs Eagle or Alex or Jason himself, and she's sure that none of the news reports mentioned him.

"Yes," Cecil replies, slightly taken aback. "Finley, his name was."

"And he died?"

"Yes, but really this was all before I knew—"

"What happened to him?"

"Oh, it was all such a long time ago," says Cecil, rubbing his head. "From what I remember, he and Jason were playing on Traveller's Bridge, you know, over on the west side of Decanten when Finley… he fell into the river."

"How awful," Lydia says. "And they couldn't save him?"

"Never found the body," says Cecil, shaking his head. "The police looked for weeks my mother said, but they never found him. Anyway, Jason thought his mother blamed him for it."

"Surely not," says Lydia. "A four-year-old child?"

Cecil shrugs and sits back in his chair, adjusting his belt. "That's what Jason used to say. That she blamed him for Finley and sometimes for his dad leaving too."

"Where did his father go?"

"No idea," says Cecil. "All I know is that wherever it was, he didn't come back."

"I see," says Lydia, her pen skimming across the surface of her notepad. "Then what about Jason? What was he like as a child?"

Cecil slowly crosses one leg over the other and puts his hands on his knees, looking upward as though searching for a memory. "He was a quiet boy. Serious. But funny sometimes too, when no one else was around. He was clever, but never had any time for schoolwork or the teachers. Came to a point where he was getting into trouble every day."

"What kind of trouble?"

"Oh bullying, drugs, theft," says Cecil, with a wave of his hand so as to suggest that the list goes on and on. "He fell in with a bad crowd. That's when our friendship became…" he looks pointedly at Lydia, "strained."

"Was he violent?" asks Lydia.

"Not exactly," says Cecil. "Not at that time, anyway. But he used to draw some very weird things."

"What kind of things?" Lydia asks, a note of excitement in her voice. The psychology of art was a fascinating pool that she had delved into on several occasions.

"Animals, people," says Cecil, "but twisted, you know, grotesque. *They* were violent, those pictures." His voice quivers, and Lydia recognises it straight away as the unmistakable distortion of fear.

"I don't suppose you have any of them?"

"Gosh, no!" He looks at her like she's crazy. "Even if I did, I would have thrown them away a long time ago. They were creepy. Especially after, you know, what happened."

"Of course." Lydia can't hide her disappointment.

"Besides," Cecil continues, "it was around that time I was barred from visiting his house."

"By Jason?"

"His mother," says Cecil. "Jason would invite me, but his mother would always make up some excuse why I couldn't go."

"Do you know why?" asks Lydia, momentarily distracted by a large spider loitering on a shelf at the edge of her vision. Cecil shrugs, his palms facing upwards. "What was she like, his mother?" asks Lydia.

Cecil scratches his face as he remembers. "Evelyn was her name. She was a theatre actress. Very flamboyant. His father was a costume designer. Used to make all her costumes, before he disappeared. I don't know his name." Cecil's gaze shifts to a large, free-standing globe, thick with dust like everything else, one side of it dimly illuminated by the fading light creeping in through the window. "I'm sure something awful happened to him."

"Jason's father?"

Cecil shakes his head. "Jason," he says. "He wasn't evil when I knew him. He was just a child. A strange one, sure. No angel." He looks up at Lydia, and for the first time she sees grief behind those old eyes. "But those things they said he did, in the papers... the Jason I knew could never have done that."

"What makes you so sure?" Lydia asks, but not for her benefit. She's heard this dozens of times before. People find it impossible to believe that someone they know is capable of terrible things. They rationalise that their friend or family member must have changed, or snapped. That the person who murdered somebody wasn't the same person from their memories.

"I just know," Cecil replies, simply. "Jason was, well, always Jason, but he was no killer, it just didn't seem within him. Even when he was doing bad things as a kid, there was, or rather seemed to be a degree of empathy I felt coming from him. But, people aren't born evil, are they? Something happens to make them that way. Life changes us. Tests us. Some react well to that, and some badly."

Lydia jots down the quote. It isn't exactly how she would have phrased it, but it'll do. She can clean it up later.

"Tell me, Miss Tune," Cecil says, leaning forward and peering at Lydia, "from what you've learned so far, what do you think happened?"

Lydia's skin prickles. She is suddenly on edge. Was that a question born of genuine curiosity, or is Cecil Sprinkler toying with her? Maybe he knows more than he's letting on. Maybe he and Jason aren't as estranged as she thought. *In which case*, a small voice in her head tells her, *you mustn't let your suspicion show.*

"Honestly," says Lydia with the lightest of shrugs, "I've only just begun looking into this, so I really couldn't say."

"Have you met him yet?" asks Cecil, that note of fear back in his voice.

"Briefly," says Lydia. "I'm going back there tomorrow."

"It must be lonely in that place," says Cecil, with a small shiver.

"He didn't strike me as the type who minds being alone," says Lydia.

"Yes, well," Cecil replies, somewhat sadly, "it's a little different when you don't have a choice."

The words strike at Lydia's heart like frozen daggers, and it takes her a moment to realise why. He's talking about her. Cecil is alone because his wife died. Jason is alone because Mortem keeps him locked up in solitary. Lydia is lonely by choice. She stares at Cecil Sprinkler. Does he know? But Cecil simply smiles, benignly.

"Yes," says Lydia finally, finding her voice again. "I suppose it is." She closes her notepad and slips it back into her bag, along with her phone. "Well," she rises with a muffled squeak from the leather chair, "thank you for your time."

"Oh," says Cecil, surprised. "Are you leaving already?"

"Unless you have more to tell me?"

"No, I don't think so." He scratches his face again. "I was just rather enjoying the company, that's all."

Lydia smiles. She knows people who would stay and chat

to Cecil Sprinkler, have a cup of tea and let him reminisce about happier times. But she isn't sentimental that way. She doesn't get attached. *You don't care*, a small, accusing voice bites in the back of her mind. Lydia banishes it with a shake of her head.

"Well, let me walk you out at least," he sighs.

"Thank you," Lydia says kindly, gesturing for him to lead the way.

"I hope you can figure out where it all went wrong for Jason," says Cecil as they pick their way back through the cluttered house. "It would be nice to finally find some…" he fishes for the right word.

"Closure?" Lydia offers.

"I was going to say peace," says Cecil. "But it's probably the same thing, isn't it?"

"More or less," says Lydia as they reach the front door. "Well, thank you, Cecil," she offers her hand for him to shake, "you've been most helpful."

"Not at all," Cecil replies. He's smiling, but Lydia has the distinct impression that something is still bothering him. She is halfway to her car when she hears her name. "Lydia!" Cecil hobbles over the gravel in his worn-out slippers.

"Yes?"

"He likes to play games," says Cecil. He looks anxious. For himself, or for her, Lydia wonders.

"What kind of games?"

"Mind games," Cecil replies. He glances around as though worried they might be being watched, which makes Lydia do the same. But there is no one in sight. "He likes to… to play with people."

"What do you mean?" asks Lydia, reaching into her bag for her phone. But before she can retrieve it, Cecil has begun backing away towards the house again. "Cecil?"

"Just... just be careful," he warns, before turning and disappearing back into the dusty darkness.

Eight

The Mask

The devil only does business with willing clients.

Lydia cannot remember where she first heard these words, but they swim in the forefront of her mind now as she sits opposite one of the most sadistic men the world has ever known. The Krimson Killer. Jason Devere.

Frozen air from the vent above seeps into her lungs, making each breath feel like an effort, and causing both Lydia and her lethal company to exhale thick clouds of vapour that churn and spiral. Neither has spoken for several minutes. The stark metal table between them contrasts sharply with Jason's grubby clothes and hair as he hunches over it, studying Lydia's contract. The chains around his wrists gently clink and scrape as his fingers work the paper, rubbing, creasing, betraying his inner tension. He looks up, locks eyes with Lydia and smiles, licks his thumb and slowly turns the page. No wonder Gretchen called him dangerous, Lydia thinks. He has a feral quality that's almost visceral. Cunning and powerful, with a jagged, broken aura that scrapes viciously against a reality to which he does not belong. He may be a prisoner, but he is free in ways that most people never will be.

Lydia returns the smile politely. She is frustrated with Jason's time-wasting, but knows that this is his intent and to show it would give him what he wants. It is imperative that she retain the upper hand. She remembers the warnings of Gretchen, Cecil and Alex. This monster likes to play games. Upon further evaluation, Lydia was beginning to find something strangely inauthentic about him. It felt as if he was playing a role, but who was it for? Her? The question nagged at the back of Lydia's mind like an ice pick, jabbing away at her.

Jason reaches the end of the final page and makes a performance of carefully returning the document to its original state neatly in front of him, perfectly perpendicular to the edge of the table. Then he flips to the first page and begins reading again. Lydia sighs. Only softly, but the cold air scrapes her throat, amplifying her impatience. Jason does not seem to react, but then a few moments later he begins to hum quietly. A banal tune. Lydia feels her eye twitch.

"What do you think?" she asks finally, unable to contain herself any longer. Jason holds up a hand signalling for her to wait. He reads on for another minute or so before finally granting her his attention.

"I like to be thorough." He smiles, then glances down at the paper again as his lips curl into a smirk. "Very pointed your notes, aren't they? Very cold and clinical. There's no poetry to them, they're not lyrical, they don't sing off the page."

"Is everything to your liking?" asks Lydia, business-like, denying his clumsy attempt to take control of the conversation.

"For the moment." Jason extends an open hand towards Lydia as far as his shackles will allow, and she flinches at the unexpected motion. He smiles, slowly. "Do you have a pen?"

Lydia reaches down, fishes a slim silver pen from her bag and looks over to the guard watching them through the window for permission. He eyes the pen warily, but jerks his head in agreement.

"Who do you think I am?" Jason asks, accepting the pen with a deliberate, slow movement. "Houdini?"

"Their house," says Lydia, inclining her head towards the guard, "their rules."

"Interesting," says Jason, scratching a jagged, staccato signature on the paper.

"What is?"

"You don't seem like the type to follow rules," he says, his cold eyes twinkling as he hands the pen back to her. Lydia shivers involuntarily. Is he flirting with her? Is this part of the game?

"Shall we begin now?" she asks, choosing to ignore the compliment.

"Whatever you like," Jason replies. "I have no pressing engagements."

Lydia sets her phone on the table, out of his reach, and taps it to begin a new recording. "Tell me about your childhood," she says, sitting back to observe her subject.

"Oh, we're starting from the top, are we?" Jason asks, sounding suddenly bored. "Well alright, but there really isn't much to tell."

"Really?" Lydia asks, surprised.

"Yep, pretty ordinary." Jason sits back as well, mirroring Lydia's posture. "Why, what were you expecting?"

He's challenging me, she thinks. He knows that I know something.

"Alright," Lydia presses on. "What about your family? Parents? Brother?"

Jason shrugs. "What about them?"

"Can you tell me anything about them?" Lydia asks, patiently.

"Not much to tell," Jason replies.

"I see," says Lydia. She pauses for a moment, then reaches back into her bag to retrieve something. She keeps the object deliberately hidden in her hand, and notices with satisfaction that Jason cranes his neck to try to see what it is. "Perhaps I can help jog your memory."

"Brought some toys, did you?" Jason asks, his chains clinking as he shifts, agitated, in his seat. "A taser, is it? Well, you needn't bother. They've already tortured me here more times than I can count."

"I'm sorry to hear that," says Lydia, sliding the object onto the table, visible but still guarded by those scarlet talons. It's a bar of chocolate. Jason stares at it for a few seconds, confused, then he laughs and shakes his head.

"You're a funny girl, Lyd."

"Why's that?" asks Lydia, innocently.

"You think you can get inside my head?" says Jason. "With pretty eyes and props?"

"Tell me about your childhood, Jason," Lydia asks again.

"Alright, alright," he says, tugging his manacled wrists away from the table in a gesture that Lydia interprets as frustration. "You want to know about my family?" He mimics Lydia's voice. "My parents? My brother?"

"If you don't mind."

"Well, here it is," says Jason, leaning onto the table and speaking in a low, animated voice as though relating a thrilling tale. "My parents got themselves into a load of debt, so they sold my brother to the mob to pay—"

"I think I've heard this one before," says Lydia, pretending to search her recollection. "Oh yes, didn't it get three stars in this morning's newspaper?"

Jason grins and leans back again, his hands raised as far as his restraints allow. "You got me."

"Look, Jason," says Lydia in a bored sort of way, "I've come a long way to see you, but if you're not going to cooperate, there are plenty of other lunatics I could write a book about."

Jason's grin fades. For one mad moment, Lydia thinks he might make a lunge for her. But then he glances down, as if lowering a small degree of the façade he was previously wearing.

"Why don't you tell me about your brother?" says Lydia, pressing her advantage.

"What about him?"

"I heard that he died," says Lydia, forcefully.

"Yeah, so what?" Jason snaps defensively, yanking at his chains again, so hard this time that the iron bolts securing the table to the floor creak.

"So that must have been very upsetting for you," says Lydia, softening her tone a little.

"It was." Jason glares at her. Lydia thinks for a moment

that his eyes have turned more blue, like ice. *It must be the cool lighting in the room.*

"How do you feel about it now?" she asks. Jason shrugs. "You don't feel anything about it?" Lydia persists, clearly dubious.

"People come and go every day," Jason turns away and replies, matter-of-factly. "My brother drew the short straw, that's all. It was his turn. That's life."

"Some people would call that a very rational response," Lydia suggests. The uneven grin spreads across Jason's face again. He's taken it as a compliment. Lydia purses her lips to suppress her satisfaction.

"Yeah, well," he says, "maybe I'm the only rational guy left in this mad world."

"Maybe you are," says Lydia, offering him a smile. A treat for the good boy. "How did he die?" she asks quickly.

"He fell," Jason replies, just as quickly. The words are out of his mouth before his grin has had a chance to fade.

"From where?"

"From the bridge."

"You were there?"

"Of course I was," says Jason, clearly irritated. "It was right next to our house, we always played there. Our mother told us not to, but we did."

"How did he fall?" Lydia asks.

"We were fighting," says Jason, his dirty, shaggy hair falling over his face. "Not for real fighting, just playing, you know. And I guess we got too close to the edge, and the next thing I knew I was falling."

Lydia hesitates. "*You* fell?"

"Yeah."

"You *both* fell?"

"That's what I said, isn't it?" Jason scowls at her. Lydia raises her eyebrows as she puts pen to notepad. "You don't believe me?" Jason growls. Lydia remembers Alex's words. *He's an animal.*

"I believe you," she says.

"I got the scar to prove it," says Jason, twisting in his chair and pulling up his dirty shirt to reveal a nasty scar about five inches long. "Hit a rock on the riverbed," he says, seemingly pleased by the disconcerted look on Lydia's face. "Needed ten stitches." He lets the shirt fall and sits straight in his seat again. "Fin wasn't so fortunate."

Lydia looks right at Jason, who moistens his lips with a few flicks of his tongue, and smiles. "Do you blame yourself?" she asks as he clenches his jaw.

"It was an accident."

"Did your mother blame you?"

Jason's eyes narrow. Lydia meets them with her best bland expression, as though she had just asked if he would like a cup of tea.

"Yeah," says Jason. "Yeah, she did. How did you know that?"

"How did that make you feel?" Lydia asks, ignoring his question.

"It didn't make me feel anything," says Jason quietly, looking. That's the truth, Lydia thinks to herself. There was more to explore here, she realised, but which nerve to trigger?

"And was this before or after your father left?" she asks

in a casual manner, making a show of taking notes on her pad again.

"What difference does that make?" Jason snaps.

"Did he leave because of what happened to Finley?"

"How should I know? I was just a kid."

"Did he leave because of what you did?"

"I didn't do anything!" Jason slams his manacles down on the table with a crash, causing Lydia to drop her pen and lean sharply away from him, and the guard in the room next door to get to his feet.

"Did you love your brother?" Lydia asks, tilting her head to peer into Jason's eyes, half hidden by his matted hair.

"Of course I did," he replies, metal scraping on metal as his manacled hands slide from the table. "I'm not a monster."

"And your father?" asks Lydia.

"Yes."

"Even after he walked out on you?"

"Love is unconditional," Jason replies, eyes down, hands in his lap. This answer takes Lydia by surprise.

"So you understand love?" she asks, after a moment. Jason slowly raises his head to look at her, his lips widening into a smile. Then he laughs. "What's so funny?" asks Lydia, shortly.

"You've no idea what to make of me, do you?"

"I'm not here to diagnose you, Jason," Lydia replies, coolly.

"That's a shame," says Jason. "I'd quite like a second opinion. Not convinced the docs around here are up to much."

He's enjoying himself, Lydia thinks. *This wasn't part of the plan.*

"Go on," says Jason. "Just for fun, tell me what you think."

"Alright," says Lydia, hotly. Her temper is getting the better of her. She knows she should pull back but giving in feels so satisfying. "You blame yourself for your brother's death, and for your father leaving, but you repressed those feelings for so long that they exploded violently when you killed those people."

"Wrong," said Jason, forcefully.

"Your mother blames you too," Lydia continues, "and you know it, and it makes you wonder if she loves you, if she ever really loved you."

"Nope." Jason shakes his head.

"You have all these feelings tearing you up inside," Lydia leans on the table now, pressing her point home, "but you never learned how to deal with them, like a normal person would. You only know one way to express yourself and that's—"

"You." Jason interrupts. Lydia stares at him. "You're talking about yourself."

"Excuse me?" Lydia looks like she's been slapped.

"You're the one with the repressed guilt, Lydia Tune. You're the one who doesn't know how to deal with her feelings. It's plain as day." He sounds bored, as if he's had enough of this conversation.

"You don't know—" Lydia begins.

"I know all about you," Jason corrects her, impatiently. "Do you think I would have agreed to meet without knowing all about you?"

"That's not possible," says Lydia.

"You had your heart broken, am I right?" Jason asks, but doesn't wait for an answer. "And I'm not talking in the romantic sense. You're running away from your pain; you've been running a long time, searching for answers in people like me."

"You're raving," Lydia snaps.

"You may be this big celebrity, but you're bitterly disappointed with the way your life has turned out and you don't know how to fix it, so you keep writing books about people you consider more damaged than you in the hope that it'll make you feel better, or lead you to some epiphany about how to save yourself. Well it won't," Jason bitterly remarks, noting the angry expression on Lydia's face.

"We're done for today," she says flatly, sweeping her phone and notebook into her bag.

"Oh, I'm sorry," says Jason, "have I hurt your feelings?"

"Not at all," Lydia replies, rising and sweeping her golden locks back over her shoulder. "You're obviously tired. We can continue this tomorrow."

"Oh no, please stay!" says Jason, sarcastically. "I felt like we were really connecting."

"Yeah?" says Lydia. "What else are you feeling right now?" She slides the chocolate bar across the table. Jason covers it with his hand.

"Pity," Jason says, seriously.

"For me?" asks Lydia, equal parts amused and outraged.

"Absolutely," says Jason. "At least I know what I am. You're still in denial."

"Even if that were true," says Lydia, swinging her bag over her shoulder, "and it's not, I wouldn't warrant your pity, Jason. After all, I'm the one who gets to walk out this door."

"Well now," Jason growls, leaning over the table towards her, "that just shows how wrong you really are." He fixes her with a smile. "Have you not considered that maybe I'm exactly where I want to be?"

Lydia doesn't answer. Instead she turns away to hide her face. If Jason sees that she's confused, he has won. She can't stop him from playing games, but she mustn't let him win. She crosses to the exit, the knock of those high heels echoing around the empty room.

"Goodbye, Jason," she says, pushing the heavy metal door open. The last thing she hears before it closes behind her is laughter. Cruel, cackling, triumphant laughter.

Nine

Blood Stone

An empty husk of a woman cradles her legs amidst bundled bed sheets, soaked in self-loathing. She will find no comfort in herself, alone in this dark room. No soothing words or warm hugs to nurse her wounded pride. She is sick of the people, all of them, their vanity, their noise. Sick of this act. Sick of this life.

Her spine juts out from her curved back, her weary skin melting from her bones as time, like a fire, consumes it. Eyes glazed over, eyelids drooping, unblinking. Is she human, she wonders, or something less than that? Is this normal?

The words of a monster, a murderer, ring in her ears, slice through her like knives, finding old wounds long forgotten. Scar tissue buried beneath decades of pain and anguish. She fixates on the wall opposite, where the last watered-down slivers of daylight have slipped through a gap in the heavy curtains. What comes next? What does she want?

At the edge of her consciousness floats an idea, unformed, uncapturable. The dream of another life. The taste of happiness. Every time she reaches for it, it dissipates like smoke. There's something more she needs to do. But what? Helplessness blankets her like a heavy duvet, smothering, suffocating, rendering her incapable of movement. Paralysed in her own mind.

Images flicker in her mind's eye, like a reel of old, grainy film. A baby in the arms of a beautiful woman, both of them bathed in golden light. Long, blonde hair, fresh face, a loving smile but such sad, green eyes. The light fades and shimmers, grows darker, orange like fire. And now the baby is a little girl, maybe eight years old, standing in a doorway, tears in her eyes. A man stands before her, his back turned, naked, ruddy skin covered with thick, black hair, muscles tensed. He raises his right arm, fist clenched, and the little girl screams. And suddenly Lydia is inside her body, screaming too, as the fist disappears with a sickening thump like a joint of meat hitting the floor. She sees her mother through her father's legs, cowering in a heap on the floor, hiding her broken face. The memory hurt like a symphony of nightmares; her mother was too trusting, timid and willing to be blind to her father's faults. That fact had always stained itself onto Lydia's perception of how a woman should not be, even though she deeply loved her mother, her weaknesses included.

The light pulses and fades again, almost to black. The little girl is a teenager, sixteen maybe, recognisably Lydia now. Kneeling on wet grass at the foot of a grave topped with a small bouquet of white lilies. A small, black granite headstone reads, "Rebecca Tune, 1960–1996. Beloved mother. Rest in peace."

In a blaze of hot, red light the scene changes again.

An empty whisky bottle crashes into a wall, narrowly missing teenage Lydia's head. She flinches and then glares. Daggers in her eyes, at the man who threw it. Her father yells something in her direction, foaming spittle spraying through the air, but in this dream state she cannot hear it. She sprints upstairs to her room, rips open a battered old wardrobe, and begins throwing clothes into a sports bag.

She crosses to the nightstand, where a ruby ring lies next to a photograph of her mother. Her mother's ring. Amidst the muted tones of this memory, it shines as bright as a red-hot star. Lydia picks it up tenderly and slips it on her finger for the first time. It is a perfect fit. She shivers as a warm sensation flows from her hand right through her body. She has never felt stronger or more in tune with the world around her. This is her touchstone, the moment she will always return to in times of doubt and difficulty. The moment she shed the part of herself that no longer felt right. Priest, her father's name. Priest, the mark of the monster. She renounced it the day her mother passed. She didn't want it. It was just the two of them now, bound by spirit, by blood, her own flesh tethered to the ethereal plane by this dark gem. The timid girl, Lydia Priest, was no more. Lydia Tune had arrived.

The image flickers and dies, overwhelmed by Lydia's waking consciousness. The voices in her head keep multiplying, evil words both real and imagined, conjured and remembered, calling to her in synchrony like a choir. Their voices growing, swelling, deafening, drowning.

With great effort, she raises her hand before her face and gazes through acidic tears at the ruby ring upon it. The crystallised essence of a mother's love, the only thing she has left to remember her by. Even in darkness it glows, as if the gem contains a life of its own. She is hypnotised, like the victim of a scarlet-eyed snake. To her, it contains the seed of her creation, a mirror of her beginning. The essence of herself. Her family. Her blood. The only voice that she wants or needs to hear: her mother's. She strokes it tenderly with the side of her thumb as if it were the cheek of a lover.

Keep going, her mother whispers. *We're almost there. We've come too far to give up now.* Lydia nods, slowly, sombrely, a single tear forming in the corner of her eye. *Never let them see your pain*, chides the voice. She wipes the tear away and swallows her sadness just as she has a thousand times before. You are ready.

"Yes," she whispers as the last of the light is swallowed by the jewel's black heart. "I am ready."

Ten

Nobody's Fault

A boozy musk drifts around O'Neal's bar, scattered with small, dim lamps and shady patrons. At the worn, wooden bar, Lydia is trying to fit in, wearing her black leather jacket over a red top, a tasteful black skirt and sturdy black boots. Nevertheless, her natural poise and golden curls attract ardent glances from all around.

She has been here for almost an hour already, sipping neat whisky and indulging in one of her guilty pleasures: looking up old acquaintances on social media and extrapolating lives from profiles. Her conclusions are never generous. Getting lost inside the sad lives of others is her favourite way to ward off her own unhappiness. She swipes away from one profile with disgust and takes another drink, noticing as she does two men watching her by the emerald pool table. One says something to the other, then they both nod, and laugh, before returning to their game. To the other side of her, on a small, barely raised stage, a tired woman is slurring the words to a Nina Simone song.

Lydia wonders why nobody has used the jukebox in the corner of the room to end the torment. Her ears ring with each screeching, misplaced note. As she contemplates doing it herself, a heavily tattooed man wearing a cheap, knitted cap enters the bar. A walking doodle. But when he removes it and mounts a bar stool, she catches sight of his pale blue eyes and feels warmth spread through her that has nothing to do with the whisky. *Dangerous handsome*, she thinks, returning to her phone. Some of the most terrible men she had studied for her books were the same. Perhaps that's how they managed to hide their wickedness for so long. *Dangerous handsome.*

"Of all the gin joints in all the world," says a familiar voice nearby. Lydia looks up, surprised, to find Alex's soft, brown eyes gazing back at her. He is wearing the same jacket from the other night over a plain white T-shirt.

"Alex," she says in a coy manner, hiding her surprise before realising she is actually strangely excited to see him. "What are you doing here?"

"Waiting for my date," Alex replies. Is he blushing? It's difficult to tell in the low light.

"Oh," Lydia replies, airily, regaining control of herself. "First date?"

"Yeah, friend of a friend at work. Her name's Sarah."

"How nice," says Lydia, taking another sip of whisky.

"How about you?" asks Alex, sliding onto the seat next to her and gesturing to the bartender. "I thought you'd be locked in your hotel room, writing."

"Needed a break," says Lydia, absently checking her phone again. She is irritated with Alex, but can't tell exactly why. Perhaps the alcohol is pulling her emotions out of their comfort zone.

"Writer's block?" asks Alex, smiling. Lydia cringes. Only someone who wasn't a writer could deploy that term so cheerfully.

"Something like that."

"And whisky helps you think?"

Lydia grips her glass, resisting the strong urge to fling its contents in Alex's smirking face. The bartender sets a cold bottle of beer atop a napkin in front of him.

"Mind if I keep you company while I wait?" asks Alex, taking a swig from the bottle.

"Sure," says Lydia. In her head it sounds like "no". She is annoyed with herself for being such a pushover, but then again knows that she could certainly use a distraction.

"So, how's it going?"

"Yeah, great," Lydia lies. "Making good progress, few chapters down already."

"You're lying."

"Excuse me?" Lydia glares at him.

"I can tell," he points the neck of his bottle towards her face. "You disengage when you're lying."

"I what?"

"All your facial features kind of reset, like a mask. I noticed it the other night." He takes another drink.

"*You're* going to teach *me* about reading people?" asks Lydia, incredulously.

"Woah, settle down, Lyd," he says, holding up his free hand in apology. "I didn't mean anything by it."

Lydia turns back to the bar. She picks up her phone,

hovers her thumb over the home button but sets it down again.

"Something bothering you?" asks Alex, tentatively. Lydia shrugs. "Did you... see Devere again?"

"This afternoon," she says, tipping back the last of her drink and ordering another.

"How did that go?"

"It was fine," Lydia replies. She doesn't want to give him the satisfaction of knowing that Jason got to her, just as Alex said he would.

"Okay."

"What does that mean?"

"It means okay, Lydia, what?" Alex looks hurt, and Lydia feels as guilty as if she had just kicked a puppy. There's a long pause.

"He got under my skin," she says finally. "Just a little bit."

"Well," says Alex seriously, "that *is* bad news."

"Why?" Lydia frowns.

"It means you're only human." He looks her right in the eyes, the hint of a smile twitching the corners of his mouth. Lydia can't help herself. She laughs.

"Asshole..."

"I'll drink to that." He raises his bottle as the bartender refills Lydia's glass.

"To assholes?" asks Lydia, one eyebrow raised.

"To liars," says Alex, brazenly. Lydia glares at him again, but she's smiling. Somewhere deep inside her she feels a release, like a dam breaking and washing all of her tension away. She raises her glass and clinks it gently against the bottle.

"What kinda music d'ya like?" Alex's speech had grown increasingly slurred over the past hour. Thankfully the wailing woman had retired from the stage and the old jukebox in the corner had taken over her duties.

"I hate that question," Lydia replies. She goes to take another sip of whisky but thinks better of it and puts the glass down. A sick feeling in her stomach is threatening to bubble over. "What kind of movies do you like? What kind of food do you enjoy?" She waves a dismissive hand. "As if you can learn anything about a person by generalising and compartmentalising their tastes."

"Woah," says Alex, "didn't mean to offend the psychoanalyst." Lydia gives him a look. Oh please. "Why don't you show me instead, then?" He nods towards the jukebox.

"Alright," says Lydia, pushing herself off the bar stool and then grabbing it again to steady herself as her heels hit the floor. Alex takes her arm. "I'm fine," she snaps, jerking it away. Alex turns away as he gets to his feet, so Lydia can't quite make out what he's mouthing to himself, but she's sure it isn't complimentary. She follows him unsteadily over to the music's source.

"You pick one, I pick one," says Alex, pushing a few coins into the slot.

"You first," says Lydia. Even in her high heels, Alex is a full foot taller than her and standing so close to him makes her feel girlish. Young. Safe. She inhales his cologne, that subtle, flowery scent, and feels a tingle inside.

"Aha," says Alex, pushing the thick, mechanical buttons, "a classic." Lydia watches him select 'Come Get Your Love' by Redbone and nods approvingly. "Your turn." He slides over to give her room. Lydia flips back and forth through the albums before settling on 'Under My Skin'. "You like Sinatra?" asks Alex, surprised.

"Who doesn't?" she replies, hazily.

"Good girl. Two spiced rums over here," Alex calls to the bartender. She makes a face.

"I hate rum."

"You're gonna love this rum," he insists. A flash of anger makes Lydia's pale cheeks warm. *Why are men like this?* she wonders, the thought almost forcing itself from her lips. The bartender pours the shots and Lydia sniffs hers doubtfully, recoiling immediately.

"It smells disgusting."

"Trust me." Alex laughs, picking his up and motioning for Lydia to do the same.

"Ugh," she sighs. "Really?"

"C'mon, Lyd," he teases, "where's your sense of adventure?"

"Fine." Lydia picks up the shot.

"On three," says Alex. "One..." Lydia's glass is already at her lips before he can finish. Taken by surprise, he raises his own quickly and tips it back.

"Ergh!" Lydia splutters, gagging and sticking out her tongue. "That's horrible."

"Really?" asks Alex, his face crinkled from the harshness of the alcohol.

"Tastes like shit and shoe polish," says Lydia, gesturing for the bartender to bring her a glass of water.

"Oh come on!"

"It does," Lydia insists, her eyes wandering to the large analogue clock behind the bar. "Hey, where's your date?"

Alex follows her gaze. "Huh," he says, quietly. "Guess I've been stood up."

"Oh come on, Alex," says Lydia, impatiently.

"What?"

"There is no date, is there?" she says. Alex looks like he's about to protest, but withers beneath Lydia's penetrating eyes.

"Alright, you got me. There's no date."

Lydia nods thoughtfully, then leans in towards him. "So why are you really here?" she whispers. Alex looks at her, then to the bartender, then around the room.

"Not in here," he whispers back, jerking his head towards the door. Then without another word he gets up and heads outside. Blindsided and bewildered, Lydia grabs her leather jacket from the back of her stool and follows.

The frozen air hits her like a wall of ice. Her heel slides and she wobbles, catching hold of Alex's arm to steady herself.

"Oh *now* it's okay," he teases.

"Shut up," Lydia replies, grumpily. "What are we doing out here?"

"Okay," says Alex, lowering his voice conspiratorially, "this is going to sound crazy but hear me out." Lydia stares at him impatiently. "Right, well the thing is, I've been here the past few nights looking for a guy."

Lydia's eyebrow rises.

"Not like that! He's a fence for a crime lord round these parts, name of Falcone."

"How dramatic," says Lydia, intrigued but trying not to sound it. "And what is it exactly you want from him?"

"Information."

"That isn't very exact, Alex," says Lydia, stuffing her hands in her pockets and pulling the jacket tight around her.

"I can't tell you everything, Lydia, you're not a cop."

"Are you afraid I'm going to run off to all my criminal friends and warn them?"

"Of course not."

"Then what's the problem?"

"I'd be breaking the law, for a start."

"Oh come on." Lydia gives him a withering look.

"I would!"

"You break laws every day for pity's sake, we all do. The reason you don't want to tell me," she steps closer, looking him right in the eyes, "is that information is power, and you like the feeling of having power over me."

"Bullshit."

Lydia grins. "So tell me."

"You think your amateur psychologist routine is going to work on me?"

"No." Lydia bites her lip and tilts her head just a little. "I know it is."

Alex stares at her for a moment, then forces himself to look away. "Fine. I'll tell you. But not because of that little performance," he adds as Lydia spins away, laughing. "I'll tell you because I trust you."

"Thank you, Alex." Lydia looks comically over-serious. "Thank you for trusting me."

"Forget it."

She starts laughing again. "I'm sorry, come on, tell me. What's the information?"

Alex rolls his eyes. "Fine. It's no big deal anyway. They're making over stolen cars someplace and I'd like to know where, so we can get eyes on their people more easily."

"Okay," Lydia nods, "that wasn't so hard, was it?"

"Oh shut up."

"So is he here tonight, your fence?"

"I'm not sure," Alex replies, sheepishly. "I've been a bit... distracted." He meets Lydia's eye and then looks away quickly.

"Well, go look, dumbass!" Lydia fans him inside with her hands, still stuffed in her pockets. "Go!"

Alex stumbles back inside and the heavy door closes behind him, shutting out the sounds of the bar completely. The silence is quite pleasant. It reminds Lydia of her childhood, walking home from school alone in the winter. What she would give for life to be that simple again. Then the door opens again and Alex spills out into the snow.

"He's in there," he says, unhappily.

"So go get your information, you idiot!" says Lydia, staring at him in disbelief. How she could ever have thought this man smart seemed, in this moment, completely beyond her.

"I can't," he sighs. "I'm too drunk now."

"Oh, don't be ridiculous," says Lydia impatiently. "Just go and get it."

Alex looks away, then walks away a few paces and stands with his back to her. Lydia marches after him, heels knocking the ground, grabs his shoulder and hauls him around to face her. The effort almost topples her over. "Pull yourself together, for god's sake!" she says, forcefully. "This is your job, isn't it?"

"Not the part I'm good at."

"What part is that?"

"Getting people to talk." Alex sighs. "I don't have the patience for it, or the empathy, or whatever it is that you need to get people to like you. I just lose my temper and then they shut down." He stares at the ground. "That's why Devere was on the run for so long."

Lydia frowns. "What are you talking about?"

"The motherfucker got to me. Got in my head," he waves a hand at her, "like you did just now. And I lost my cool. And our leads started drying up."

"Oh, Alex," says Lydia, annoyed but also feeling a little sorry for him. "Getting people to talk is easy."

"For you, maybe."

Lydia thinks for a moment, her face struggling with itself, as though trying to decide something. "Fine," she says eventually. "I'll show you. Come on." She grabs his sleeve and leads him back towards the door.

"Wait," Alex calls out, jerking his coat from her grasp. "Lydia, I can't let you do this. It might be dangerous."

"Alex," says Lydia, whipping around to face him, "I sat alone in a room this afternoon with a murdering psychopath, asking him at what point his life went looney tunes. I can handle a bog-standard mobster!" Alex stared at her sheepishly, like a little boy being told off by the teacher. "Okay then," Lydia says, impatiently. "Let's go back in, and you point him out to me and I'll find out where the dodgy dealings are being done with these cars."

"Far side of the bar," says Alex, not moving. "Black shirt, silver tie, moustache."

"Got it." Lydia grasps the door handle, freezes for

a moment, then stops and turns. "If I get you what you need…"

"Uh-oh…"

"If I get it for you—"

"No."

"I want to see those crime scene reports."

"I can't!"

"Okay, but you see I know that you can."

"How on earth would you know that?"

"Because I've done this—"

"You've done this before," Alex finishes for her. "Of course you have."

"So how about it?" Lydia bites her lip and cocks her head, leaning towards him while keeping one hand on the door handle, and the other lightly on his strong arm. Alex watches her for a moment and a smile spreads across his face. He knows he's being played, but it's different this time. She's putting on the performance for him, not with him.

"Fine," he says finally. "You scratch my back, and I'll scratch yours."

"Ooh!" Lydia curls her slender fingers through the air like a claw.

"Will you get in there already before he leaves?"

"Alright, I'm going!" She pulls herself back towards the door and turns the handle as she does so, tumbling through it back into the hazy bar.

She squints as her eyes re-adjust to the yellow-orange light, and spots her mark at once; a heavy-set man in his forties with tanned, leathery skin and bushy eyebrows. As Alex said, he's sitting at the far end of the bar, alone. Lydia takes a breath to compose herself, then marches right up next to him.

"Beer and a shot," she barks at the bartender, then waits just a moment for the mark to take her in before making eye contact with him. "Some asshole smashed my tail light," she says, breaking the eye contact. *Don't let him read you.* "You believe that?"

"In this city?" the heavy-set man replies. "Sure."

"I'm not from around here," she says, downing the shot and then putting the beer bottle to her lips and tipping it back. As she lowers it again, the liquor spills unseen from her mouth into the bottle.

"Yeah? Where you from?"

"New York," she replies, sliding onto the stool next to him.

"Shoulda guessed."

Lydia smiles. "Why'd you say that?"

"You got an attitude about you."

"Only when some punk messes with my goddamn car." She takes another phantom swig of beer.

"What do you drive?"

"Mustang."

"New or classic?"

"New."

"Damn." The man shakes his head.

"What?" Lydia stares him down.

"Here I took you for a real classy kind of girl."

"What would a real classy kind of girl be doing in a dump like this?" She waves a hand at their surroundings.

"Good point." The mark's eyes linger on her chest. "You need a ride then?"

"Nah, I'll risk it."

"You sure? Asshole cops in this city are happy to pull you for a broken tail light."

"I'm staying just down the way," Lydia replies, gesturing vaguely, "it's not far. I'll sort it tomorrow." She sighs. "If I can find a repair shop around here."

"Take it to Red's, over on Lincoln Avenue," the man replies. "Tell 'em Joe sent you, they'll fix you right up."

"Yeah?" Lydia wears a mask of grateful surprise that hides her triumphant glee. "Joe, huh."

"That's me."

"Sarah." She offers her hand, and leans right into him as he takes it. "Lemme buy you a drink, to say thanks." She beckons the bartender over.

"I won't say no to that."

"Two beers," she says, pulling her phone from her pocket and pretending to check it. "I should let my friend know I'm gonna be a while... damn."

"What's up?"

"I got no reception in here." Lydia makes a show of waving the phone around, looking for a signal. "I'll be right back." She slides off the stool and calmly, confidently makes for the exit.

Outside in the snow, the door bangs open loudly, and Lydia comes marching through it. "Red's on Lincoln Avenue," she says, with a smug smile. "Oh yeah, and here you go." She produces a thick, brown leather wallet from her pocket and tosses it to Alex.

"How the hell did you do that?!" Alex stares at it, then at her.

"Like this," says Lydia, stepping close to him, shifting her weight to her hip and tilting her face up towards his. She runs her hand along his arm giving it a gentle squeeze, smiles, and flutters her eyelashes just a little bit, then sheepishly bites her plump, ruby red bottom lip and moves her face even closer to his, almost to the point of a kiss. Then suddenly she lets the mask slip and takes a step back.

Alex snaps out of his trance. "What the hell was that?"

"Ta-da!" she says, presenting a watch theatrically as if it were a prize. Alex looks down at his wrist, where the watch used to be.

"Where did you learn that?" he says, impressed.

"Flirting?" Lydia asks, innocently.

"Sleight of hand," says Alex. "I knew you could flirt from the other night."

"Hey!" says Lydia, feigning outrage. "That was barely flirting."

"That's kind of cheap, Lydia," says Alex, snatching back his watch and slipping it onto his wrist.

"What did you call me?" says Lydia, indignantly.

"Not you," he replies, "the trick."

"The end justifies the means," she says, nonchalantly. "So said Ovid in Heroides."

"Stop showing off, Tune."

"*Heroides* means *the heroines*," says Lydia, smiling, her eyes twinkling.

"Are you flirting with me right now?" asks Alex, grinning back at her.

"Why," Lydia replies, "do you have something I want?"

Alex's grin fades. "That isn't funny."

"Oh lighten up, Gilbey," says Lydia. She looks up and down the street. "You know another bar around here?"

"Yeah," he says cautiously, "there's a hotel around the corner. Why?"

"Well we can hardly return to the scene of the crime," says Lydia, jerking her head back towards the door. "And I think you owe me a drink. As well as—"

"Let's start with a drink."

"Not gonna welch on our deal, are you?" Lydia looks pointedly at him.

"Come on," he replies, already walking away. Lydia's eyes narrow, but she follows without pushing it further.

The bar at the Marriott is contemporary; half sports, half not, big screens inside, fire pits and square sofas outside. Tonight, there's a game on, so it's pretty full. Lydia and Alex are perched on tall, round, red stools nursing near-spent drinks.

"How about a game?" Lydia suggests. "Since we're in a sports bar."

"What kind of game?" asks Alex, warily.

"Who can get the most phone numbers in thirty minutes," says Lydia, a twinkle in her eye.

"You'll win that easily," says Alex, dismissively.

"Well thank you," says Lydia, accepting the accidental compliment. "But let's play anyway. It'll give you a chance to practise your people skills."

"Alright," says Alex, "what are the stakes?"

"Stakes?"

"I find sports a lot more interesting when I have something riding on them," says Alex.

"Whatever you like," says Lydia, waving a hand.

"Deal," says Alex quickly, grinning. "Whoever wins has to give the other whatever they like."

"We already played that game. I won, remember?"

"Double or quits."

"Hey I didn't agree..." Lydia begins, but Alex is already making a beeline for an older woman sitting by herself at a table. "Fine," she says, scanning the room for her first target. For the next half hour, the two of them circle the room, stopping every few minutes to make flirtatious small talk with anyone who will listen. Once time is up, they rendezvous back at the bar.

"How many do you have?" asks Lydia, with almost childlike excitement.

"Two," says Alex.

"Six!" Lydia thrusts her hands into the air. "I win!"

"Congratulations," says Alex, sarcastically. "What do you want then?"

"Hmm..." Lydia considers for a moment. "I think I want... another drink."

"I think you've had enough," says Alex.

"But I didn't even tell you what kind of drink I want," says Lydia, sulkily.

"Fine," says Alex, "what kind of drink do you want?"

"Water please," she calls to the bartender. "Oh, and another whisky!"

Alex rolls his eyes. "Make it two whiskies."

"I'm sorry," says Lydia, giving his arm a squeeze.

"For what?" asks Alex.

"That you're such a loser."

"That depends on your point of view, I guess," says Alex.

"What do you mean?" asks Lydia, peering at him through her blonde curls.

"Well," says Alex, "I got the information I needed, and I got to know you a little better." He smiles at her. "I'd call that a win, to be honest."

Lydia peers into his soft, brown eyes as the bartender sets up their drinks. "You're cute," she says finally, pinching Alex's cheek before picking up her whisky and tossing it back in one go.

"Alright," says Alex, blushing, "you've definitely had enough now."

"You know what?" says Lydia, leaning into him. "This is the most fun I've had in forever."

"You don't have a lot of fun writing about murderous assholes?" asks Alex, feigning surprise. "That is a shock. I'm shocked."

"That is fun actually," says Lydia defensively. "Or well, interesting at least. But I meant more like... I don't have fun with people. You know?"

"Yeah," says Alex, nodding. "Me neither." He picks up his own whisky and sinks it. "I hate people."

"Why is that?" Lydia props her elbow on the bar and her cheek on her hand, peering up at him. "What's your story, Alex Gilbey?"

"I don't know," Alex shrugs, "I don't think I have a story. Least not much of one."

"Everyone has a story," says Lydia, tucking her hair behind her ear.

"I mean I've seen what I've seen, and done what I've done," says Alex, fighting his intoxication to find the right words. "But ain't no rhyme or reason to it. No thread. No sense. You know?"

"Not really," says Lydia.

"Maybe I'm just weird," says Alex, looking away. "Or maybe I'm just drunk."

"Or maybe both," says Lydia, taking his hand and smiling sympathetically. "But hey what do I know? I spend my days hanging out with psychos."

"Is that your story?" asks Alex, looking back at her.

"Eh…" says Lydia softly. "I have a lot of stories, but none of them ever end well."

"Why do you think that is?"

"I guess life just has it in for me," says Lydia, sadly.

"Maybe you just need to take control of your own story?" Alex offers. "You know, be the… what do they call it? The leader?"

"Protagonist?" Lydia offers.

"Yeah, that."

"After what you've seen tonight," says Lydia, one eyebrow raised, "you think I'm too passive?"

"Maybe not passive, exactly…"

"Trust me," says Lydia, her eyes floating around the room. "You wouldn't believe the things I've done."

"Yeah, well," says Alex, "there's doing things, and then there's doing things for yourself, isn't there?"

"This is depressing," says Lydia suddenly. "Let's talk about something else."

"I'm sorry," says Alex. "I get maudlin when I drink." He thinks for a moment. "Alright, how about another game?"

Lydia perks up. "What do you have in mind?"

"Did you ever play 'Would you rather'?" asks Alex.

"Uh, yeah," says Lydia, "at school."

"Let's play."

Lydia looks dubious. "You first."

"Okay," says Alex. "Would you rather... know you're going to die in ten years' time, or live forever?"

"Live forever," says Lydia without hesitation.

"Really?"

"Absolutely! You'd never have to worry about dying; never have to worry about wasting time or running out of it. You'd have forever to do all the things you want to do."

"But everyone you cared about would die," says Alex. "Don't you think you'd be lonely?"

Lydia thinks about it for a moment, then shrugs. "Hey, that was a pretty morbid question."

"I told you I get maudlin when I drink," he replies. "Your turn."

"Hmm..." Lydia thinks hard. "Would you rather... know *where* you're going to die, or *how* you're going to die?"

"How," says Alex after a moment's thought. "Because you'd be less paranoid probably."

"Me too," says Lydia.

"Hey that was a pretty morbid question," Alex teases.

"I'm just following your lead. Anyway, it's your turn."

"Would you rather... drink spiced rum or vomit?"

"Vomit," says Lydia, completely deadpan. "Without a doubt."

"You're so stubborn," Alex laughs.

"Shit," says Lydia, catching sight of a clock on the wall, "is that really the time? I'd better go. I have an early start tomorrow." She slips from the stool and starts pulling on her leather jacket.

"I'll get us a cab," says Alex, rising with her.

"It's okay," says Lydia, "I can get my own."

"This isn't your city," says Alex holding her by the arm gently, as he tips her chin up to meet him, "and I want to make sure you get back in one piece. I won't sleep otherwise."

Lydia looks up into his eyes, those big, brown eyes, and she can't help but blush. It's been a long time since she experienced the feeling of having someone who wanted to look after her, and she likes it. But a quiet voice in the back of her mind is wondering what Alex Gilbey really wants. *They all want something.*

Eleven

The Sun's Cold Rise

Lydia stares up at the faded, off-white ceiling, her head both buzzing and pounding, every painful throb loaded with regret. Every rattling breath feels like an effort. The room is roasting hot. She feels like her skin is about to catch fire, steaming, soaking the sheets with sweat that cools and makes her shiver. When she moves, her bones feel like they might snap. Everything at the periphery of her vision is out of focus, shimmering in the dusty sunlight that sneaks in through ill-fitting curtains.

Nausea churns violently in her stomach and she panics, rolling to the edge of the bed and letting her legs fall out. Her feet hit the thick carpet with a soft thump. This isn't her hotel room with its thin, worn-out floor. Where is she? She scans the room, heart pumping so fiercely it makes her vision swim in pulses, the rhythm of her pain.

A clock radio on the bedside table shows ten twenty-one. There's somewhere she needs to be. Lydia tries to remember. Mortem. Jason. Two o'clock. She needs to get back to the hotel and straighten herself out. Sober and clear-headed, Jason Devere had got the better of her. In this state...

Lydia swivels her sore neck around and sees a foot protruding from the sheets at the far corner of the bed. With a soft groan, she shifts her body and turns the other way to find the back of Alex's head half-buried in a pillow, fast asleep. He looks so at peace, the opposite of how she feels. Next to him on his bedside table, a tatty piece of paper bearing what is unmistakably her handwriting. As her eyes slowly focus, Lydia recognises it as a list of songs. She remembers. She wrote down her favourite songs in the cab on the way home. She cringes at the adolescence of it even as she deciphers the drunken scrawl.

'Under My Skin', Frank Sinatra

'Mr Sandman', Nan Vernon version

'If I Can Dream', Elvis

'Come Get Your Love', Redbone

'Only You', Elvis

'Hooked on a Feeling', Blue Swede

'Bohemian Rhapsody', Queen

'I Don't Want to Set the World on Fire', Ink Spots

If she heard any of those songs at this moment, Lydia thinks, she would hate them for the rest of her days. How could she have been so stupid? This isn't her.

Focus, she tells herself, closing her eyes. First things first. Get the hell out of here.

As gently as she can manage in her unbalanced state, Lydia eases herself up off the bed, snatches what clothes she recognises, including her heels, and creeps to the bedroom door. Before she leaves, she takes one last look at the man in the bed, still dead to the world. Was he her conquest, or she his? Some small part of her knows that this is a ridiculous distinction to care about in a moment like this. But to Lydia, it matters. To Lydia, it always matters.

Twelve

Quiet Minds

Jason Devere is bound to his cold steel throne with heavy chains, observed by two guards facing him in the corners of the stark room. He shifts his weight lazily and lifts his head to peer through greasy hair at the clock on the wall as the second hand ticks rhythmically towards two o'clock. He licks his lips in anticipation.

On the stroke of two, as if summoned by the clock, Lydia sweeps breezily into the room, wearing a sleek black suit over a white blouse and carrying a blue box. Jason's lips twist into a grin when he sees her. Lydia does not say a word to the guards or even acknowledge them, but they animate together like statues given life and walk to the door. Lydia waits until they are gone, then crosses the floor to the chair on the opposite side of the table to Jason's, her high heels clicking on the polished floor and echoing around the bare walls. Eyes fixed on Jason; she places the blue box on the table, and takes her seat.

"I've been thinking," says Lydia casually, taking her

phone from her bag, tapping the screen and setting it down on the table, "about how this is going to end. Who is going to win this little game of ours?" She watches Jason, but beyond the smirk playing around the edge of his mouth he shows her no reaction. "Maybe you?" she continues. "Maybe me? Maybe we will both be winners. Or both losers. Who knows?"

"You're persistent," says Jason, amused, "I'll give you that."

Lydia smiles at him pleasantly. "Did you get the items you requested?"

"I did!" Jason replies, cheerily. "My penmanship is becoming a sight to behold." He raises his manacled hands with a clatter and mimes writing in the air with long, elegant strokes.

"Good," says Lydia. "So, today I thought we would try something different."

"Variety is the spice of life," says Jason, with another wave of his hands. He seems in good spirits today, Lydia thinks. Is it genuine, or an act? And if an act, to what purpose? Only one way to find out.

"As you can see, I've brought something with me." She motions to the blue box with an open palm. "A gift."

"What kind of gift?" asks Jason, peering at the box curiously.

"You'll find out," says Lydia, "if you answer one simple question for me." She holds up a lily-white finger.

"Which is?" asks Jason.

"Why do you kill?" asks Lydia, simply.

Jason considers the question for a moment, then shrugs his shoulders. "Fish gotta swim," he says, brazenly.

"I need a better answer than that, Jason," says Lydia. Her voice is measured, calm. She sees the flash in his eyes and it gives her a warm feeling of triumph in her heart.

"It's my nature," says Jason, as if forcing himself. "I'm just not like other people."

"Why do you think that is?" Lydia asks, flipping open her notebook.

"Oh, I don't know." Jason sits back, his chains clinking. "Suppose I wasn't wired up the same as the rest of you."

"You think you were born this way?" Lydia asks, a note of scepticism in her voice.

"Yeah," Jason replies. "Sure. Why not?"

"Well," says Lydia, scratching her nose with her pen, "in all my years studying people like you, I've never found one I thought was born evil."

"Yeah?" Jason asks, as if only mildly curious.

"Their behaviour is always caused by some sort of trigger," says Lydia, peering at Jason and pursing her scarlet lips just a little.

"In your opinion," says Jason, politely.

"Let's not play games anymore, Jason," says Lydia with a demure smile. "I told you there were only a few different ways this could end. Why don't you help me to help you?"

"And just how do you propose to do that?" asks Jason, leaning towards her.

"Tell me what you're hiding," says Lydia, calm yet forceful.

"I'm not hiding anything," Jason growls softly. "Not anymore."

"I see," says Lydia, frostily. She slides the blue box towards her, opens the lid and begins to retrieve items from within, lining them up neatly on the table between herself and Jason. A creased photograph, a comb, a mirror, and a silver, heart-shaped locket inlaid with sapphires. Jason eyes them greedily. He licks his lips. "Your personal effects," says Lydia. "As requested."

Jason can't help himself. He lunges across the table and there's a loud clang as his steel chains hold him back. He snarls in frustration.

"You see, Jason," says Lydia, unmoved, "I always keep my word. If you keep yours, there's a lot that I can do for you." Jason doesn't answer, but stares at her, seething, his eyes fierce behind that matted curtain of hair. "Now tell me," says Lydia, "what is the significance of these items to you?"

Again, Jason remains silent. Lydia nods and turns her head slightly towards the observation window without actually looking at it. A moment later, a fire alarm bursts into life, filling the room with an unbearable cacophony. Lydia doesn't flinch. She is expecting it. But Jason jerks upright in his chair, his wild eyes flying straight to the silver locket.

Lydia holds up one hand, and the alarm ceases immediately. "Thank you, Jason," she says, with a small smile. He looks confused and furious. "Upon hearing an alarm," Lydia explains, "a person will usually look to the thing most important to them. Like a loved one," she reaches out and picks up the locket, "or a prized possession. So tell me." She meets his burning gaze and dangles the locket in the air by its silver chain. "Why is this so important to you?"

Jason stares at the locket as it swings lazily back and forth, jewels glimmering and dancing even in this harsh, artificial light. He looks transfixed. "It was my mother's," he says finally.

"Was?" says Lydia. "Is your mother gone?"

"She's…" Jason grits his teeth. "She's in the hospital."

"Why is she in the hospital?" asks Lydia. Jason doesn't answer. He seems to be lost in his own thoughts. "She fell down the stairs, didn't she, Jason?" Lydia prompts, gently.

"Yes," says Jason quietly. "While I was in here."

"She used to visit you in here, didn't she?" asks Lydia. Her voice is quiet, warm, empathetic.

"Yes," says Jason. "But she can't now."

"Tell me why this locket means so much to you," says Lydia, placing it gently down on the table and pushing it towards him. Within his reach. Hesitantly, he reaches out and takes it, holds it, runs his fingers over it. Just for a second, Lydia sees Jason Devere's mask slip, and there is a completely different man sitting across from her. But then just as quickly the other side of him is back. "Why does it mean so much to you, Jason?" Lydia asks again.

"It just does," says Jason, flatly. Lydia half turns towards the window again, and within seconds the two guards burst into the room, making straight for Jason and slamming his face down on the table, his arms pinned behind his back. "Get off me!" He growls. One of the guards wrenches the locket from his shaking fingers and throws it back to Lydia. "Give it back," Jason spits, resisting his captors with all of his might even though it is hopeless.

"That's enough," says Lydia calmly, and the guards immediately release Jason. "Thank you." They leave the room again without a word.

"You're a fucking sadist," Jason growls, chains clinking as he wipes saliva from his face.

"And you're a murderer," Lydia retorts. "So I guess neither of us is going to heaven."

"Why did you do that?" Jason demands, slamming his manacles on the table.

"Because you weren't cooperating," Lydia replies, calmly. "Look Jason, this isn't complicated. Give me what I want and you get what you want too. It's not a trick."

"I don't know what you want from me!"

"I want to know why you are the way you are," says Lydia.

"How can I answer that?" says Jason. "Can *you* answer it? Go on, try. Why are *you* the way *you* are?"

"That's not how this works, Jason," says Lydia, shaking her head. "I'm not here to answer your questions; you're here to answer mine."

Jason scours her with his eyes, the wolf sizing its prey, circling, formulating a new plan of attack. "What was the question again?" he asks, that familiar smirk creeping back onto his face.

"Why did you kill those people?" Lydia asks.

"Just something to do." Jason shrugs. Lydia feels anger boil up inside of her, and is distantly aware that it has little to do with his stubbornness. Something about this man doesn't make sense to her and she can't figure out what it is, and it's making her mad at herself. She knows that something about this whole situation is wrong, but can't find the language to describe what it is. She's aware of it only in the abstract, like a jigsaw puzzle that doesn't quite fit together properly.

"I swear to you, Jason," she says, hotly, her own mask slipping, "you may think you've known torture in here but I can devise punishments worse than you can imagine. Mark my words if you don't start talking, I will make your life hell."

"I don't know why I killed them," says Jason, raising his voice. "I don't know what made me do it. Why don't you tell me? Huh?" He whips his chained hand in her direction. "You're the shrink. You're the expert. You tell me why I did it. Go on!"

"You don't know?" says Lydia, incredulously. "You don't know why you murdered all those people? You don't remember? Do you have amnesia or something?"

"It's the truth."

"Why did you display their bodies like you did? Like some sick kind of art?" asks Lydia fiercely, leaning towards him.

For a second, Jason looks hurt. A deep hurt, like grief, and it takes Lydia by surprise. Then a second later he's smiling, not the usual smile, but a bitter grimace of resignation. He sits back in his chair and fixes Lydia with a penetrating look. "Do you like art?"

"*Do I like art?*" She repeats the question incredulously. "Do you?"

"Sure," Lydia replies with a shrug. "I like art. Why, is that what this is all about to you? Do you think you're an artist?"

"You tell me. You're the one who's interested in my work."

"I'm interested in what makes a human being capable of

doing what you did," Lydia replies, coldly, "not to appreciate the aesthetics of torturing people."

"If their deaths hadn't been spectacular, would you be quite so interested?" There's a calm, judgemental quality to his voice that Lydia resents. Is *he* judging *me*?

"Spectacular?" she says, mastering her anger. "Is that what you wanted people to think?"

"I don't know."

"What do you mean you don't know? Don't you remember?"

"I don't know," Jason repeats, forcefully. "Maybe I was on drugs or something."

"No you weren't, Jason," says Lydia. "You weren't on anything and even if you were, there are no drugs that can make a person do those things."

"I honestly don't know what to tell you," says Jason, sitting back in his chair, suddenly calm. "It's all a blank to me."

"A blank?"

"Yeah," he says. "Like when you wake up and can't remember the dream you just had, even though you know you had it and you can sense it right there at the edges of your mind."

"You're saying these events are like a dream to you?" Lydia asks, watching him carefully.

"That's right," says Jason. "Like a dream I forgot a long time ago."

There's a long pause. Lydia is trying to decide whether she believes him or not. It doesn't seem plausible, but Jason is so defiant, so utterly impervious to her questioning that it forces her to entertain the possibility that he might be telling the truth.

"Did you know any of the victims?" Lydia asks finally. "Before you killed them, I mean."

"No," Jason replies.

"Not one?" Lydia asks, a note of surprise in her voice.

"Not one."

"Huh…" says Lydia softly, sitting back in her chair, her eyes fixed on him.

"Lemme ask you something," says Jason quietly, leaning over the table. "D'ya ever get the feeling you're being watched?"

"You are being watched," Lydia replies impatiently, gesturing to the window.

"Not me," says Jason, "you. And not just here, anywhere. Everywhere. That feeling like there are always eyes on you."

"You're talking about a manifestation of self-doubt," says Lydia. "Insecurities. I have no insecurities."

"Oh, come on," Jason grins, "everyone's insecure about something."

"If these are the games everybody warned me about," says Lydia flatly, "they've clearly grossly overestimated you."

"Funny thing to say," says Jason, his eyes flashing with annoyance, "after everything I've accomplished."

"Murder isn't an accomplishment, Jason," Lydia says, returning to her calm, patient persona.

"It's made me famous, hasn't it?"

"And is that all you want to be known for?"

"Out of my hands now, wouldn't you say?"

"It's never too late to change," says Lydia. "Never too late to start making amends, if you really want to."

"How do you suggest I do that, locked up in here?" Jason asks defiantly, holding up his shackles.

"Well," says Lydia thoughtfully, "if you did get out someday, what would you like to do?"

Jason considers the question for a moment. "I always wanted to be a teacher," he says finally.

"Really?" Lydia asks, genuinely surprised.

"Yeah," says Jason wistfully. "At a little school, someplace quiet. Wife. Two kids. One boy, one girl."

"A normal life?"

"Yup," Jason agrees. "A normal life." He looks away, straggly hair hiding his face. "But the world didn't want that for me."

"So you believe in fate?" Lydia asks, curiously.

"I think we all have our parts to play," Jason replies. "Don't you?"

"I've never really considered it," Lydia lies.

"You're not as good a liar as you think you are," says Jason, smirking.

"And you're not half as smart as you think you are."

"Yeah I believe in fate," says Jason, sitting upright, suddenly animated. "And I'll prove it to you as well."

"How are you going to do that?"

"One day soon I'm going to ask a favour from you," says Jason seriously. "A big one. And you're gonna have to do it."

"Oh I am, am I?" Lydia asks, her perfectly pencilled eyebrows raised. "Why is that?"

"Because you won't have a choice," he says, simply.

"We always have a choice, Jason."

"You'll see," says Jason, the smug smirk spreading across his lips. Lydia feels a shiver run up her spine. "You won't have a choice because you are who you are, and your impulse is to act."

"Like yours is to kill?" asks Lydia, coolly.

"Some of us are born wolves," says Jason, as though reading her mind. Lydia's uneasiness grows. "I can't help what I am."

"So you're a predator?" asks Lydia, scratching notes in her pad as she speaks.

"Naturally."

"Do you prefer to prey on men or women?" Lydia asks, casually. "Or both the same?"

"It isn't a sexual thing, darlin'," says Jason with what is unmistakably a leer. Lydia obliges him by tucking her blonde hair behind her ear with those slender fingers.

"But you do like women?" she asks, looking him straight in the eye without flinching.

"Well yeah, but…"

"Ever had a girlfriend?" she asks quickly.

"Not exactly." He frowns, retreating. "I had one, once."

"Tell me about her."

"Anna, her name was… is. We dated for a while, when we were kids. Eighteen, nineteen, I can't remember, but we had a fun time. I took her to movies, to picnics, I treated her well. I did good by her, but then I…" he breaks away, shaken slightly, as if he was recalling a painful memory. "I broke up with her, got bored," says Jason conclusively to himself as he goes to fold his arms, but the shackles prevent it. Lydia feels that familiar buzz of success in her chest. He's rattled.

"How did she make you feel?" she asks to find no reply. "Did you love her?"

"None of your business," says Jason flatly.

"Have you ever loved anyone? What about your parents?" asks Lydia. "You must love them?"

"What kinda dumbass question—"

"Did they hug you a lot? Your parents? When you were a kid?"

"Na, we weren't like that." Jason frowns. "I mean Mom, yeah, when we were little, I guess."

"But not your father?"

Jason's eyes narrow with suspicion. "Na, Dad was a hard man," he says grimly, "'n he brought us up the same way."

"You and Finley?" asks Lydia, with the casual air of somebody just helping the conversation along.

"Well I didn't have any other brothers," Jason snaps. "Are we nearly done?"

"Was your father a competitive man?"

"Yeah, he was," Jason replies. "He used to tell us that winning was everything and losers were nothing."

"What do you think he'd say if he could see you now?"

"I don't give a damn what he'd say," Jason shouts, whipping his chains against the floor with a crash, getting restless. "He's gone, ain't he?"

Lydia doesn't answer; she just stares at him long and hard, and then lowers her eyes to jot down something in her notebook.

"What are you writing?" Jason demands, irritated.

"Just what I see," Lydia replies, finishing the note before looking back up at him.

"Yeah?" says Jason, reclining in his seat, attempting to recover his lost swagger. "What do you see? Tell me what you've learned about the monster Jason Devere."

"Okay," Lydia says, calmly. "Your father taught you that the world was black and white, so when Finley died you thought he must blame you, that it was entirely your fault. You believe that you're the reason he left and therefore why your memories of your mother are all of her being sad."

"You don't know shit," Jason says casually, but Lydia sees the truth in his sad eyes.

"That's why you got into trouble at school," she presses on. "The bullying, the stealing, the drugs."

"What's your point?"

"You asked the question."

"So you know everything there is to know about me, is that it?"

"Not everything. There's still something you're not telling me."

"Yeah? What's that?"

"I don't know," Lydia replies, shaking her head. "Whatever it was that made you snap and release all that bottled up emotion in the way you did."

"You got me," says Jason, applauding her with slow, sarcastic claps that echo around the room. "I have a deep, dark secret. Is that what you're looking for? Is that what'll help sell your little book?"

"Well?" says Lydia, folding her arms. "Are you going to tell me what it is?"

"Sure."

"When?"

"When you do me that favour we talked about," says Jason. He isn't mad now, but he isn't smirking either. He looks almost sad, Lydia thinks. "That's the day you'll have your answers."

"And when will that be?" Lydia asks, impatiently.

"Soon."

Thirteen

Bed Bugs

Snow is falling heavily again as Lydia's deep red Mustang pulls into the hotel parking lot and eases to a stop. She switches off the engine, but makes no move to open the door. Snowflakes settle on the windshield. All is quiet, though not quite silent. The distant sounds of human activity are muffled, as if smothered by a vast duvet that has fallen over the world. Lydia closes her eyes and allows herself to tumble gently into that inviting space between wakefulness and not, her tired, still-hungover brain slipping away from her like a boat still tethered to a jetty let free to drift.

A loud thump on the window right next to her pulls her back to the waking world with a sharp intake of breath, her heart thumping as she whips her head around, leaning instinctively away from the sound. She can see a hand in a black leather glove emerging from the sleeve of a long, dark grey overcoat. Then the coat bends at the waist and Alex's face appears in the window.

"Jesus Christ," Lydia yells, yanking the door handle and

shoving it open hard as Alex dodges out of the way, "are you trying to give me a heart attack?"

"A little jumpy, are we?" The smirk on his face only fuels her temper.

"You get off on scaring women?"

"You wanna know what I get off on?"

Lydia glares at him so fiercely that he takes a step back, holding his hands up in apology, and Lydia notices for the first time that he's carrying a thick manila envelope. "What's that?"

"Just a little present," he says nonchalantly, "but if this is a bad time…"

"Don't play games with me," Lydia pulls her leather jacket tighter around herself, "I'm cold and tired and I just want to go inside and…" she breaks off, glancing towards the hotel entrance. "How did you know where to find me, anyway?"

Alex makes a face as though the question is beneath him.

"Did you call around all the hotels in the city or something?"

"Only the seedy ones."

Lydia shoves him hard and he takes a step back. "Asshole."

"Hey," Alex waves the envelope, "do you want your present or not?"

"Can we do this inside, Alex? It's freezing."

"That's a tempting offer," he grins, "but unfortunately I can't stay. Bad guys to catch, you know."

"Then why are you here?"

"I felt bad about this morning."

Lydia's face wrinkles in confusion. "What about it?"

"Well, you snuck out of my place without so much as a

goodbye, so I figured I must have done something to upset you."

"Is this how it's going to be?" Lydia folds her arms. "'Cause I gotta tell you, the whole clingy vibe does nothing for me."

"Clingy?"

"You're making a fuss because you didn't get a goodbye kiss?"

"Wow."

"What?"

"You're colder than this snow."

"I will be if you don't hurry this up." She nods at the envelope. "You gonna give me that or what?"

"Take it." He hands the thick package over. "No, no, don't open it now, you can thank me later."

Lydia's fingers, already half-way inside the envelope, halt and then retreat. She shrugs, smooths the flap closed, and turns towards the hotel. "Alright, see you later." After a few paces she stops, feeling Alex's eyes still on her, and looks over her shoulder. "When?"

"Huh?"

"When will I see you?"

"I, uh…"

Lydia rolls her eyes. "Tomorrow?" she flippantly remarks.

"I'm rotating to nights tomorrow." He looks disappointed.

"During the day then."

"Not going to see Devere again?" There's a definite note of jealousy in his voice, and Lydia savours it.

"There you go again." She smiles, slyly.

"What are you talking about?"

"*Clingy.*"

"You're ridiculous, you know that."

"Pick me up here around midday," she says, already walking away again.

"I haven't said yes yet!" Alex calls after her, but Lydia just waves goodbye without turning around or breaking stride until she's disappeared inside and out of sight. She knows leaving him wanting more will only work in her favour.

The heavy, brown envelope lands on Lydia's bed with a soft thump, and she throws her bag and jacket into a chair before stooping to fetch a bottle of water from the minibar. The rows of tiny liquor bottles make her shudder, and she shuts the door on them hard before twisting the bottle top and gulping down the cool liquid, its soothing properties radiating from her stomach to her brain in seconds.

Setting it down on the bedside table, she falls onto the soft mattress and pulls the envelope towards her, reaching inside with those elegant fingers and extracting the contents. It's a folder, stuffed thick with documents and worn thin at the edges, deep blue in colour, bearing upon its front the badge of the Decanten Police Department and underneath that, written in black marker pen, the name of its subject: Jason Devere. A broad smile spreads across Lydia's lips. "Thank you, Alex," she whispers, opening it up and beginning to read.

As she scans page upon page of police reports, witness statements, forensic reports and crime scene descriptions, one thing becomes crystal clear: the media coverage of the Krimson Killer didn't even begin to do justice to the full horror of these events. She knows, for example, because the papers reported it, that the eight-year-old Dimitroff twins, Ivan and Elena, had their skin flayed and swapped one with the other. But the newspaper reports never detailed the gruesome, surgical precision with which Jason Devere had carried out this task. That he had carefully removed and switched their eyes. That he had posed the children to match a photograph of them playing on the living room floor on their birthday, with the exact same toys, balloons, cards. And, Lydia physically recoils from the file as she reads, that they were both alive when the process began.

She sits back, takes a deep breath and reaches for her water. This is going to be more difficult than she thought. Not because of the death, she's written about death before. Not because of the wickedness, that was an inherent part of any premeditated murder. Not even because these were innocent children. No, there is something else here, something quite new to her. A level of pleasure that this killer seemed to take in his work. A pride he felt in its presentation. This wasn't just torture. It wasn't just murder. It was a performance, each one different, each so repulsive and sickening in its own way that it makes her uneasy in a way Lydia has never experienced before. A feeling that burrows beneath the surface of both body and mind. A discomfort of the soul.

She leans forward, turns over the page and finds herself staring at a photograph of the two children, just the way the police found them. Just the way their parents had found them. At a glance, they look quite normal, alive, posed mid-action as though playing on the floor. Only a closer look reveals the fresh scars, the ever-so-slightly sagging skin and hollow expressions. They look like badly made dolls.

They were alive when he did this to them. Lydia feels the hot sickness boil suddenly up inside of her like an erupting volcano and dashes to the bathroom just in time.

Get a grip, she chides herself, rinsing her mouth with water and then dabbing it dry with a warm hand towel. *It's not going to get any easier*. She isn't wrong. Over the next few hours, she experiences second-hand horrors that most people could not conceive of in their darkest nightmares. Human beings tortured, sliced, crushed, twisted, even liquefied, all in the most deliberately painful ways that their killer could formulate. All made an example of; a spectacle for his audience.

Me, she thinks with a pang of guilt and horror. *I'm his audience*.

The last, and most recent case in the file is that of an eighteen-year-old girl, Alice Redmond, a student at the city's art college. Alice, like the Dimitroff twins, had been flayed alive, but only her torso. Her skin, stretched and pinned like a canvas, painted upon with her own blood; a swirling pattern, a crimson void. She was probably still alive, the coroner notes, when her killer jammed the paintbrush he used through her eye, deep into her brain, and then posed her as if she had painted the picture herself, brush still protruding from her head.

Lydia closes the file and pushes it away from her. Now that she knows what it contains, the paper itself seems to exude malevolence and right now she wants to be as far away from it as possible. Sliding purposefully off the bed, she snatches it up, crosses to the dressing table, pulls open a drawer, crams the file inside and slams it shut again. It strikes Lydia suddenly, with those images staining her cranium, that the Jason she knew, that the Jason she had been questioning and examining didn't seem capable of such horrific acts. It felt... inconsistent, in a way that made her uneasy. Lydia felt she never wore self-doubt well; the shade didn't complement the rest of her character. Now looking up into the mirror, for a split second she doesn't recognise the face staring back at her. She's never seen that expression upon it before. Fear and nausea have robbed it of its usual confidence and composure. She crouches to open the minibar and retrieves two small bottles of vodka, twisting the top off one with shaking fingers and tipping it down her throat. It's empty in seconds. *I'll regret that in the morning.* But she doesn't care. She won't sleep otherwise.

Carrying the second bottle back over to the bedside table, she sets it down and then strips off her clothes, tossing them onto the chair where her jacket lies before slipping between the cool sheets. She twists open the vodka and then reaches for her phone while she drinks. No messages. She feels a pang of irritation that Alex would leave her with this package of nightmares and not even bother to check on her. *Who's clingy now?* Lydia curses herself and turns out the light as the warm tingle of the alcohol begins to numb the fringes of her consciousness.

High-heeled footsteps echo through the dark corridors of Mortem Asylum. Either side of Lydia as she walks, the walls are shifting, writhing, a fleshy tapestry of silently screaming faces. She tries not to look, her pace quickening, her footsteps growing louder. Ahead of her is a door, and through its tiny window she can see bright, white light. As she approaches it, a dark figure moves in the room beyond. Lydia hesitates. The walls begin closing in on her, stone grinding on stone, the squirming, howling faces pushing towards her. She dashes to the door, fumbling the handle and then, just as she feels the breath of those terrible faces on the back of her neck, tumbling through it and falling to the floor.

She hears the door slam shut behind her, and as she looks around a strong arm grabs her around the throat, lifting her clear off the ground. She screams, struggles, fights, kicks, claws, but it's no use. The strong figure carries her to a steel table in the centre of the room and slams her down on it, his hand pinning her down by the throat, and a bolt of fear shoots through her as she sees the wolf-like face of Jason Devere looming over her, his lips curling into a sly smile.

Lydia squirms desperately, but his grip is like a vice. He grabs one of her wrists and drags it to the edge of the table where a heavy iron manacle on a chain rests. "No!" Lydia chokes as she feels the metal close around her flesh.

"Yes," the killer growls softly in her ear as he forces her other arm to the far side of the table and clamps that one too. "You're mine now."

"Please," Lydia begs, still fighting desperately to free herself, the bloody images of the Krimson Killer's victims racing through her mind. "Please don't."

"Oh come now," Jason moves around the table so that he's looming over her head, "fair's fair. You wanted to get inside my head, didn't you?"

"No." Lydia starts to cry, her legs still twisting and kicking in vain.

"Well, now I'm going to get inside of yours." He raises

his hands high above her, and Lydia sees that he's gripping a huge meat cleaver, its polished steel glinting eerily in the bright, fluorescent light.

"NO!"

The blade plummets towards her, propelled with brutal force, and in a split second she feels its impact, feels the sharp edge cut through her, hears the sickening crunch of her own skull.

Lydia wakes, sitting bolt upright in her pitch-dark room, screaming.

Fourteen

In the Eye of the Beholder

"**S**o where are we going?"

"It's a surprise."

Lydia shifts to glare at Alex, the leather of his passenger seat squeaking beneath her. "I don't like surprises."

"You didn't like your present?" he asks, nonchalantly.

"Yeah, thanks for the nightmares."

Alex glances at her, his face a mixture of hurt and disbelief. "I thought that's what you wanted."

Lydia doesn't answer. She's still mad at him for not checking in with her last night, mad at herself for slightly caring, and to top it all off that dull thump has started up in her head again.

"You alright?" he asks. "Not still hungover, are you?" Lydia closes her eyes and presses her fingertips to her forehead. "Damn, you must be getting old." He sees her expression. "I mean we, *we* must be getting…" Lydia stares daggers at him. "Nothing. I didn't mean anything."

The car slows, and Alex pulls over to park outside a large,

concrete building. Lydia cranes her neck to peer through the driver's side window, and sees a large, bronze plaque fixed to the front of it.

DECANTEN MUSEUM OF MODERN ART

"Really?" she looks at him doubtfully.

"Yeah," Alex replied, uncertainly. "Why, you don't like art?"

"Do *you*?"

"Sure," he unfastens his seatbelt, "I come here all the time." Lydia's eyebrows almost disappear up into her blonde locks. "Alright, fine. I've never been here before in my life. Are you happy?"

"A little bit, yeah." Lydia smirks. "Are you trying to impress me?"

"Na, I just heard the restaurant here did a decent chili."

"Well in that case," Lydia unfastens her own belt and reaches for the door handle, "we'd better walk around a bit, so I can work up an appetite."

Inside the building is a series of vast, open rooms with high ceilings and polished wooden floors. The walls and fixtures, Lydia can tell, were once a crisp, clean white, but time and mild neglect have seen them fade to a slightly sour cream. There aren't many people here, but that might not be so strange. She has no idea what the average footfall of a place like this must be.

"What do you think of this?" Alex asks, standing in front of a large canvas. Lydia joins him and takes a moment to consider the mess of coloured shapes.

"I think their mother must be very proud," she says finally.

"You don't see anything of value in this picture at all?"

She peers up at him, trying to figure out if he's messing with her or not, and is surprised to find that he appears quite sincere. "What do *you* see?"

He shrugs. "I don't know, but someone did take the time to paint it; they must have been thinking about something when they did." He points to a bold, bright red brushstroke. "Maybe that represents anger. And that blue area there is like... a sea of sorrow, or something." He catches Lydia's eye, and she bursts out laughing. The sound fills the huge space, bouncing back on itself so that it sounds like there's a whole room full of women laughing. "Or not." Alex blushes. "Whatever."

"A sea of sorrow?" Lydia tries to control her cackling, but she just can't help herself.

"Hey," Alex holds his hands up, "it's not my fault if you're dead inside."

"I am not."

"If you say so." He moves along to the next painting, leaving Lydia behind.

"Hang on," she chases after him, "just because I don't see a web of deep and meaningful emotions in some childish painting, that means I'm dead inside?"

"I guess I just expected more from one of the world's foremost experts on the human mind." He looks at the painting straight ahead, a cacophony of black blots and splashes, and determinedly not at Lydia, which she interprets as a deliberate attempt to wind her up.

"I'm a psychologist," she replies flatly, "not an art critic."

"Evidently."

Lydia shoves him hard, and Alex is so surprised that he

almost falls onto the painting. "Hey!" He spins his arms in the air to steady himself. "Watch it."

"Sorry," Lydia replies, her nose in the air. "I didn't realise you were so weak."

"If I'd damaged that, you would have been paying for it."

"Do you want me to buy you a picture?" she asks, stepping slowly along to the next one, a harlequin pattern of metallic blue and silver. "Something to remember me by, after I've gone?"

"There's no need to be mean."

"You can look at it while you drown in oceans of sorrow because I'm not here."

"Stop." Alex nudges her gently, his hands in his pockets. "You'll make me cry."

"You're a sensitive soul." She looks up at him.

"More than you know," he replies, gazing right back. The softness of his eyes is disarming, making Lydia forget the snappy comeback she had already.

"Let's move along," she says briskly, snapping out of it, "I'm getting hungry." She heads through the doorway into the next room, then stops so suddenly that Alex walks straight into the back of her.

"What's wrong?" He looks past Lydia into a smaller room with only three giant paintings, one on each wall. They're all of the same theme: irregular black borders fading inward through dark shades wine-red, to crimson, to scarlet, to glimmers of palest pink, almost white. Lydia doesn't answer. She's staring at the painting straight-ahead, and starts to approach it in a kind of trance, as though drawn forward by some invisible force.

Closer up, she can see the thousands of individual strokes,

meticulously placed, a flick here, a swirl there, a flurry of movements designed, she can see as clearly as she has ever seen anything in her life, to create the impression of blood, rushing to escape a fresh wound from the inside out. But that isn't why Lydia's own blood has suddenly run cold.

"This is it," she whispers.

"Huh?" Alex stands at her shoulder.

"Don't you recognise it?"

"What are you talking about?" He looks the painting up and down. "It just looks like—"

"Blood."

"Yeah, I guess." He shrugs. "So what?"

"It's just like the painting Jason did," she hisses through gritted teeth, trying to suppress the sickness rising within her again, "on that girl. The student. Alice."

Alex's jaw falls, his eyes wide as he stares at the canvas. "Jesus Christ…"

"Who painted this?" They both dash towards a small sign hung to the right of the blood painting.

"It doesn't say." Alex frowns, scanning the words printed on it. "Don't they usually say?"

"*By a local artist*," Lydia reads. "It doesn't even say when." She turns to him. "How many people saw what happened to that girl?"

"I don't know." He shakes his head, confused. "Not many. The teacher who found her, the first officers on the scene, the detectives who worked the case…" He swallows. "Her family."

"Oh my god," Lydia mutters under her breath.

"Look, I'm sure this is just a coincidence." Lydia shoots him a warning look. "Lyd, Devere's been locked up for years. If he had painted these before then, how on earth would they have got here?"

"I don't know," she breathes, taking one last look at the monstrous image before turning and heading for the door. "But I know who will."

Fifteen

A Fallen Angel

The heavy steel door slams shut behind Lydia, making her jump, the nightmare still fresh in her memory. Taking a deep breath to compose herself, she crosses to the table in the centre of the room and takes a seat.

"Can't stay away, can you?" Jason leers at her through lank curtains of hair, slumped back in his chair. Lydia's eyes flick down to his hands, manacled together in his lap, and remembers vividly the terror she felt when he clapped them around her wrists. He didn't, she reminds herself forcefully. It didn't happen.

"Tell me about Alice Redmond," she says flatly. Jason frowns, and a startling thought occurs to Lydia. *Has he forgotten her name? After what he did?*

"Alice…" he turns the word over. "Yeah, the art student."

"That's right, the girl you tortured and murdered. Tell me about her."

Jason pauses and then shrugs. "You probably know more than me." He grins. "I just killed her."

Lydia fights to hide her hatred, her teeth gritted behind pursed lips. "Are we really not past this yet?" she says, in a bored tone. "Honestly, it's like babysitting a child."

"Tell you what," Jason lifts his bound hands onto the table with a thud, and Lydia jumps again, "you promise to read me a bedtime story, and I'll tell you all about little Alice."

"We already made a deal, Jason. I held up my end. Will you hold up yours?"

"I'd love to," he nods towards his crotch, "but you'll have to take it out for me. As you can see, I'm a little…" he pulls apart the manacles until the chain between them tightens, "tied up."

Lydia tilts back her head and eyes him with supreme disdain. "You're disgusting."

"I'm whatever you want me to be," he replies, his smile fading. "Isn't that how this works?"

"What do you mean?"

Jason looks about to elaborate, but then shrugs and shakes his head instead.

"What do you mean?" Lydia repeats more forcefully.

"You didn't come to find out who I am." Jason's eyes narrow. "You came to make up a story and put me in it."

"*Make up?*"

"That's right."

"Are you denying that you did those terrible things?"

"See," Jason says quickly.

"What?"

"You've already made up your mind. You've defined me by a handful of events."

"*Events?*" Lydia stares at him, incredulous. "*You tortured children.*"

"It's not simple like that," Jason replies, with... *is that a smile? Is he smiling, fake smiling or grimacing?* She feels a powerful urge to leap over the table and strangle him for the answer.

"Complicate it for me."

"Alright." He sits back in his chair again, like a king holding court. "I will. You see, none of us is ultimately responsible for the things that we do—"

"Of course we are," Lydia interrupts, dismissively. "Who else is responsible for your actions if not you?"

"You're not seeing the big picture." He shakes his head. "We are all of us part of something much greater than ourselves. A chain of events, set in motion long before we existed and whose conclusion none of us will live to see."

"Determinism?" Lydia says, scathingly. "That's your excuse? Well it's hardly an original one." Lydia looks closer and notices Jason's now twitchy demeanour as he lowers his chin, and knows exactly what it indicates. "You don't really believe that, do you?"

"No one's truly good," he bitterly murmurs with a hint of regret.

"Most people are."

"No," Jason shakes his head sadly. "No, they're not. People are good and bad, at different times and in different ways, but the balance doesn't tip to one side. Our nature is far more mixed than we care to admit."

"You've lost me." Lydia is frowning, but less out of frustration now. Her anger has ebbed. She's genuinely curious.

"Well," Jason gazes at her, his eyes bright, "you know that Lucifer was a fallen angel, right?"

"So the story goes."

"More than a story." Jason smiles. "Why do you think we've clung on to these ideas for so long, even while technology puts them beyond credulity?"

"Tell me."

"Because on some level, we understand that they're about us." He leans forward, his voice becoming more urgent. "They explain us. The Devil used to be an angel, and God is capable of terrible things. A bringer of death. These are the dual, interchangeable characters upon which we imprint our image of ourselves. The Devil, evil. And God, good. They're one and the same. They are us."

Lydia stares at Jason Devere, as though seeing him clearly for the first time. How did this person do those things? How is he not the monster she expected him to be? How was she managing to see this humanity in a killer who had done such awful heartless things? What did it say about her?

"What were you asking me about?" Jason leans back, the expression on his face one of satisfaction, but not triumph.

"Alice Redmond," Lydia replies, the name catching in her throat. She feels like she's doing the poor girl a disservice with this whole conversation, but has no idea what to do about it.

"Ah," Jason's head falls. "Yes. Alice." He thinks for a moment, uncomfortably, then looks Lydia right in the eye as he suddenly shifted gears, now nonchalant, or at least trying to be. "I wanted to make something terrible out of something beautiful."

Crime scene photographs fresh in her mind, Lydia thinks

this is maybe the most revolting thing she has ever heard. More disgusting than the detailed coroner's reports, more disgusting even than the photographs she has seen. To hear that justification, calm, defiant, righteous even. It made her feel sick to her soul.

"You think that's art?" she asks, through gritted teeth.

"Sure," Jason replies somewhat unconvincingly now, the deep growl returning. "All art is a reflection of the artist. The girl inspired something in me, and I expressed it as best I could. Just as your work is an expression of who you are."

"No," Lydia replies flatly, getting to her feet. She's had enough. "They're just books." She turns and heads for the door.

"Oh, Lydia." Jason's voice is almost melodic as it drifts after her. "Nothing is *just* anything…"

Sixteen

New Friend

Lydia stalks through the dark, sinful corridors of Mortem Asylum that silently scream neglect and torment as though built from the living flesh of its inhabitants. Jason Devere's voice twists and turns in her mind, folding over and over itself like a writhing ball of worms as she battles to make sense of the wolf's riddles.

A shout bursts through the cacophony, ringing around the ancient building, and Lydia's eyes snap to the source of it; exactly the place that she is heading. Gretchen's office. She slows as she reaches the half-open door, stepping lightly to muffle the click of her heels on the floor, and comes to a halt just outside, out of sight, ears pricked.

"This is ridiculous," a low voice trembles. Lydia recognises the fear and disbelief it carries. From her hidden vantage, she can just make out the stout silhouette of a man.

"No," says another voice. *Gretchen*, Lydia thinks immediately. "What's ridiculous is that you're the one who's supposed to be running this institution!"

"I thought you were a doctor!" the unseen man hisses.

"I am a doctor!" Gretchen cries.

"You're not behaving very rationally," says the low voice. "I might expect this hysteria from some of the other imbeciles, but I would think you of all people might see that I am doing my best to rescue this godforsaken place."

"Doing your best?!" Gretchen's voice rises with incredulity. "Tell me one single thing you've done to help us?"

Lydia waits, but the man does not reply. Deciding that it would be unwise to get caught eavesdropping, she steps casually forward and knocks on the door. "Hello?"

"Who is it?" Gretchen snaps. Lydia moves inside the room. "Oh, Lydia," says Gretchen, her whole body relaxing. "I'm sorry; I didn't recognise your voice."

"That's quite alright," Lydia replies, eyeing up the mysterious stranger; a large, round man in a dark, pin-striped suit, polished black shoes and round, wiry spectacles perched upon a crooked nose. What little hair he has left atop his shiny head is grey and lifeless.

"Oh," says Gretchen, following Lydia's eyes. "This is Winston... I mean Mr Shade, the warden."

"Nice to meet you," says Lydia pleasantly, offering her hand. Winston Shade takes his time appraising Lydia with stern, hawk-like eyes before finally accepting it. His handshake is brief, and limp. Not a sign of weakness, but of disinterest. Of a man whose substantial body is infused with an unshakable sense of his own importance. His own superiority. A man who dominates people through sheer force of will. An alpha bully.

"The famous Lydia Tune," he replies, evidently

unimpressed. "Yes, of course. I understand you're interrogating one of our ingrates for some... book." He spits the final word with such disdain Lydia feels she ought to take it as an insult.

"That's right," she replies, pleasantly.

"Well?" asks Shade, impatiently.

"Well... what?" asks Lydia, politely confused.

"How are you getting on with it?" asks Shade, raising his voice and enunciating his words bluntly as though dealing with a stupid person.

"Um," says Lydia, blindsided by the man's shameless rudeness. "Slowly."

The warden rolls his eyes, glares at Gretchen, and makes for the door, brushing Lydia aside with his belly.

"I couldn't help but overhear," says Lydia quickly. Shade stops dead in his tracks. "I understand that Mortem has something of a troubled reputation," Lydia goes on, choosing her words carefully. "I would hate for my book to have to reinforce that."

Winston Shade turns his head towards her slowly, his face a mask of supreme indifference. "Miss Tune," he replies, "I highly doubt that anybody whose opinion matters to me would so much as glance at one of your books." Lydia's eyebrows raise halfway up her forehead. "I will speak to *you* later," Shade says to Gretchen before striding from the room, snapping the door shut behind him.

"Charming fellow," says Lydia, turning to Gretchen. The doctor blinks, then laughs.

"You don't know the half of it," she says, removing her glasses to rub her tired eyes. "You caught him on one of his better days."

"Goodness," says Lydia, glancing towards the door, wondering with modest alarm what Winston Shade might be like on one of his bad days.

"How did your interview with Jason go?" Gretchen asks, replacing her glasses. "Sorry I couldn't be there."

"It was…" Lydia considers the question, "good. Better than the first one anyway. I think we're making progress."

"I think he likes you, you know."

"He talked to you about me?" Lydia asks, surprised.

"Oh, yes. Nice trick with the fire alarm by the way. Where did you pick that up?"

"I can't even remember," says Lydia with a smile. "I believe it's a trick the police like to use when they're interviewing suspects."

Gretchen nods approvingly. "I might pinch that one myself." She reaches for a heavy green coat on the back of the door and pulls it on.

"Off home?"

"Yeah, have to relieve the sitter and I'm already…" she checks the time on her phone, "damn, he knew I was in a hurry and he still…" she sighs through clenched teeth. "I'd better call." Gretchen lifts the phone to her ear with one hand and holds the office door open for Lydia with the other. "Hey Laurie, I'm sorry, I'm running a little bit late." She closes the door behind the both of them and fishes a bunch of keys from her pocket with which to lock it. "I know, I know, I'm sorry. I'll be there as soon as I can and I'll pay you for an extra two hours, okay?" She sets off down the corridor so quickly that Lydia has to break into a trot to catch up. "Okay, see you soon. Sorry again." She hangs up and stuffs the phone into her pocket as the two women enter the elevator and Gretchen pulls the heavy metal gate across with a loud rattle and a clang.

"Everything okay?" Lydia asks, cautiously.

"No." Gretchen sighs, falling back against the wall as the metal box shudders and begins to sink slowly. "I mean yes, it's just, this is the second time this week I've been late home. If I lose another babysitter..."

"Surely she expects you to be a little late now and then?"

"Ha!"

"No?"

"She's a teenager. She thinks the whole world is conspiring to piss her off." Gretchen looks over at Lydia. "Don't you remember being a teenager?"

"I try not to."

Gretchen smiles. "Yeah? Not me." She stares down at the ground, her eyes distant. "Happiest time of my life."

Lydia instinctively finds this a bizarre notion, but then she thinks about the building they're in and what it contains, looks at the doctor with her tired face and slumped shoulders, and tries to imagine living her life. Day in, day out, working a job she clearly resents in this hell-hole of a building to support children who probably don't even appreciate it. She shudders involuntarily as the elevator creaks to a halt and Gretchen heaves open the gate.

Once again Lydia finds herself left behind as Gretchen crosses the reception area and pulls open the great wooden door. The frozen talons of winter night sink themselves into Lydia's flesh before she even steps outside.

"Are you here tomorrow?" Gretchen asks as the gravel crunches loudly underneath their feet.

"I don't know yet. I should start writing or Donna will be on my back again."

"Donna?" Gretchen looks confused.

"My agent."

"How glamorous." Gretchen fishes her car keys from her pocket and makes for a little brown hatchback that has seen considerably better days. "Well, see you then maybe."

"See you."

Lydia hears Gretchen's car door open and close as she heads for her Mustang, then the loud, hoarse wretch of an engine struggling to start. It chokes and splutters for a few seconds, falls silent, and then tries again with the same result. She looks around, then walks back towards the stricken vehicle as its increasingly frantic owner attempts to coax it into life for the third time.

"Battery?" Lydia asks as a miserable Gretchen winds down her window.

"No, it had a new one last year. God damn it." She slams the steering wheel with her wrist and grimaces in pain.

"Want a ride?"

"Really?" The doctor looks so pathetically grateful that it makes Lydia laugh.

"Sure. Come on."

Seventeen

Girl Talk

The floor of Gretchen's living room is covered with toys, books, and the occasional garish, plastic dish or cup. Lydia stands by the door in her coat, trying to decide whether to pick her way through the wreckage to the couch or stay where she is. Out in the hall, she can hear Gretchen still apologising to the teenage babysitter.

"Sorry again. I'll see you tomorrow, right?" The response is mumbled, and a moment later the front door closes.

"Everything okay?" Lydia calls over her shoulder.

"Yes, thank god." Gretchen appears beside her and starts picking up bits and pieces of clutter and throwing them into a large, rectangular fabric container to the side of the room. "I don't know what I would have done if she'd said no. It's not like I can just take a day off. We're severely understaffed as it is."

"Is that what you were arguing with the warden about?" Gretchen's head snaps around to look at her, and Lydia realises she may have overstepped her bounds. She always has trouble in social situations. If Gretchen were a subject she was interviewing, Lydia would instinctively know where the boundaries were, when she could push or break them and when to pull back. Not now. *You're in her home,* she scolds herself. *The rules are different.* "Sorry, I didn't mean to pry."

"No, it's okay." Gretchen sets the small stack of books in her hands down on the coffee table. "It's just a bit... you know."

"Yeah." Lydia understands. To be overheard receiving a dressing-down from your boss is embarrassing. She had accidentally robbed Gretchen of her professional dignity, and now here she was intruding on the chaos of her private life too. "I'm sorry, I should go."

"No, please," Gretchen looks at her earnestly, "at least stay for dinner. It's the least I can do."

She doesn't really want to, but the poor woman's eyes are pleading and her voice sincere, and together they conspire to melt Lydia's frozen heart just enough. "Alright. Sure."

"Great." Gretchen beams. "I hope you like reheated lasagne."

An hour, two plates of pretty decent lasagne and half a bottle of wine later, Gretchen pinches the stem of her glass between finger and thumb and swirls the deep red liquid within gently as she talks. "So then after he left, I didn't really have much of a choice. Mortgage to pay and two kids to feed."

"You never thought about applying for a job somewhere else? Someplace a little less..."

"Nightmarish?"

"I was going to say depressing, but..."

"Please, I work there. I know what it's like." Gretchen takes another sip of wine. "I mean I do my best to keep both parts of my life separate, you know? Like, work Gretchen and home Gretchen. Doctor and mom. But the human brain doesn't work that way. You can't voluntarily compartmentalise stuff."

"It must be hard." Lydia sips from a glass of water and resists the urge to check her phone for messages from Alex.

"You know what the worst part is?" Gretchen sits back and looks her right in the eye. "I'm terrified that I'm going to bring some of that evil, some of the wickedness that infects that place home with me, and pass it on to them." She nods towards the ceiling.

"How would you even do that?"

"I don't know." Gretchen shakes her head. "It sounds crazy, doesn't it? But I swear, some days I feel like I'm carrying something around with me. Clinging to me. Something dark."

"If you like, I could put a good word in for you at this private hospital in New York? I'm sure with your experience they could find a place for you."

"Really?" Gretchen's whole face lights up, and Lydia catches a glimpse of how beautiful she must have been before life extracted its terrible toll.

"Sure, I'll call them tomorrow."

Gretchen's eyes drift lazily off to one side and slip out of focus, and Lydia knows why. She's imagining another life. A better life. A parallel universe where she's happy again.

Then her smile disappears, and her face falls. "No," she says quietly. "It wouldn't work."

"Why not?"

"I'm already underwater on this house, bills, a pile of credit card debt. I'd have to pull together the deposit for a new place, and in *New York*? I mean…" She waves a hand helplessly.

"New York's more than the Upper East Side and Carnegie Hill, you know. I'm sure we could find you someplace."

"We?" Gretchen grins at her. "What, are you my realtor now?"

"I'm just saying—"

"Thanks," Gretchen stops her. "I appreciate it, I do. But it's…" a strange look overtakes her face, a haunted look that Lydia has seen somewhere before. "It's not a good time."

Lydia hesitates. "Something else going on at Mortem I should know about?"

"The less you know about that place the better," Gretchen replied firmly. "Trust me, if you have any sense, you'll chalk this whole trip down to experience and go write your book about something else."

"That's what he said," Lydia mutters, rolling her eyes. "Everyone knows what's best for me except me, I guess."

"Who?"

"Huh?"

"You said that's what he said. Who is he?"

"Oh," Lydia's hand moves instinctively towards her chest, fidgeting when she thinks of Alex, but she checks herself. "Just this detective I spoke to about Jason's—"

"Horrendous trail of gore and misery?"

"Case."

"Right." Gretchen's green eyes twinkle. "Tall fella? Brown eyes?"

"Yeah…" Lydia frowns. "How did you know?"

"I remember him visiting Jason a lot when he first arrived. Alex, right?"

"That's him."

"He's cute."

Lydia fixes Gretchen with a look, but she can't help cracking a smile and Gretchen grins back. "Actually we went to school together, back in Philly."

"Small world."

"Yeah." Lydia's phone rings, and her hand shoots to her bag to fetch it out. "Speak of the devil," she says, seeing Alex's name on the screen. "Do you mind?" Gretchen waves an open hand, still grinning like a schoolgirl, and Lydia is torn between amusement and mild irritation as she lifts the phone to her ear. "Hey, we were just talking abo—"

"Lydia," Alex interrupts her, his voice strained and distant. Is that the line, or is that him? "Something's happened."

Lydia's expression tightens, her voice suddenly sharp. "What? What's wrong? Are you okay?"

"I'm fine, but you need to see… you need to come…"

"You're breaking up." Lydia stands up, frowning. "Where am I supposed to come?"

"The museum."

"The museum… where we were today?" She sounds surprised. What the hell is going on?

"Yes. Come to the front entrance. Tell them I asked for you."

"Alex, what's going on?"

"Please," the line crackles. "Just come."

"Alright." She hangs up.

"What's going on?" asks Gretchen.

"I don't know." Lydia lifts her leather jacket off the back of her chair and pulls it on. "He wants me to come to the museum."

"Of modern art?" Gretchen looks as confused as Lydia feels.

"Yeah, we were there today and…" She frowns. "I don't know, I guess something happened. I'm sorry to dash off like this."

"No, it's fine." Gretchen gets up and walks her to the door. "I hope everything's okay."

"I'm sure it is." Lydia pauses on the threshold. "I mean, why else would a man I've barely seen in twenty years demand that I meet him at a creepy museum in the middle of the night?"

"You know what men are like," Gretchen replies, casually. "Maybe it's some ill-conceived romantic gesture."

"Maybe." Lydia considers the proposition. "You know," she eyes Gretchen suspiciously, "for a woman who does what you do, you have a remarkable talent for optimism."

"I know. It's my best quality." Gretchen beams, and once again, for just a second, she looks ten years younger. "Take care, and thanks for the ride."

Lydia's thoughts have already turned to Alex before she reaches her car, running through various scenarios that might lead him to summon her to the museum in the middle of the night, each more unlikely than the last. But amidst her worry and confusion, she is distantly aware that Gretchen is still standing in the doorway watching her even as the red sports car pulls into the street and, with a low growl, accelerates off into the winter night.

Eighteen

An Artistic Endeavour

The pulse of eerie blue light in the atmosphere gives Lydia advance warning of the police presence long before she arrives, but the size of it still gives her an unpleasant shock. Five cars and two vans are blocking the street and at least a dozen officers, some ushering a crowd of curious bystanders away but most just standing around. As her Mustang crawls towards the barricade, one of them, a young man with neat blond hair, approaches her window.

"Have to take the long way around." He gestures back the way she's come from and then off to the left.

"I'm here to see Detective Gilbey," Lydia replies. "I'm Lydia Tune."

"Who?" The officer frowns.

"Lydia Tune." Lydia feels her cheeks warm with embarrassment. "I'm a writer."

"No press allowed right now." Again, he points back down the road.

"He's expecting me."

The young officer crouches and peers at her, then reaches for a radio on his belt. "Sarge, you got the detective with you?"

Silence, then the radio hisses. "Yeah."

"There's a woman here says he's expecting her."

"Tell her to meet him at the Motel 6 like the rest of 'em."

The officer smirks, his eyes travelling down Lydia's front, and she has to bite back the urge to snap at him. The radio hisses again, but this time the voice coming from it is Alex's. "Let her in."

"Copy that," the officer replies, still smirking. "Go ahead." He jerks his thumb towards the entrance and walks away. As Lydia parks, she sees him rejoin his group, who all laugh and look over at her. She mutters a curse under her breath, gets out of the car, pulls her leather jacket tight around her and heads for the entrance, ducking underneath hastily erected black and yellow crime scene tape.

Inside, the building has a very different atmosphere than earlier in the day. Lit only by dim emergency lights, the rooms feel smaller, the ceilings lower. Large, boxy stands and cases cast dark shadows, and paintings that were bright and colourful look drained and melancholy. *Where is everybody? Where am I supposed to go?*

Following the same path that she and Alex took through the exhibits, she catches the swinging beam of a flashlight and hears low voices through a doorway ahead. *The blood room.* Lydia's heart beats faster as she moves towards it, then explodes in a frenzy when she sees what lies beyond.

In the middle of the room, faced by all three giant paintings that remind Lydia of gushing wounds, a new display has been erected. Atop a cylindrical plinth, a grotesque creature posed in a crouched position. Its body is human; loose, greying skin hanging and folding, pierced all over with giant, plucked feathers. Arms outstretched like sick parodies of wings. And where a human head used to be, the head of a golden eagle skewered onto the top of the spine, beak wide open, black eyes bulging.

Lydia retches violently, her legs giving way beneath her, and a strong hand catches her arm as she begins to fall.

"I got you."

Before she knows what is happening, Alex's arms are around her. She closes her eyes and breathes deeply. "I'm okay." He releases his grip, and she looks around at him. "Who..." She can't bring herself to finish the question, or look around again at the mutilated body.

Alex looks at her for a long moment, as if trying to decide how to answer. Then his eyes move up and to the left, and he jerks his head slightly. Lydia looks, a sucking void in the pit of her stomach.

Above the door she came in through, a human head has been mounted like a trophy, its eyes and mouth wide mirroring the expression of the bird. Lydia recognises it at once as Dorothy Eagle.

"She's—" she begins.

"Devere's old teacher," Alex finishes. "I know."

"I met her." The sight of the old woman's gaping face causes cold waves of horror to crash over Lydia, but she can't tear her eyes away from it. "Three days ago."

"Yeah, we're gonna need to talk about that." Alex puts a hand on her shoulder to bring her attention back to him. "On the record, you understand?"

Lydia blinks at him. "Of course. Now?"

"If you're up to it. The quicker we can gather information, the better our chances of catching whoever did this before they strike again."

"Again?" Lydia's eyes dart involuntarily to the half-human, half-bird monstrosity, crouched in a pool of congealing blood.

"I'm sure it's a copycat." Alex follows her gaze, a grim look on his face. "Some sick freak picking up where Devere left off. Happens more than you'd think, idiots trying to glorify killers as if they're celebrities or something. Like they have a fan base!"

A thought occurs to Lydia that makes her already-chilled blood freeze. "Why her?" she asks, looking at Alex, her eyes wide. "Why now? Do you think they know that I…"

"I don't know." He shakes his head. "But you're not going anywhere without a police escort for a while."

"Alex." Even in these circumstances, Lydia bucks at the notion of having to be protected. "That's not—"

"Negotiable. So get used to the idea."

"I'm not some damsel in distress you have to save, Alex!"

"I know you're not. You're about one of the only few people I actually do consider my equal."

Lydia's jaw tenses. "I can handle myself."

"I know you can!" Alex states, gripping her by the shoulders now. "But, I just don't want you to have to be put in that sort of situation, any situation." Lydia notes the sincerity in his tone as he gazes away, letting her go. "I'll have a couple of officers take you back to the station and then, when we're done, to a hotel. A different one."

"But—"

"I'll have someone fetch your things. You can't go

back there. If whoever did this has been watching you…"
He doesn't finish the thought. He doesn't have to. Lydia
remembers her dream, being bound to that table, the
glinting steel blade rushing towards her eyes.

"Alright." She looks down at the floor, visions of this
poor woman's final moments flashing through her brain at
lightning speed, like an old projector.

A stocky, grey-haired officer enters the room and approaches
them, unnerved eyes fixed upon the grim spectacle, and
murmurs in Alex's ear. "Forensics here."

"Okay," Alex replies, then as the man starts to walk
away, "oh hey, Jack, can you take Lydia back to the
station and get her some coffee? I'll be along soon."

"You bet." He puts a large, gentle hand on Lydia's arm
and gestures towards the door with the other.

"Soon?" Lydia looks back towards Alex as she lets the
officer guide her towards the exit.

"You're going to be alright," he says, summoning a forced
smile. "I promise."

The hollow words echo inside Lydia's head as she turns
and leaves the room, spilling out into the dim, cavernous
halls of the museum as she passes through, fading, dispersing,
until finally escaping like smoke into the black night.

Nineteen

An Early Christmas Gift

It's still dark when Lydia emerges from the police station next morning, but a deep grey dark rather than pitch black. Dawn approaches. The young officer with blond hair follows her out, swinging a set of keys in his hand.

"Four Seasons, miss?" He tips an imaginary hat as he opens the rear door of the police car. *Is he still mocking me?*

"I have to go somewhere else first."

He frowns. "The detective said—"

"I heard what he said. We'll go to the hotel, but I need to check on a friend of mine first."

"Who?"

"I'll tell you on the way." She climbs into the back seat, and the young man mouths a silent curse before closing the door after her.

The roads are quiet as they head north out of the city. High-rise blocks become terraces, terraces become detached houses and bungalows, all sprinkled with the colourful trappings of the season. *Gaudy never sleeps.* On Lydia's instruction, the car bears right and then along a winding road lined with wrought-iron gates and homes set back out of sight. "Here," she says, leaning forward and pointing to an entrance ahead and to the left.

The gravel of the driveway crunches under the tyres, then under Lydia's feet as she pushes open the door and steps out even before the car has come to a complete stop. "Hey," the officer calls after her, "hang on." But she's already hopping up the rotten, wooden steps to Cecil Sprinkler's front door. She knocks with bony knuckles, and presses the bell firmly with a crimson-clawed finger.

"Cecil?" Lydia calls towards the nearest window.

"He's probably asleep," says the officer in a weary voice, catching up with her. His eyes are sleepy, his movements sluggish. Thanks for the bodyguard, Alex, she thinks, rolling her eyes.

"Cecil!" Lydia shouts louder this time, hammering on the door again.

"Steady." The officer makes a grab for her hand, but Lydia whips it away in time. "You'll wake the whole street."

"I don't care. We're not leaving until I see him, so either help or get out of my way."

The young man looks annoyed, but seems to decide that arguing will only keep him from his bed longer, because he sighs and then calls out, "Mr. Sprinkler? Are you there? It's Decanten PD."

"Cecil!" Lydia stabs at the doorbell again once, twice, three times.

"Maybe he's not home."

"This man hasn't left his house in years," Lydia mutters, leaning to the window on the other side of the door and rapping on it hard.

"What's so urgent anyway? Does he know something about what's happened?"

Lydia doesn't reply. She doesn't want to voice her fears out loud, that would only make them more real. Instead she crouches down by the door and fishes the slim, metal lockpick from her purse.

"What the hell are you doing?" The officer stares in disbelief as she jams the instrument into the lock and manoeuvres it just-so. "You wanna go back to the station in cuffs?"

"I'm sure you've let worse slide."

"Well, yeah," he admits, "but usually I get something out of it."

"I'll buy you an ice cream." The lock clicks and Lydia wrenches the handle, darting inside before the young man can try to stop her. She heads down the hall into the living room, eyes peeled for any sign of trouble, anything that looks out of place. But everything from the books on the floor to the photographs on the shelves seems to still be covered by that thick layer of dust. She opens the study door and looks inside. No sign of life. No sign of a struggle.

"I swear if you steal anything, I'm bringing you in," says the officer, hot on her heels. Lydia turns and brushes past him on her way back to the hall. She looks up the stairs to the dark landing above and steels herself. Every one creaks loudly, as she knew they would, but she takes them quickly and in a moment is on a narrow landing with three doors off it.

She tries the first, a small bathroom with olive green

fixtures. Clean, but musty-smelling. Ancient soaps wrapped in a dish on the sink. Lydia backs out and opens the second door into a room with two slim, single beds covered in boxes full of clutter. This must be the spare room. Lydia scans it for anything odd before retreating and moving to the third room.

She takes a deep breath before pushing open the door, and a shock of fear rips up her spine. The silence is oppressive, gnawing at her nerves. She steps forward into the room, fumbling for the light switch as she does so. It clicks, and for a second the warm yellow light is blinding. Then as her eyes adjust, she sees a neat, perfectly made bed with a folded green towel on top and a pair of slippers on the floor next to it. On the bedside table sits an old carriage clock, its hands unmoving, alongside a photograph of Cecil and his wife, again thick with the dust. Lydia stretches out a hand to pick it up, when a loud noise makes her scream and spin around.

On the window ledge, a Christmas ornament, a snow globe on a stand about the size of a cantaloupe, is lit up and playing music, rotating slowly as it does so. Lydia's eyes dart around the room, to the door, and then back to the globe. *White Christmas*, she thinks, the object's hollow, metallic chimes barely recognisable as the warm, comforting tune that she knows.

"What's going on up there?" the officer calls up the stairs. Lydia doesn't answer. She can't find her voice. Instead she inches closer to the ornament, staring at it, the hair on the back of her neck prickling. Inside the glass sphere is a house made of red brick, with a pointed roof and tall, arched windows like eyes.

A creak on the landing sends a fresh chill rippling across Lydia's skin, but she can't tear her eyes away from the house. "What did you find?" The young officer steps into the room behind her. "Is he here? What's that?" Lydia reaches out and picks up the ornament. It's warm to the touch. "What did I say about stealing?" He moves to her shoulder. "Go on then, give it a shake."

Every fibre of Lydia's being is screaming at her not to, but her hands seem to be acting of their own free will. As though in slow motion, they tip the globe back and then jerk it sharply upright again. Instead of snow, thick, blood-red clouds engulf the tiny house, spreading quickly to fill the glass sphere as the eerie music scrapes out of tune, then grinds to a halt.

Twenty

Against the World

"I want to go to Mortem." Lydia leans forward between the front seats of the police car, trying not to look at the blood-filled globe lying on the passenger seat.

"I'm taking you to the hotel," the young officer replies. He looks shaken.

"I need to talk to—"

"I have orders to put you in your hotel room and that's what I'm going to do." He puts his foot down and the car accelerates smoothly along the downtown street. The traffic is picking up now as people start to head out to work.

"Take me to my car then, I'll drive myself."

"Did you hear what I said?" He glances at her with a fed-up expression.

"I'll just get a cab then." Lydia falls back onto the seat, arms folded.

"They won't let you into that place today anyway, it's on lockdown." He turns down the main street.

"What do you mean?"

"I mean the detective's going there to see Devere, and nobody else will be getting in until he says so."

Lydia pulls her phone from her bag and dials Alex's number. It goes straight to voicemail. She remembers the thick, stone walls and heavy steel doors of Mortem. If he's already in there, she won't be able to reach him. Fuck.

The car pulls over in front of the Four Seasons, a decadent hotel clad in gold and marble, and Lydia throws open the door.

"Don't try running," the officer calls, unfastening his seatbelt, "I'm really not in the mood." He tries leading her by the arm, but Lydia shakes him off with a glare. "Fine, follow me then."

Inside, two more officers are waiting for them; the older man Lydia recognises from the museum, and a squat young woman with short hair she doesn't know. "Miss Tune," her bodyguard announces, "this is Officer Zeiss and Officer Ramirez; they'll do their best to keep you alive while you're here. You can help them by staying in your room and not going off playing detective anymore. We've got real detectives for that." He exchanges smirks with his colleagues.

"Room 212." The female officer hands Lydia a key attached to a heavy block of wood about the size of a candy bar. "We'll be right outside, so if you need anything just ask."

"Am I under arrest?"

"Think of it as protective custody." The officer smiles. Lydia rolls her eyes and heads for the elevator.

*

The bed in Lydia's room is vast and soft, and sinks invitingly when she falls onto it, but her brain is far too busy for sleep. So much has happened in the last twenty-four hours and she feels like the pieces of the puzzle are so close to fitting together if she can only organise her thoughts. She heaves herself up and fetches her suitcase from where the officers have left it near the door, lifting it up and onto the bed and zipping it open. Sitting right there on top of a messy wad of clothes and shoes is her laptop. She carries it to a table by the window, sits down, and opens it up.

I should start writing, or Donna will be on my back again. Lydia's own words come drifting back to her, and she pops open her word processor. Maybe if she orders events on the page, the links will become clearer. She rests her fingers on the keys and begins to type, remembering her arrival at Mortem that first night in as much detail as she can, her impression of the building as a living, breathing organism with a malevolent spirit, the people inside of it; Charlotte, the receptionist and Gretchen, both women drained of their youth and vitality by a force more potent than age or exhaustion. It was that place. As if it was feeding on them.

Lydia's fingers skim the keys rapidly, the soft clicking soothing her like raindrops on a windowsill. She renders the events, the descriptions, the feelings as vividly as she can, but tiredness is pressing on her mind and she begins to slow, to struggle. *I need coffee. And food.* She glances towards the phone. *Room service?* No, they won't have what she's craving. Then her eyes slide to the door. *We'll be right outside if you need anything.* A slow smile creeps across Lydia's face. *May as well make the best of this.*

An hour later, Lydia crumples the greasy, empty wrapper

of a double cheeseburger and tosses it into the trash before picking up a massive cup of coffee and taking a big gulp. That's better. Junk food has healing properties. She sets the coffee down and turns her attention back to the screen.

Her tale has stalled on the second day, because every time she tries to recall her meeting with Dorothy Eagle, she relives the horror of seeing her mutilated corpse. Only in Lydia's mind, the severed bird's head turns to stare at her, its eyes accusing, its mouth screaming a silent curse. Was it her fault? If she had never come here, never met with the teacher, would Dorothy still be alive? Would Cecil Sprinkler be at home right now, making himself tea and toast in his musty kitchen or polishing those green apples for the hundredth time? Is she the catalyst for what's happening? What is happening?

In search of distraction, she checks her phone. Nothing. Should she try calling again? If Alex gets out of Mortem and sees a dozen missed calls, he might think something's wrong. *Leave it. He'll call when he can. He does care.* She picks up the remote that's lying on the table and flicks it at the television on the wall, scanning the listings for a local news channel. Are they covering the murder? Nope, nothing. The citizens of Decanten have no idea that the Krimson Killer Mark Two is on the loose. Maybe they're better off not knowing.

Lydia mutes the TV and turns her attention back to her computer. The cursor blinks at her impatiently, right where she left off. She begins a new sentence just to make it stop, but the words are all wrong and the ring finger of her right hand stretches for the backspace key. Why is this so difficult? *Just write it like it happened.* But her own brain is fighting her now, stubbornly refusing to finish a thought, drowning in ideas and theories. And fears. That's new. She flexes her fingers, and her ruby ring glimmers darkly, catching her eye. And then she is lost in it, drawn right into the gemstone, its interior an endless, shapeless expanse of deep reds that flow and shift like the clouds of blood in the snow globe. It speaks to her in a language no human being ever uttered, but she understands. She is not a victim. That's not her role. This is wrong. She needs to be out. She needs to hunt.

Her head snaps back, eyes wide as she frees herself violently from the creeping tendrils of sleep and tries to focus again upon the words on the screen, forcing her mind to seek the thread of the story and pick it up again. But it is elusive. So much of writing is momentum. Once you lose it, you're lost.

Idly, Lydia's fingers slide the cursor over to her browser icon. She pops it open and navigates to her Facebook page. She rarely posts herself, but the lure of other people's lives is irresistible. She begins to scroll, every photograph an opportunity to silently judge somebody she once knew for their life choices. *He married her? Talk about settling, that won't last.* Or maybe it will. Easier to make do when you've given up. Everyone reaches that point eventually. *Even me. I wonder when that will be.* Picture after picture of identical babies with their stupid, blank expressions. Why are people so proud of these things? It's hardly a challenge to make one; they cost a fortune, shit themselves and wake you up in the middle of the night. Of the human minds' many quirks and intricacies, the desire to have children is perhaps the one she understands the least.

Lydia taps in the search box and enters Alex's name,

scrolling the profiles until she sees his picture. Like her, he doesn't post much. Just a handful of pictures; first day in uniform, a vacation in Mexico. That must be his wife. Ex-wife. She's pretty. Not as pretty as me. Lydia smiles and takes another sip of coffee. After the shock of the last twenty-four hours, her confidence is returning. She's remembering who she is, and what she's capable of. A strange warmth spreading into her fingers, she swaps back to her manuscript and begins to type.

It's hours later when the sharp beep of a text message breaks Lydia's trance, yanking her abruptly out of her story. For a second, as she reaches for the phone, she even forgets that she was desperate to make contact with Alex, but seeing his name on the screen brings a rush of excitement with it. She slides her finger across to read the message.

Hope you're okay. Done here soon. Meet you at the hotel.

Hmm, she thinks, with a sly smile. That's nice, but I have a better idea. Alex may be the law, but he isn't in charge of her. This weak sideshow has gone on long enough, and a plan is hatching in her devious mind. She opens her contacts and taps the 'AAA' right at the top.

"Hello? Yes, my car broke down. I need it towed from outside of the Decanten Museum of Modern Art to Mortem Asylum as soon as possible. It's a red Mustang…" She crosses to the door as she gives the details, picking her coat up from a chair on the way, and opens it to find the two police officers leaning against the hallway wall, mid-conversation.

"You need something, Miss Tune?" the old man asks,

noticing her first. Lydia holds up one finger while she finishes her call.

"Okay, great. Thanks." She hangs up. "I just spoke to Detective Gilbey," she tells them, straight-faced. "He wants me to meet him at Mortem."

The police officers exchange doubtful looks. "The detective gave us strict orders to stay here," says the plump woman. "I don't think—"

"Call him." Lydia bluffs. The officer looks at her, shrugs and takes out her phone. "Voicemail," she says a moment later to her colleague, and they both look at Lydia again.

"It's important," Lydia says, pulling on her coat and closing the hotel room door behind her. "Shall we?"

The older officer puffs out his cheeks with a sigh. "I guess…"

"Wonderful." Lydia heads towards the elevator, making sure that she's past them both before she allows herself a smirk.

Twenty-One

Creature of the Night

"Is Doctor Engel here?" Lydia asks in a hushed voice, leaning across the reception desk.

"Yes," Charlotte replies, "would you like me to call her down?"

"No, that's okay. I know my way to her office."

"Guests aren't really allowed—" the receptionist begins, frowning.

"She's expecting me." Lydia looks back into Charlotte's face, trying to gauge her reaction. "You could let her know I'm on my way up, if you like." She turns away before the girl can answer, and crosses to the two officers waiting by the door. "You're off the hook," she says, with the air of someone presenting a generous gift. "I'll get a ride back with Alex."

Again, they exchange looks. "We should really wait," says the female officer.

"How long have you been on duty?" Lydia asks the man,

who looks the more exhausted of the two. He checks his watch.

"About eighteen hours now."

"And how much overtime do you think they're going to kick out for sitting around here waiting for me?"

"She's got a point," says the woman.

"Alright," the man agrees, somewhat reluctantly. "If the detective changes his mind, he can call us. We have to go back to the station first anyway."

"Thanks again," Lydia calls over her shoulder, already on her way to the elevator.

Gretchen's office door is closed, but there's light spilling from underneath. Pressing her ear gently to it, Lydia can hear muffled voices within; one male, one female. The warden again? No, a younger voice. It's Alex. She listens hard.

"It's the same shit all over again," Alex complains. "I can't tell whether he knows anything or not."

"How could he?" asks Gretchen, sounding quite exasperated. "He doesn't have contact with the outside world, no newspapers, no television, letters, phone calls, nothing."

"What if someone here is passing messages for him?"

"What are you suggesting?" Gretchen's voice rises. "That one of our staff murdered this woman?" Alex doesn't reply, at least audibly. "Do you think I killed her? Because I have a witness who was with me all night."

"That's true." Lydia opens the door, knocking on it as an afterthought. "She was with me yesterday evening when you called."

"What the hell are you doing here?" Alex rounds on her at once. "I said I'd meet you at the hotel. Where are the officers who were supposed to be watching you?"

"I sent them home," she replies coolly, stepping into the room and perching herself on the corner of Gretchen's desk, facing him.

"What do you mean you sent them home?" Alex looks incredulous. "They're supposed to take their orders from me, not you. I swear—"

"They've been on for eighteen hours, Alex, they need to sleep."

"So do I, but I'm not about to just wander off and abandon my responsibilities." He's practically yelling now.

"They didn't abandon anything," Lydia says, calmly. "I said I sent them away. I'm not under arrest and I'm not a prisoner, and you need to calm down." She turns to Gretchen before Alex has a chance to reply. "Can I see Jason?"

"He's been in the interview room for hours already today," Gretchen replies, eyeing Alex warily. Is he giving her a warning look? Lydia feels a rush of contempt for him. "I don't know how far we should push him."

"It won't take long." Lydia moves towards her, looking directly into the doctor's eyes and summoning as much earnestness as she can. "Please. It's important."

Gretchen sighs. She looks from Lydia to Alex and back again as though trying to decide who she least wishes to anger, then says finally, "Alright. Ten minutes."

"Thank you." Lydia beams.

"Do I get a say in this?" asks Alex, brusquely.

"Why would you?" Lydia gives him a cool look. She

does like him, but the macho protector routine is kind of a turn-off.

"Because it's my investigation."

"Oh, is he a suspect?" Lydia turns towards him, arms folded. "I'm sure we'd both be interested to hear your theory about how he broke out of here, murdered a woman, staged a display of frankly pretty sloppy taxidermy and then snuck back in completely unnoticed."

Gretchen covers her mouth with her hand and looks away quickly.

"Fine," Alex replies, spreading his hands to signal that he's had enough. "Get yourself killed. You're all as stubborn as each other."

"All who, exactly?" Lydia glares at him dangerously, but Alex seems to know better than to answer that. Instead he leaves the room without another word, slamming the door behind him.

"Speaking of stubborn," Gretchen murmurs.

"Seriously." Lydia turns to her. "Thank you for this."

"No problem." Gretchen smiles. "But let's get on with it before Shade finds out." Lydia frowns at her, confused. "The warden," Gretchen explains, fetching her keys from a drawer. "He's not happy about all this attention. I think he'd rather like to see the back of you."

Jason Devere tugs restlessly at his chains as Lydia enters the cold, white room. He stops when he sees her, that familiar wolf smile creeping across his face. "Well well," he growls softly. "Here comes the good cop."

"Why would you think that?" Lydia asks, taking the seat opposite and looking calmly back at him.

"Because that cop doesn't have the temperament for it." Lydia grins before she can catch herself. She looks away, but it's too late. "Aha," Jason's voice is smooth and gleeful, "you two know each other." He leans forward over the table and whispers, "How well, I wonder?"

"Don't play the shrink, Jason." Lydia gives him a pitying look. "You don't have the training."

"How do you know?"

"I know all about you." She leans forward, knowing by now that his chains aren't long enough to let him reach her. "I spoke to your teacher, remember? The one who was killed last night."

"Not by me," he shows off his manacles, "if that's what you're implying."

"Of course not. But you do know who did it."

"How would I?"

Lydia looks placidly back at him. She doesn't know that yet, so the question is best left unanswered. "I presume Detective Gilbey told you what happened to her?"

"Do you call him detective in the bedroom, too?" Jason sneers.

"Jealous?" Lydia smirks.

"Don't flatter yourself."

"You didn't answer the question."

"Neither did you." Jason stares her down, defiantly.

"You were fond of her, weren't you?"

"Not especially." He slumps back and looks around, his foot tapping on the smooth, grey floor. He is tired. "Besides, that was a long time ago."

"What about your friend, Cecil?" Lydia watches him closely for a reaction, and she gets it. For a split second Jason's pupils dilate. Fear. He's worried about his old friend. He's not directing this show. *She knew it*. But he does know something he's not telling.

"What about him?"

"I went to see him this morning," Lydia replies, casually.

"So what?"

"He wasn't home."

"That's a great story, Lydia, truly. No wonder you sell so many books."

"It's a little odd, actually," Lydia presses on, ignoring the sarcasm. "Because I got the distinct impression that he'd hardly left his house for years. Did you know that?"

"I didn't know, and I don't care," Jason replies, irritably. "Listen, if you're the good cop aren't you supposed to offer me a drink, or a blowjob or something?" He leers at her.

"I'm not a cop," Lydia replies with her sweetest smile. "If you're thirsty, you should let a guard know."

"I like you less every time we meet," he growls.

"I have that effect on people." She smiles, getting to her feet. "Goodnight, Jason."

"Hey," he calls after her as she heads for the door. "Tell your boyfriend I don't know anything."

"That makes two of you," she replies, without looking back.

Lydia makes quick time through Mortem's maze of haunted corridors, back towards the cavernous foyer where she finds a man sitting in the waiting area. He is wearing a smart grey suit and his posture is upright and elegant. An immaculately groomed moustache that harks back to the turn of the century; cigarette cases and old sepia photographs. As she passes, he lifts his head and meets her eyes with his pale blue ones. His gaze is powerful, so much so that it causes Lydia's breath to catch in her throat. She returns his polite smile, and continues on her way outside.

Sheet ice covers the car park under a thick, grey sky, snow falling heavily as Lydia picks her way carefully to the car that she is relieved to find has arrived safely. The lamp posts that line the drive are flickering, and the vines coiling and grasping around the building seem to be pulsing, shifting, tightening their grip. The world is on edge. A shape at the very top of Mortem catches her eye, something shifting atop the roof, a figure she can't quite make out in the darkness. Its shadow ripples and expands, like a vast bird stretching its wings, and then in a moment it is gone.

Do you ever feel like you're being watched?

Jason's words echo in Lydia's mind and she glances around, fishing in her pocket for her keys. But her hands fumble in the cold and she drops them next to the front wheel of the car.

You're being paranoid, she scolds herself as she feels her fight or flight reflex kick in, her heart race, her breath quicken. She bends down and reaches for the keys with quaking fingers, when something heavy cracks her hard around the back of her head. Her brain lurches. Her eyes darken. Deep within her core, sparks fly briefly, then fizzle and die.

Twenty-Two

Her Handsome Hero

Light filters slowly through Lydia's heavy eyelids, her own personal sunrise, penetrating gradually, painfully, cruelly all the way into her skull. She tries to turn her head away from its source, but her neck is stiff, frozen. Then suddenly the pain retreats. The light blocked. She senses a presence looming over her.

"Awake at last, Miss Tune," says an unfamiliar voice. "How are you feeling?"

Lydia blinks, and the room swims into view. Bare, white, stark. A hospital ward. The man standing over her in his long, white coat waits patiently for her to get her bearings.

"What happened?" Lydia croaks finally. Her mouth is so dry, the words cut on their way out and she winces.

"I was hoping you could tell me," the doctor replies, making a note on his clipboard and then dropping it to his side. "Doctor Engel found you lying face-down in the car park and brought you inside. Lucky she did, too. Another couple of hours and you would have been completely buried by the snow."

"I don't..." Lydia swallows painfully. She tries to reach for the pitcher of water on her bedside table, but her arms feel too heavy to lift. She feels like a bird with broken wings.

"Let me," says the doctor, pouring her a glass and bringing it to her cracked lips. She drinks greedily, feeling the life force flowing back into her as she does so.

"Thank you," she croaks.

"You're welcome." The doctor sets the glass back down. "So you don't remember anything?"

"I remember getting hit on the back of the head," says Lydia. She can feel the dull throb now from the site of the wound. "Then... I don't know." She looks around again, her eyes processing more details as they acclimatise. The floor tiles are off-white and dirty. Flies congregate in the corners of the room. There are six beds, but only one opposite is occupied, by an old lady who seems to be asleep. Lydia hopes she is asleep. "Where am I?"

"Still at Mortem," says the doctor. "In the medical wing. Doctor Engel thought it best to bring you inside and warm you up rather than wait for an ambulance. Besides, you're not too badly hurt. You'll have a nasty bruise, a hefty bump and a cracking headache for a while, but you'll live."

"Where is she?"

"She had to go home to her children. But she'll be back first thing in the morning."

"I should..." Lydia tries to get up, but the doctor lays a heavy hand on her shoulder.

"You should get some rest," he says. "A nurse will bring you something to eat, and then you need to sleep. We can't just let you go home after a bang on the head like that." He smiles, and Lydia notices how young he looks. Late twenties, maybe, with wavy, dark brown hair and large, dark green eyes. She feels a warmth within her, not enough to thaw her frozen core but sufficient to reassure her that this man means her no harm.

"Okay," she mumbles sleepily, letting her head fall back onto the pillow. "Thank you, doctor." She listens as his footsteps fade and disappear into the asylum's long, winding corridors. Her headache intensifies, and with each painful thump inside her head she visualises the blood pumping violently through every vein, every artery in her body. The throbbing agony echoes inside of her, bouncing back and forth over itself and building to a crescendo of searing torture. She opens her mouth to scream, but there is something else now beyond the rhythmic drum of pain. Another sound. More footsteps. Is the doctor back so soon? With a soft wail she lifts her head and shoulders from the bed and faces the door.

Alex bursts into the room, his old, worn leather jacket flapping behind him, clutching a raggedy bunch of daffodils in one hand and a box of chocolates in the other. "Lydia!" he says, breathlessly, as he catches sight of her and makes a beeline for the bed. "Jesus, Lydia! Are you alright?"

"What are you doing here?" Lydia's voice slides from surprise to anger over the course of the question as her pounding head evokes the fresh memory of creeping from Alex's room that morning.

"They just called me," he replies, somewhat taken aback by her hostility. "I came to make sure you're alright."

"I bet you did," she hisses, falling back onto the bed.

"What does that mean?" Alex asks. Lydia can hear the hurt in his voice and it just makes her angrier. *You are not the victim here*, she thinks.

"It means you don't have to act like you're my boyfriend or something just because we slept together." Lydia keeps her eyes closed. It's easier to say what she feels if she doesn't have to look at him. "I don't need protecting, and I sure as shit don't need those." She waves a hand at the flowers.

"Woah, woah," says Alex softly, as though soothing a skittish horse, "Lydia, we didn't sleep together."

"What do you mean?" She squints at him.

"I mean you were too drunk to remember the name of your hotel, so you came back to mine and passed out on my bed." He takes a cautious step forward and lays the flowers gently at the foot of the bed. "You don't remember?"

"I…" Lydia tries to remember, but inside her head it's so loud. "But you were…" She glares at him.

"Oh," he says sheepishly, looking down at the ground. "Well, it's only a small place, you know, I don't have a spare room and the couch is too small to sleep on, so…"

"Nothing happened?" Lydia asks. She wants to believe him.

"Nothing, I swear."

"You better not be lying."

"Hey, you're the expert," Alex says somewhat defensively. "If I were lying, you'd be able to tell, right?"

Lydia looks him right in the eyes, and Alex looks right back, and after a long moment she seems to decide that he's telling the truth. Or at least that she's prepared to believe it, for now.

"So what happened to you?" he asks. "The girl who called said you slipped on the ice?"

"I didn't slip," Lydia snaps. "Somebody hit me."

"What?!"

"I dropped my keys..." Lydia grimaces as she tried to remember. "And when I bent down to pick them up, somebody hit me on the back of the head." She leans forward and turns her head to show him the injury. "See?"

"But who would—"

"Jason," Lydia says, so quickly that she surprises even herself.

"But..." Alex says gently, "he's—"

"Locked up, I know," she says, impatiently. "He didn't actually do it. I don't even think he's causing all of this. But it has something to do with him, I know it does." Lydia squirms as though trying to sit up, and Alex places a hand on her shoulder.

"I'll look into it."

"What about Cecil Sprinkler? Did you find—"

"Nothing," Alex replies, quietly. "We're having the blood tested in that thing you found, but it's going to take a while."

Lydia sighs and thumps her head back against the pillow. "I won't be able to sleep, Alex. I need to do something."

"Here," says Alex, laying the box of chocolates next to her. "Eat these."

"Oh, yes," Lydia replies sarcastically, "a rush of sugar and endorphins is just what I need right now." She pushes the box away and closes her eyes, missing the fleeting look of disappointment on Alex's face.

"Alright," he says quietly after a moment, "I'll go and

speak to that doctor. Then tomorrow you're coming to stay with me until we've figured this out."

"I told you I don't need protecting. I don't need a bodyguard."

"Evidently."

"Don't be…" Lydia begins, trying to sit up again.

"No arguments," says Alex, touching her wrist this time. The touch of skin on skin sends a shock that pierces Lydia's consciousness and immediately clears the fog engulfing her brain. "Your safety is the most important thing here."

Lydia looks up into his kind eyes, and then quickly away for fear that he will see the truth in hers. "Whoever did this obviously doesn't want me dead," she says. "They wanted to make a point."

"What point?"

"You'd have to ask Jason, I guess."

"But he's—"

"I KNOW." Lydia winces again as the reverberations inside her own head from her raised voice set it thumping again. She hears a buzzing sound and wonders for a moment whether her blood might be pounding so hard that it is making the bed itself vibrate. Then she opens her eyes and sees Alex retrieving something from his coat pocket. A pager.

"I have to go," he says, frustrated. "I'll see the doctor on my way out and be back as soon as I can."

"Alright."

"Save me a caramel," he says, smiling, already halfway to the door.

"I won't," Lydia replies shortly, feeling around for the chocolates she rejected a moment ago. Then she laughs at her own childishness and looks up to see if Alex is laughing too. But the room is empty.

Hours later, Lydia is still awake and more agitated than ever. She picks her phone up from the bed next to her and then sets it down again. She has already been in touch with Donna to let her know what's happened. Alex sent a few texts just to check in, but she figured he must have long since fallen asleep. There is nobody else in the world that she can tell, who might care, about what has happened. Lydia is used to solitude. She has fashioned her life around it. Fashioned herself around it. But now it bothers her, and she can't figure out why.

Mostly as a distraction, she makes a list in her head, a plan for what she is going to do when she gets out of here. As the list grows, and the complexities multiply, she picks up her phone again and starts writing it down, thick, crimson nails tapping on the glass like an agitated bird pecking at a window.

"For God's sake, child, will you please go to sleep already?" Lydia jumps. She drops the phone, and in its glow glint two small, black eyes peering at her from across the room. The elderly lady was alive after all.

"I'm sorry," says Lydia, "I didn't know you were…" *Alive?* "Awake."

"How could I not be with you flapping and tapping over there?"

"I'm sorry," Lydia repeats, sounding more annoyed than apologetic. She isn't used to sharing space with people. It bothers her. "It's not like I want to be here, I got hit over the head and—"

"Oh yes, you've had a rough day," says the old woman, sarcastically. "I heard all about it when you were complaining to your poor boyfriend."

"My..." It takes Lydia a moment to realise who she means. "He's not my boyfriend, he's a detective."

"Oh, okay." The woman laughs a wheezing laugh. "Lots of detectives bring you flowers and chocolates, do they?"

"We went to school together," says Lydia defensively, picking up her phone to resume her task. "That's all."

"If you say so, sweetheart."

"I have to finish this, if you don't mind," says Lydia coldly.

"But I do mind," says the woman, sitting up a little and rolling her weight to one side. "There's a time to work and a time to sleep, you know."

"Well, I'm always working," Lydia snaps.

"Ooooh!" says the woman. Lydia can't see her mouth in the darkness, but her eyes are sneering. "Think you're special, do you? What kind of work is that you're doing?"

"I'm a writer," says Lydia flatly. "My name's Lydia Tune."

"Never heard of you."

"Well as devastating as that is," says Lydia, "I still have to get this done."

"Of course you do," says the woman, her thin, nasty voice wearing on Lydia's every nerve. "I'm sure it's very important."

"I don't expect you to understand," she snaps.

"Oh, but I do," the woman whispers. "I used to be you."

"Shall I summon the nurse?" Lydia asks sharply. "Clearly you're in need of a little something to settle your nerves."

"Listen you tight-arsed, control freak little bitch," the

woman spits, "you think you're so clever, but you don't even realise that nobody gives a shit about you or your precious work."

"Nurse!" Lydia cries out in a strangled voice.

"And you don't give a shit about them either," the woman carries on undeterred. "Oh you can take your mind off it with work or whatever other crap you tell yourself is important, but you can't stop the clock. One day it's going to catch up with you, and all you'll have to show for your petty life is a stack of pointless old books and a sack of regrets weighing you down. One day real soon."

"Nurse!" Lydia calls again, louder this time.

"Don't bother," says the woman. "I'm done. And besides," her eyes disappear as she falls back onto the bed. "Nobody can hear you anyway. Take it from someone who knows."

Lydia's phone goes dark, and a chill creeps up her spine that will hold its icy grip on her until the sun rises. She closes her eyes and feels exhaustion begin to overwhelm her, her consciousness drifting against its will, fighting like a fish caught on a line. Eventually she succumbs to sleep, but not to rest. Until this mystery is solved, there will be no rest.

Twenty-Three

Best Laid Plans

Lydia stands before a mirror in the cold, grey ward, fully dressed. She tries to summon her usual, confident smile but those crimson lips remain mutinously unturned. Even her own body, it seems, has lost faith in her. She glances over to the elderly woman, now sound asleep. She looks peaceful, kindly even. For a moment Lydia wonders whether she imagined their conversation. Perhaps whatever drugs the doctor administered had caused her to have a vivid nightmare. She raises her phone and taps to check her notes. The to-do list is there, just as she wrote last night. She looks up into the eyes of her own reflection. Are they... afraid?

"You've been given the all clear."

Lydia whips around to find Alex standing in the doorway. He looks tired, but smiles as she meets his gaze. "Did you speak to Doctor Engel?" Lydia asks.

"Some nurse," says Alex. "Said the doc's on her morning rounds." He walks over to Lydia's bed and picks up her bag. "Shall we go?"

"Not yet." Lydia snaps her lipstick closed and checks her hair in the mirror one last time. "I need to see him first."

"See who?"

"Jason," says Lydia, snatching her bag from Alex on her way to the door, heels clicking against the cold floor with each long, purposeful stride.

"Now wait a second," says Alex, chasing after her, "I don't think you're in any condition to be—"

"Oh, are you a doctor now too?" she asks, without slowing down.

"You can't just go barging in there."

"Who's going to stop me?" She glances at him over her shoulder. "You?"

"Hold on," Alex pleads, reaching out to grab her arm. "This isn't you."

"Oh really?" She stops and spins around, jerking her arm out of his grasp. "Who is it?"

"I mean…" Alex scrambles for the right words, "without a plan. Do you even know what you're going to say?"

"I'm a smart woman, Alex," says Lydia, setting off down the corridor again. "I'm sure I'll manage to put some words in an appropriate order."

"You're being emotional."

She shoots him a withering look.

"That's not what I meant," Alex says, frustrated. "Look, this isn't what you would usually do."

"I wouldn't usually get beaten around the head in a car park either," she snaps, "but it happened and I'm going to find out why."

"Fine," Alex says loudly, sprinting to get ahead of her and block the corridor. "Fine, okay, if that's what you want."

"I wasn't asking for your approval, Alex," says Lydia shortly. "Please get out of my way."

"I will when you tell me what your plan is."

Lydia glares at him, but she's more annoyed with herself for not having an answer.

"Listen," says Alex, holding up his hands in an appeasing fashion, "one of the guards here is an old friend of mine."

"A friend?" Lydia raises an immaculately-pencilled eyebrow.

"Well, acquaintance," says Alex, sheepishly. "Whatever, why don't you let me talk to him? Maybe I can work something out."

"Like what?" Lydia asks, half curious, half incredulous.

"You have your ways," he grins, "I have mine." She stares at him with a mixture of scepticism and irritation. "Look," he says, "if I can't stop you, at least let me help you. Okay?"

"I can handle myself," she remarks, pulling away.

A long-frustrated sigh bellows from Alex's chest, "Fine." He suddenly smiles with what appears to be a thought. "I'll see you later."

Before Lydia can add anything, he turns away and starts walking down the corridor with what is unmistakably a swagger in his step. She stares, open-mouthed, wondering why, and then leaves to go and see Jason.

Twenty-Four

Cat and Mouse

Nightmares lurk within the shadows that haunt every corner of this high, grey room. A small window far out of reach allows the sun's tired rays to spill over its three, thick bars and cast down a spotlight upon a single cell, a cell in the centre of several others that remain empty and embedded into the old cracking grey walls. This one cell was purposed to contain the mad dog serial killer and his meagre furnishings: bed, toilet, and a pale blue yoga mat, the scene's only colour. Jason Devere, in loose grey pants and vest, angles his body into a perfect downward dog, heels flat, arms straight, flexed muscles remembering their old strength.

"I told you I keep my word," says a woman's voice above him. Jason's torso flattens to the mat in an instant, back arched, head raised like a cobra ready to strike. "So this is your place, huh?"

"It's just like the Ritz," he growls softly. "I guess I forgot to hang that 'do not disturb' sign on the door."

"Funny you should mention privacy," Lydia says, stepping right up to the cell and laying her hands upon its cold, steel bars. "The other day, you asked me if I ever felt like I'm being watched."

"Yeah," Jason replies, slowly raising to his feet. For the first time, she realises how tall he is. A powerful figure. "So?"

"Tell me why."

Jason just stands for a moment, watching her with his piercing eyes, head slightly tilted. He's only a few feet away. If he lunges now, she probably won't be able to react in time. Every fibre of Lydia's being is screaming for her to get away, to run, but her brain warns her not to back down, not to show weakness, and Lydia's brain always wins.

"Just making conversation," says Jason finally.

"You're lying," says Lydia quickly. "Why did you say it?"

Jason approaches her slowly. "The real question is," he says quietly, his bright eyes locked on hers, "why you didn't listen?" He's almost at the bars now, within reach. Lydia lets go and begins to pace slowly in front of the cell, the click of her long heels echoing up to the ceiling high above, past thin metal walkways where guards are perched silently like bats in the rafters of an old mansion.

"Enough games," she says, "you know why I'm here."

"I heard through the grapevine that you had an accident." Jason presses his face to the bars, his eyes following her.

"It was no accident, was it, Jason?" Lydia asks, snapping around to look at him. Jason pulls back from the bars, a feral smirk creeping over his face, and begins to walk towards her.

"I don't know what you're talking about," he growls.

Lydia turns and walks back towards him. "I think you do," she hisses, leaning towards the cell as she slowly paces by. Jason gets a fleeting, close look at her face, catches the scent of her perfume. Involuntarily, his tongue slides forth to moisten his lips.

"You're lonely, aren't you?" he asks, following her again within his cell, right to left.

"I'm not playing your games today, Jason," Lydia lies. She's making him chase her. Frustrating the beast so that he'll make a mistake. Does he realise?

"We're more alike than you know," he says. "Both at home in solitary confinement. Only your life-sentence is self-inflicted, isn't it?"

"How did you contact your accomplice?" Lydia asks, calmly.

"I didn't contact anyone," Jason replies.

"Stop lying." Lydia gives him a withering look.

"You know that I'm not," he smirks. "The great Lydia Tune, expert in human behaviour. If I were really lying, you'd know." He pauses to enjoy the flicker of irritation on her face. "Is that what's bothering you?" He leans forward into the bars again. "Or is it something else?"

"Who did it?" Lydia snaps.

"Could it be," Jason continues his thought, undeterred, "that you thought yourself untouchable?" Lydia doesn't answer. She's trying to read him, but in this fading light the nuances of Jason's expression are cloaked in shadow. The only features she can clearly see are those hungry eyes, and yellowing teeth when the wolf smile appears as it does right now. "You must know by now, no one is untouchable," he says with a touch of sadness.

"Who did it?" Lydia hisses like steam venting from the fury within her.

"You should never have gotten involved, Lydia," says Jason, twisting his arms around the cell bars like impatient snakes.

"*Who did it?*"

"That's for you to find out."

"Okay!" Lydia says, sharply. She spins on her heel and makes for the door across the room.

"See you around," says Jason, his energy diffused in a heartbeat, slumping back onto his bed.

"Oh, we're not finished," says a low bearing voice in the far right hand corner of the room where a figure lurks in the shadows beside another locked entrance. Jason squints towards it, his body arching as a creature to danger. Suddenly the figure moves, advancing upon his barred room rapidly. Lydia stops and turns in shock.

"Alex."

"Detective!" Jason exclaims, beaming. "Goodness, you're stealthier than I remember. Back for more, are we?"

Alex doesn't reply. His eyes are burning. His breath audible. Producing a long, steel key from his pocket, he unlocks the cell door, steps inside and pulls it shut behind him with a crash.

"What'll it be today?" asks Jason, cheerily. "A little good cop, bad cop?" Alex springs and holds Jason firmly against the wall, towering over him as Lydia watches on in frozen disbelief.

"Alex!" she calls, edging closer to the bars.

"Who was it?" asks Alex, clenching the inmate tight.

Jason laughs. "Oh, I like him!" he says to Lydia, then

focuses back onto his assailant. "Do you hear that? I like you!"

Alex's grip tightens on the inmate's shoulder. "Who was it?"

"Christ, you're stupid." He grins. "I think that maybe you're just mad... because you couldn't catch me."

"Alex, listen to me," Lydia pleads.

"Who was it?" Alex demands, applying more pressure, now around his neck.

"Because I..." Jason sneers, "turned myself in..."

"WHO WAS IT?" Alex yells, gritting his teeth, slamming Jason against the wall again.

"Alex!" Lydia hisses, knowing this intimidation act is now going too far. "That's enough!"

Alex backs away, letting Jason go, who coughs slightly. "Jeez, at least buy a boy a drink first!" Jason manages, rubbing his neck.

As the red mist clears from Alex, he feels a sickness rise from the pit of his stomach. He turns away quickly, retreating from the cell and locking the door behind him, trying to avoid eye contact.

"Are you alright?" Lydia asks, appearing at his side and laying a hand on his arm.

"I..." he says quietly, not looking at her, "I shouldn't have..."

"It's okay," she whispers, "I understand, we'll talk about it later."

"It's rude to whisper when you have company."

Lydia whips her head around to see Jason staring at her. His face pink, but he's still smirking. "It's rude to deny your guests," she replies, coolly.

"Should've said please," Jason croaks. "Would've been a lot easier than setting your dog on me."

"I didn't…" Lydia feels Alex's bicep tense beneath her fingers, and she gives it a gentle squeeze. "Never mind," she says, "I'm done here. I'll write about somebody else."

"I don't know who attacked you," says Jason quickly. "That's the truth."

"Bullshit," Alex mutters under his breath.

"I can take a guess though," Jason offers, struggling painfully to his feet.

"Go on then," says Lydia.

"Well," he says, spitting out a little blood, "I hear you have some pretty twisted fans. Maybe one of them tried to abduct you."

"That's ridiculous," Lydia replies, contemptuously. "Whoever it was didn't try to abduct me, they just left me there."

"Maybe they got scared," says Jason, feeling the faint burn of the law man's grip around his neck still. "Had second thoughts. It's not easy to go through with something like that. You have to be brave."

"You're not brave," Alex snarls, glaring at him.

"And you are?" Jason snaps, his voice strained for the first time. "I mean, I gathered that you were a dirty player, Lyd, but using this lug to beat up a prisoner for information? Oh, such a hero." He turns to Lydia whose dagger eyes penetrate into his. "But then again, with that said, I can see what you see in him."

"Let's go," says Alex, grabbing Lydia's wrist and starting towards the door.

"Maybe you just slipped on the ice," Jason calls out, "and the concussion made you forget."

"You said," Lydia turns back to him, yanking her wrist from Alex's grip, "you said I was being watched."

"Did I?" Jason makes a show of scratching his chin, pretending to think about it. "I don't think I did, you know."

"You said…"

"I believe I asked if you *knew what it felt like* to be watched," he says, innocently. "You know, because you're so famous and all."

"That's *not* how you said it," Lydia glares at him.

"Are you sure?" Jason asks, calmly. "You did just hit your head you know, maybe you don't remember…"

"I remember everything."

"Maybe…" That smile spreads across his face again, eyes glowing softly in the fast-fading light. "Maybe you're going a little crazy." He lifts a finger to his temple and moves it in slow, deliberate circles.

"Lyd!" Alex pleads. "Let's go."

Lydia glares at Jason for a moment longer, then turns and strides purposefully from the room.

"See you soon," Jason calls out in a musical tone. Alex shoots him a filthy look before following Lydia out.

The wolf, alone again, weary from the hunt, sinks onto his bed.

Twenty-Five

Watcher in the Wings

"**A**re you alright?"

Even as the heavy steel door shuts behind them, Alex catches Lydia's arm and spins her around to face him. A neon light above buzzes and flickers, echoing her chaotic thoughts.

"I'm fine," she replies, absently.

"Listen, I'm sorry about what happened in there, I- I just couldn't help myself—"

"It's fine." She cuts him off. "What did you find out about that teacher?"

"I can't talk to you about it," he replies sheepishly. "Not right now."

"You invited me to the crime scene!" Lydia blinks at him in disbelief.

"I shouldn't have done that. I wanted to make sure you were safe, and I couldn't leave."

"So you have no idea who attacked me?"

"If someone attacked you," Alex says gently, moving

to hold her again. Lydia shakes him off with a piercing look.

"You think I'm lying?"

"Of course not!" Alex pleads. "But you have to understand how this all sounds. You didn't see anyone; you don't remember what happened and the doctor says you had quite a concussion. You could have been out for hours. I mean..."

"Don't say it, Alex," Lydia warns.

"Are you sure you didn't just slip, and you're paranoid because of what's happened?"

She takes a step away from him, the colour draining from her already pale face, eyes wide with shock.

"Lydia, please don't be mad," Alex says. "I'm just trying to figure it out. And I mean, wouldn't that be better? If it was an accident?" He makes a movement towards her again, but Lydia raises a straight arm, her hand flat against his chest.

"Maybe you're right," she says, her voice empty as though her mind is elsewhere.

"I can still look out for you," he says. "If that's what you want?" Lydia doesn't reply. She sways unsteadily and for a moment looks like she might topple over. "Lydia?" Alex goes to catch her, but she regains her balance at the last moment.

"I'm fine," she says quietly. "I just feel a little strange."

"Do you want me to take you back to the hotel?" asks Alex. "Or..."

"Your place?" Lydia narrows her eyes at him.

"I was going to say 'to get something to eat'," says Alex. "But I like your idea too." He catches her eye and she smiles.

She can't help herself. Being desired makes her feel good, makes her feel strong and purposeful again, even if she knows it's only for a fleeting moment with her handsome toy. In a way, Alex is the only thing in this troublesome time keeping Lydia together; she feels safe with him strangely, though she would never admit that to herself, much less to anyone else.

"Food sounds good," she says. "Where shall we go?"

"I'll surprise you." Alex grins.

"I hate surprises," says Lydia with a frown.

"You'll like this one."

Lydia opens her mouth to say that she doubts it, but decides that she doesn't have the energy for this small talk right now. "I'd like to go back and change first," she says, "take a bath; get his... scent out of my nostrils." She makes a face.

"I'll give you a ride," says Alex.

"Don't be silly." She waves him away. "My car's here."

Alex stares at her. "How did your car get here? I thought it was still—"

"You're not the only one with a few tricks up their sleeve."

"Are you sure you're okay to drive?" he asks, looking somewhat alarmed. "The doctor said—"

"I know what she said," Lydia says flatly. "I am saying that I'm fine."

"Alright," says Alex. He doesn't look happy, but he doesn't want an argument either. "Then I'll pick you up around... eight?"

"Perfect." Lydia smiles an unsteady smile. Usually false sincerity comes as easily to her as breathing, but this definitely feels forced, and she can tell from the look on Alex's face that he's noticed it too. "Let's get out of here," she says quickly. "Come o—"

"Miss Tune!"

Lydia turns to see the tyrannical Warden Shade marching down the corridor towards them.

"You'd better go," she murmurs to Alex. "He won't be happy when he hears what you did to Jason. I'll smooth him over, but best you're not here."

"Sure?" asks Alex, uncertainly.

"Positive." Lydia smiles. That one was easier. Just a temporary lapse. "I'll see you at eight."

"Alright," says Alex, and he turns and heads in the opposite direction, back towards the entrance to the asylum.

"Is Detective Gilbey in a hurry to be somewhere?" asks the warden, brusquely.

"Work," Lydia replies, simply.

"I see," says Shade. "Tell me, does his work usually involve assaulting his suspects?"

He knows, Lydia thinks. One of the guards must have gone straight to tell him. *Of course he had a spy. He's just the sort.* "I expect that depends on the suspect," Lydia replies, coolly.

"Indeed," says the warden. His tone is conversational, but his eyes are dark and menacing. "I must say I'm surprised that you approved such a course of action."

"Why so?" Lydia asks, politely.

"I had heard that you were a woman of many subtle talents," says Shade. "I thought you would find Detective Gilbey's approach crude and unsatisfactory." Lydia peers at him curiously. Was that an insult or a compliment? Perhaps both? "Still," the warden continues, "if it gets results, I suppose. So our boy knows nothing about your situation, eh? That is unfortunate."

Lydia feels a chill creep up her spine. Could Warden Shade be Jason's accomplice? Was she standing here alone with the man who had knocked her out and left her for dead in the snow? "I wouldn't be so sure about that," she says, the coolness in her voice turning to ice.

"No?" says Shade. "Well I'm sure about this; you and your damn book are going to get this place shut down if this carries on. And I'm afraid I can't allow that."

"I assure you, warden," says Lydia quickly, preservation instincts kicking in. "You may see me as a problem, but I can also be a solution."

The warden peers at her over the top of his spectacles. "Go on…"

"Allow me to continue my work undisturbed," says Lydia smoothly, "and I guarantee you Mortem will receive nothing but praise from me."

"I see," says Shade, thinking it over. "That's all very well, but why should I trust you when I can save myself the bother and just kick you out now?"

"If you were going to do that," says Lydia, taking a subtle step towards him and pushing out her chest a little, "you would have done it before now. I already have more than enough material for a story."

"Hmmm…" Shade's piercing eyes fix upon her as though trying to see through her veneer of deceit. "I'd like to show you something," he says finally.

"Of course," Lydia replies, somewhat taken aback. Alarm bells are ringing in her head, and it takes her a second to realise why. There is a battle of wills being waged, and she is losing. The sensation feels like a distant memory to her. Is she doing something wrong? Is she in danger?

"This way." He gestures down the corridor that Alex took, and together they make their way back towards the entrance to Mortem Asylum.

The cage-like elevator shudders as Warden Shade pulls the grate shut, and the vibration travels through Lydia like a wave of anxiety. Shade pushes the button marked with a downward arrow and it lights up as, with another quaking shudder, the contraption begins to descend into the bowels of the asylum.

"You see, Miss Tune," he says, looking straight ahead, "people see themselves as entitled to things they have not earned. They believe that they can achieve anything they set their minds to." He smooths his walrus moustache. "Having borne witness to more failures of the human experiment than I care to count, I have to disagree. A person's birthright is not the moon and stars; it is nothing but ash and dirt. The chance at a life, nothing more." The elevator slows, and grinds to a standstill. "Please," he says, heaving the grate aside. "After you."

Lydia steps out into a pristine, white, well-lit corridor. "Where are we?" she asks, uncertainly. Just hearing the question come out of her mouth makes her heart race. She can hear the fear in her own voice, a quavering that echoes the crawling of her skin. And now the doubts begin to stack upon themselves, the thread of sanity slipping between her fingers. Panic. A synapse that, once triggered, cannot be undone. Something feels different about this part of the building, a tremor in the air itself that sets her teeth on edge.

"The basement," replies the warden. "Where we carry out our electroshock treatment program." He motions down the corridor and they proceed. Lydia notices the network of pipes and cables along the ceiling all snaking towards their destinations in a twisted, convoluted manner.

"So, do we have a deal?" she asks, a futile attempt to wrestle the situation back onto her terms. But she is out on a limb, and she knows it.

"We do," Shade replies, peering at her for the briefest moment. "You will return to Devere as many times as necessary to write your book, and you will have the full cooperation of my staff. In return," he lets the words linger a moment, "you will put Mortem Asylum back on the map, for the right reasons. And you will give me full and final approval of your manuscript."

They reach a door with a glass window, through which Lydia can see a figure in a white coat. Doctor Engel? No, a man. He steps aside, and her heart stops. A patient is strapped to a chair, belts tight around his wrists and ankles, and a twisted crown of metal upon his head. His mouth is gagged, but his eyes are screaming.

Shade opens the door. "After you."

"I never offered you approval," Lydia says, frozen to the spot.

"Nevertheless," the warden replies with a nasty smile, "that is the deal."

"What if I refuse?" Lydia asks. She knows she is in danger, but her curiosity gets the better of her. Who is this man?

"Then I'm sure we will find other uses for you," says

Shade, stepping inside the room himself and holding the door for her. If Lydia is going to bolt, she knows this is the moment. But before she knows it, she is inside, and the door has closed behind her. *Reckless*. She imagines Alex's face if he could see this. He would be furious. Maybe she will tell him, she thinks, when it suits her purpose.

"Uses?" she asks, snapping back into the moment.

"Like our friend here," Shade gestures to the man in the chair. "Nasty piece of work. Enjoys the taste of human flesh. Can you imagine?" He wrinkles his nose in disgust, but his gleeful eyes suggest to Lydia that Shade doesn't need to imagine. She tastes bitterness at the back of her throat as the panic rises from deep within her. She badly underestimated the warden, and now finds herself at the mercy of a monster.

"You see," Shade continues, giving no sign as to having noticed Lydia's discomfort, "our friend here can no longer contribute to society, so now he contributes to our research effort instead. *Don't you?*" Shade smacks the helpless man upside his head, and Lydia watches tears form in the tortured, barely alive creature's eyes.

"I hope you're not threatening me," she says sharply, summoning as much bravery as she can muster and rounding on the warden as he makes his way to the computer bank where two doctors are poring over their data. Both are old, and frail, and neither says a word to their guests. It's almost as if she and Shade are ghosts visiting a spirit world, Lydia thinks.

"My dear, I have no reason to threaten you," says Shade, poking one of the scientists and pointing to a switch. "I have the utmost confidence that you will not betray my trust."

Lydia opens her mouth to reply, but as she does so the doctor reaches for the switch and turns it hard to the right. The lights dim and a deafening buzz fills the room, followed by blood-curdling screams as thousands of volts of electricity surge through the wretched young man's already fried brain. Lydia feels all of the strength leave her body in an instant, and has to grab on to a table to stop herself from falling.

A moment later, the screaming stops. The lights return to their original brightness. The buzz is gone. A sudden, eerie peace.

"Electricity is a reliable force," says Shade, with the air of an English general casually explaining the destructive power of a new weapon to a stunned civilian. "No matter who we put in that chair, it will break their mind as surely as stone breaks glass. Even a brilliant individual," he turns to Lydia, black eyes twinkling with malice, "such as yourself. We could fry your brain in seconds, toss you in a cell and just tell people you went mad writing about all these freaks."

Lydia stares at the broken test subject, his eyes rolling independently in their sockets, drool running down his face and neck, hollow cheeks, wasted flesh. She is frozen, unable to move, or speak, or even to breathe. This is what pure terror feels like.

"Do we understand one another?" Shade's voice reverberates through her very soul, a deep and timeless evil.

Lydia nods weakly, still winded from shock.

"Excellent," says Shade, smoothly. "Now, would you like to stay a while and watch? It's really rather fascinating."

Lydia shakes her head, her eyes fixed upon the victim in the centre of the room, slumped, twitching, broken. *This is the heart of darkness*, she thinks. *This is worse than death.*

Twenty-Six

Heart of Ice

Howling winds churn falling snow against the black night, swallowing everything in a thick, wet, suffocating cold. Frost creeps down the window of Lydia's hotel room, hiding the worst of the storm from her as she hurries to dress. Here in the warmth, within these four reassuring walls, the warden of Mortem's threats feel almost like a dream. But a dream that she knows will haunt her every waking moment until this story is put to bed one way or another. And in order to do that, she will have to return to the asylum. The very thought makes her feel sick.

Alex will be here soon, she tells herself. He will protect me. She believes it too, up to a point. Alex is strong, and capable, and smart. Not smart like her, but savvy. He thinks like a cop. That can be useful. But Lydia thinks like bad people do, and the man in the cage whom she needs to break, bested Alex for a long time.

A gentle knock bounces off the door and Lydia jumps.

She's not ready. Bare feet skim over the carpet to the door, which she opens with a coy flourish.

"Hi." She smiles.

"Wow…" Alex replies. He's wearing that same leather jacket over a clean, white shirt and black jeans. For him, Lydia knows by now, this is dressed to impress. Simple, but, she admits to herself with a tremor of pleasure, pretty attractive nonetheless.

"I'll take that as a compliment." She blushes, looking down and shaking her luxurious blonde curls before flicking her eyes back up to him. She's wearing a fitted two-piece bodice of rich ebony-hued fabric, with hints of an intricate swirling pattern in dark purple embroidery. Lacing of the same rich, royal shade cinches it closed at the back, perfectly enclosing her breasts and revealing a small area of toned stomach. The bottom section flares over her hips, below which a midnight blue skirt, slit front and back, falls elegantly to the floor. Clear crystals encircle her neck, and the ever-present ruby ring.

Alex mouths a response, but finds his lungs suddenly devoid of air and unable to project it. Lydia grins and motions for him to come in. "I just need a moment to finish my make-up," she says, heading for the bathroom. "Make yourself at home."

"You look amazing as you are," he calls after her, relocating his voice.

"You're sweet," she replies through the half-open door. Alex sinks gingerly onto the foot of the bed and picks up the nearby TV remote. He points and clicks, and a local weather report appears on screen. The volume is low, but it serves to settle his nerves a little. His leg is twitching, restless, venting off some excess tension. He hasn't spoken to Lydia since the incident with Jason. What does she think about that? About him? Has it changed? Would she even say if it had? His eyes dart around the room, seeking comfort but finding only an unsettling order everywhere they alight. Everything is too straight, too perfect, from the radio on the bedside table to the shoes arranged perfectly next to the wardrobe, and finally the desk; a closed laptop, pens laid neatly together and a small notebook. Alex glances quickly towards the bathroom and then back to the book. He hesitates, then snatches it up like a cobra seizing its prey. Eagerly, he flips to the most recent entries.

What is evil? Reference historical figures.
Focus: Jason's family history, genetics, ancestors – looking for psychopathic tendencies.
Birth of twin brothers – colour, relatable.
Childhood – relationship with brother (Finley), how does death affect Jason? Blame from father? Guilt for mother?
School with Cecil – friends? Bullied? Grades?
Teen years – romantic relationships? Hostile ones?
Young adult – drug abuse, theft, peer pressure, circumstance, home environment.
First kill – how, why?
Birth of the Krimson Killer – influences, inspirations? What do his methods tell us about him? What about his targets?
Downfall – confession, guilt?
Mortem – my POV.

A toilet flushes, ripping Alex from his trance. In a panic, he throws the notebook onto the desk and then, eyes flicking back and forth between it and the bathroom door, lunges to correct its position, perfectly aligned to the right of the laptop, and centred beneath the pens.

"Hoped it was my diary, did you?" asks Lydia. Alex snatches his hands away from the desk and whips around to face her.

"I just…" he stammers.

"It's okay, Alex." She smiles, leaning against the frame of the door. "Curiosity is a normal human trait; I'm not going to punish you for it." She walks towards him, hips swaying meticulously. "Unless you want me to?"

"I, uh…" Alex swallows, his mouth suddenly dry. "Sure."

Lydia takes a moment to enjoy the thrall that she has over him. She does like him. He's kind, funny, good company. But first and foremost, right now he is useful as a bodyguard and source of information. She doesn't feel bad about using him. This is the way the world works. Human beings are inherently selfish and self-serving. She's only obeying her natural instincts, using the tools that Mother Nature has gifted her.

"I'm kidding, you dope." Lydia turns and snatches up a pair of black heels from the floor, then sinks into a chair to put them on. "Well, what did you think?"

"Of what?" asks Alex, confused.

"Whatever it was you read in there," she says, nodding towards the desk.

"Oh." Alex glances at the notebook. "Well I guess… it was interesting to see your thought process. The way you structure things, you know, plan them."

"They're just bullet points." Lydia smiles. She likes that he admires her mind, but doesn't wish to seem arrogant. Or at least, any more arrogant than might be strictly necessary.

"Well," says Alex awkwardly, "they're very neat bullet points."

"Thank you," Lydia laughs, standing up. "Shall we?"

"Sure." Alex jumps up.

"I still don't know where we're going," she says in a deliberately breezy fashion, grabbing her coat from the back of the door.

"I told you," Alex replies, "it's a surprise."

Lydia's instinct is to be irritated, but she isn't. She hates surprises, doesn't she? Always has. Could it be that she doesn't mind the uncertainty when she's with him? Could it be that she's changing? Is the ice queen melting?

This is a surprise.

Twenty-Seven

Winter's Waltz

A small, silver car ploughs through winter's wrath, wheels skidding on the icy road, headlight's dipped against blinding banks of snow. Behind the wheel, Alex Gilbey concentrates hard while attempting to convey an impression otherwise. His gently misting breath gives him away, however, as it forms and swirls with increasing force and frequency. Lydia sees it.

"So," she says, casually, "where are we going?"

"Nice try." Alex grins, snapping his eyes off the road for a split second, just long enough to capture a fleeting image of Lydia's twinkling eyes, framed by those shining blonde curls.

"It is safe, right?" she asks, uncertainly. Alex wasn't stupid, but he was still a man and might easily underestimate Lydia's insecurity in light of recent events. Especially as he hadn't been privy to all of them.

"Of course it's safe," he replies, genuine. "I'm looking after you, aren't I?" With a cheeky, boyish smirk he rests his hand upon hers for a sweet moment, then Alex proceeds to steer the vehicle's wheel, steadily moving them past a struggling blue hatchback. Red tail lights from another car ahead flare up, and he eases onto his own brakes, slowing then turning left.

"Is it… public?" Lydia prodded.

"No," Alex deadpans, "I'm taking you to the field where I buried all my other bodies."

"That's not funny," Lydia scolds. Alex grins at her.

"Come on, Lyd, we're just going to dinner. No one's going to knock you out in the car park, I promise."

"Is it loud?" she asks. She feels like swimming in a sea of noise and life might wash away some of this terrible tension.

"What is this, twenty questions?"

"It can be less," she says pointedly, "if you tell me where we're going."

"Do you make an effort not to have any fun?" asks Alex with another quick glance at her.

"I find knowledge fun," she replies. "And you didn't answer the question."

"Maybe," says Alex, lifting his chin as though daring her to play the game.

"You can't say maybe!"

"Why not?" Alex's concentration lapses for a split second and the car wobbles on the ice. Lydia grabs his arm and he looks smugly at her. She releases it at once. "Why can't I say maybe?"

"Because that's not how twenty questions works!" Lydia replies, exasperated. "Yes or no?"

Alex pretends to think hard. "Perhaps," he says finally.

"God, it's a real battle of wits with you, isn't it?" Lydia rolls her eyes and sits back in her seat, facing straight ahead.

"You're just mad because you're losing."

Lydia ignores him and reaches to push the power button on the stereo.

Here comes Santa Claus,
Here comes Santa Cl—

"Ergh…" Lydia growls, stabbing the button again with a crimson talon. "No."

"Got a problem with Santa Claus?" asks Alex, one eyebrow raised, trying not to laugh. Lydia opens her mouth to reply, but Alex spots their destination up ahead. "Murray's!" he announces cheerfully. "Here we are."

Lydia peers through the windscreen at the front of the restaurant. It looks nice, sophisticated. Simple signage with flowing lettering, and through the window the soft glow of chandeliers illuminating crisp, white tablecloths. It seems pretty full of well-dressed clientele. Lydia eyes Alex's jeans uncertainly.

"Looks nice," she says, hopefully.

"I've only been once before," Alex replies, "but it was great. They have singers, dancing, drinks, a little bit of everything. You can have whatever kind of night you fancy."

"Very thoughtful," she says with a smile.

"I have my moments." Alex grins back.

"There's a space!" says Lydia suddenly, one slender finger shooting out to indicate a gap between two parked cars. Alex slows down and swings wide to approach it, but a sleek, black car sweeps in front of him to steal it. Lydia sees his knuckles turn white against the steering wheel. "Dick!" she yells at the car.

"Wow." Alex peers at her, surprised. "You're really serious about your parking spa—"

"There's one!" Lydia's finger jabs again towards another spot across the road, then she grins at the look on Alex's face. "What?" she asks, innocently. "Everyone has a talent, don't they?"

"Sure," Alex agrees, manoeuvring into the space, "I just thought yours was, you know, writing."

"That's just my day job," says Lydia, unbuckling her seatbelt as the car comes to a halt.

"You're in a funny mood."

"Probably just the hunger talking." She pushes the door open and slides out, elegantly. "Careful," she calls out as Alex emerges from the other side of the car, "the ground's icy."

"I know." He boggles at her. "I was just driving on it." He comes around the back of the car and offers her his arm. "Besides, you're the one in ten-inch heels."

"Okay," Lydia says, taking his arm. "Well, these are four-inch heels. There's no such thing as ten-inch heels unless you're a stripping giant."

"Only on the weekends," Alex replies, as they navigate their way across the slippery tarmac. "Weather's supposed to get worse tomorrow too," he mutters, with a glance up to the sky.

"You're a glass half full type, aren't you?" Lydia observes.

"Depends what's in the glass." Alex grins. "Speaking of

which." They reach the door of the restaurant and he holds it open for her. A blast of warm, delicious air hits Lydia's face and she begins to salivate.

"Thank you, sir," she says, and makes a point of touching her necklace as she passes him.

Murray's is even grander than it looks from the outside. A large stage at the back hosts an entire orchestra of musicians and singers entertaining a packed dance floor. Above the revellers a giant crystal chandelier sparkles, while candles flicker on the tables all around. There is an upper balcony too, over which beautiful faces peer down at the revelry, and dark corners and crannies where those less inclined to the limelight might lurk. Every inch of the place is rich with cream and gold, warmth and comfort.

"Welcome to Murray's," purrs an impeccably presented maître d', appearing beside them.

"Table for Gilbey," says Alex.

"Of course, sir, right this way." They follow him through a sea of fine suits, fur and feathers to an immaculate little table with a perfect view of the stage. "May I take your coats?"

"Thank you," says Lydia, slipping her long, cherry coat from her shoulders and offering it to him. She notices several men seated nearby glance up from their food and conversations, and enjoys their lingering eyes upon her. Alex notices them too, but he seems less pleased.

"Thanks," he says, handing over his leather jacket.

"A waiter will be along directly to take your drinks order," says the maître d', holding Lydia's chair for her.

"Thank you." She smiles, settling herself. "Gosh, it's lovely here," she says to Alex across the table.

"Yeah," he agrees, looking around. "Just how I remember it."

"What made you think of this place?"

Alex shrugs. "I just have this memory of a perfect night here," he says a touch wistfully, "and that's what I wanted tonight to be."

"A perfect night with your wife?" Lydia asks gently. Alex looks down at the table.

"Yeah..."

"I'm sorry," Lydia says, somewhat uncomfortable, "I shouldn't have mentioned... I'm stupid."

"We both know that's not true," he replies, looking up with a small smile. "It's okay, Lydia, yes I came here with my wife before she ran off with a bartender and it was great."

"That she ran off with—"

"The night here was great." He raises an eyebrow at her. "Though you're doing your best to ruin my happy memories."

"So make new ones," she says, a twinkle in her eye.

"May I get you some drinks?" asks a young, penguin-like waiter at Lydia's shoulder.

"Gin Martini," Lydia replies, smiling up at him. "And Jack Daniel's and Coke for the gentleman."

"Very good, madam." The waiter gives a curt nod and disappears back into the shimmering haze of luxury.

"You remembered," says Alex.

"I'm not a goldfish."

"What kind of fish are you?" he asks.

"The curious kind," Lydia replies, leaning forward a little. "Tell me why Jason thinks you would be so annoyed about him turning himself in."

Alex's face darkens. "I thought we'd come here to get away from all that."

"I need to figure this out," Lydia says firmly. "I'm sorry, but I won't have any peace until I do."

Alex sighs, leans back in his chair and looks over at the people dancing. This isn't the start to the evening he was hoping for. "Alright," he says finally. "Well, it wasn't long after we'd started putting the pieces together and connecting all of his murders. The ones with bodies were easy, but the disappearances... we couldn't be sure if those people were dead or alive, so..."

"Oh, they're dead," says Lydia flatly.

"Probably," says Alex, peering at her uncomfortably.

"Of course they are." She waves a hand dismissively. "The Krimson Killer obviously likes to play with his food, but when he gets hungry enough, he'll eat it."

"That's a charming metaphor to deploy in a restaurant."

"Sorry." Lydia smiles, glancing at her menu. "I might get the shrimp..."

"Seriously," says Alex, himself leaning across the table now, "what if they are still alive? I mean most of the missing victims are younger women, what if—"

"There's absolutely no reason to believe those girls are anything other than dead and gone."

"The thing is..."

Before long, their waiter appears from seemingly nowhere with their drinks; Lydia smiles as he lowers them before hastily scampering off back to the bar.

"The thing is," says Alex, lowering his voice slightly, looking and sounding a little frustrated, "the last few disappeared right before he walked into the station."

"So?"

"So what if he was, I don't know," Alex fishes for the right words, "banking some leverage or something."

"That doesn't make any sense," says Lydia. "Jason didn't even confess to those murders, did he? The ones you never found?"

"No, but…"

"And he's been in that hellhole for years now. If he had leverage, if he had – I can't believe we're even talking about this – if he had *hostages*, he would have mentioned them. Hell, they'd be long dead anyway, right? Unless…"

"What?" Alex seizes on her uncertainty.

"I mean unless he had an accomplice," Lydia finishes the thought.

"*That's* crazy."

"We're dealing with crazy people," says Lydia, matter-of-factly. "What if Dorothy Eagle wasn't a copycat? What if there were two of them the whole time? What if that's who's been stalking me?"

"I suppose you have some notion as to who this secret psychopath – who, by the way, none of us saw even a trace of at the time – might be?" asks Alex, sarcastically.

"Not yet," she replies, holding up her menu a little higher, "but I'll figure it out. Maybe I'll ask his mother."

"What?"

"I'm going to visit her tomorrow," says Lydia, perusing the lavish dishes, "at the hospital."

"How do you know she's in the hospital?"

"Because I'm good at my job," Lydia replies without looking up. Alex opens his mouth to reply, but then correctly interprets Lydia's demeanour as a warning not to, and picks up his own menu instead. After a moment, Lydia sits back in her chair and watches the figures on the dance floor swaying gently to the music.

"So I was wondering," Alex says with a note of forced brightness. "How do you go about writing your books? I mean, what's your process?"

"Well," Lydia replies, setting down her menu and accepting the implicit request to move the conversation along, "first I decide on a concept. Something that interests me. So, for *The Masks We Wear*, for example, it was the social constructs as well as the different personas we use and we instinctively pick up on, form and put in place in order to thrive in our modern-day society. With this book, I want to examine what evil is, how it happens and what it's for."

"Okay."

"Then I discuss it with my agent and we decide if there's a market for it. If the answer is yes, I start looking for promising subjects to base the narrative around."

"And this time you picked Devere?" Alex asks.

"I mean," Lydia shrugs, "he wasn't the first, but he's the most promising so far."

Alex makes a face that makes it clear he wishes she had picked literally anyone else. "So," he says, trying to keep the conversation rolling, "when do you actually start writing?"

Lydia smiles an indulgent smile that makes him feel a little silly. "It's all writing, Alex," she says. "But if you mean actually chained to my desk and bashing out pages, I started this morning, but it won't be finished for months yet."

"Seems like a long time."

"You can't rush a good thing. Besides," she strokes her

ruby ring absently as it glints in the flickering candlelight, "I get lost in the stories. It's kind of therapeutic, you know?"

"I get my catharsis when we lock them up," Alex replies.

"Are you ready to order?" Their cherubic waiter has reappeared, pad in hand.

"I'll have the shrimp," says Lydia confidently, handing him her menu, "and then the filet, rare."

"I knew there was a reason I liked you," says Alex, his grin returning. "I'll have the filet too, same way, and the pate."

"Very good, sir." The waiter stabs the pad with his pencil and disappears again.

"Damn," says Alex, picking up his near-empty drink. "I forgot to ask him for another." He makes a half-hearted attempt to attract the attention of a waitress loitering nearby, but fails.

"You're too polite," Lydia teases.

"That's a problem?" he flares, indignantly.

"It can be," she says with a shrug. "Watch and learn." Lydia stretches out her hand and catches a fast-moving waiter by the arm. "Excuse me," she purrs, smiling broadly at him, "could we get another round of drinks please?"

"Of course, madam," he replies, turning on a well-polished heel and heading back towards the bar.

"That's how you do that." She grins like a Cheshire cat, sitting back in her chair. Alex takes in the spectacle hungrily. Her confidence, arrogance even, is intoxicating. Lydia's eyes linger on his as she picks up her glass and tips back what's left.

"I've never liked gin," says Alex, making a face. "Always thought it tasted like nail polish."

"Why were you drinking nail polish?"

"You know what I mean," he says. "It tastes like nail polish smells."

"I see," says Lydia. "Well I've never liked Jack Daniel's. It smells and tastes sickly." She makes a face.

"Anything can be sickly if you have too much," says Alex, then tips back his own drink to muffle the words, "like you did the other night."

"What was that?" Lydia puts a hand to her ear. "I didn't quite catch that."

"Oh, nothing," says Alex, sweetly.

"Something about the other night?"

"No, no…"

"God, that was embarrassing." She slumps onto the table. "Please don't let me get like that again. I don't even remember half of that night."

"Evidently," says Alex, "since you accused me of taking advantage of you."

"I did not!" Lydia protests confidently, "I didn't accuse you of anything, I just didn't know if—"

"Lydia," says Alex calmly, "I'm kidding."

"Seriously," she says, leaning towards him and speaking in a conspiratorial whisper, "did I say or do anything stupid?"

"No," replies Alex reassuringly. "No, of course not. Stupid? No, no, no. I mean…" he pauses for effect, enjoying the look of dawning horror on her face.

"What?"

"You *did* do the crab in front of a packed bar."

"I did not!" Lydia claps a hand over her mouth.

"Nah," Alex laughs, "you didn't."

"Asshole…" Lydia shoots him a dirty look and tosses her napkin at him just as the waiter returns with their drinks.

"I apologise for my companion's behaviour," Alex says to him. "She's from little Philly, you know." The waiter looks mortified, but not as much as Lydia.

"Would you bring me another one of these, please?" she asks, picking up her fresh martini. "My… companion here is going to be wearing this one any second now."

"Very good, madam," says the young man, relieved to be given an opportunity to flee.

"I think you scared him," says Alex, sipping his drink.

"Yes, well," says Lydia, "that just goes to show, doesn't it?"

"Show what?"

"That there's a monster in all of us." She grins wickedly, eyes sparkling.

"I'll drink to that," says Alex, reaching out with his glass. Sealed with a clink, an unspoken pact to swallow their respective pasts, at least for now.

"Well that was something else." Alex lets his delicate silver spoon drop onto a plate streaked with the remnants of a chocolate torte and sits back in his chair.

"Mmmm…" agrees Lydia, her own spoon still in her mouth, savouring the last bite of a decadent caramel soufflé. Bursts of sugar-fuelled energy pop and fizz inside her like tiny explosions.

"Wow," says Alex, watching her with a smile playing about his lips.

"Mmm?" Lydia asks, the question muffled by her spoon.

"Are you actually speechless?" He feigns amazement, puffed cheeks and wide eyes.

"Dessert doesn't say dumb things," says Lydia, finally releasing the spoon and placing it carefully down next to her dish, "so I never need to set it straight."

"I see," says Alex, nodding, "so most of the time you're talking, it's because you're..."

"Correcting stupid people," Lydia nods, "that's right."

Alex rolls his eyes.

"Honestly though," says Lydia, "I think that was the best meal I've ever had." She smiles and plays with her necklace demurely. "Thank you."

"My pleasure," Alex replies. "I'm just happy to cross something off my bucket list."

"Excuse me?" Lydia asks, eyes wide.

"Impress a successful, beautiful novelist in a fine restaurant," he replies.

"That's on your bucket list?" Lydia laughs. "Is it right above *give a sceptical woman a contrived, cack-handed compliment?*"

"Two birds..." Alex shrugs.

"Who has a bucket list anyway?" Lydia scoffs at the idea.

"You don't?"

"Like, what," Lydia waves a hand, "see the seven wonders of the world? Run a marathon? Jump out of a plane? Please..."

"You don't want to do those things?" Alex asks, sounding a little disappointed.

"I don't think about them," Lydia replies dismissively. "I'm too busy with my job to daydream."

"Pity," says Alex, taking a sip of his fifth drink of the evening. "I think it's good to daydream now and again."

"Don't tell me you actually have a list?" asks Lydia, incredulous.

"Yeah," he replies, unashamed.

"What's on it?"

"It's a secret." He grins at the reaction he knows this will get.

"Oh don't be ridiculous!" Lydia explodes. "Are we children again? You don't have secrets like that."

"I don't?"

"Tell me."

Alex shakes his head. Lydia exhales forcefully and tosses her napkin in the air to vent her frustration. "You're really frustrating sometimes, you know that?"

"I've been told," Alex nods solemnly. His eyes wander to the dance floor, which has gradually thinned out over the course of the evening, though the music is still in full swing. "Wanna dance?"

"Oh," says Lydia, looking horrified, "no, I'm a writer, not a dancer."

"Come on," says Alex, sliding out of his seat and holding out his hand to her. "It'll be funny."

"I don't want to," Lydia snaps, hiding behind her fourth martini.

"Please?" asks Alex, with his most practised puppy dog eyes. "Just one dance. If you hate it, I'll never ask you to do it again."

"I've heard that before," Lydia mutters.

"I don't even want to—"

"Fine," she says suddenly, pushing her drink away and

taking his hand. "One dance. But I'm warning you, I'm really bad."

"That's what I'm counting on," Alex purrs softly in her ear as he pulls her up. He leads her along a snaking path between tables to the smooth, wooden dance floor and they find a space. Amongst the twirling of feathers and fur to a lively jazz beat, Lydia looks completely out of place. She wobbles awkwardly from side to side, heels clicking out of time with the beat.

"Did no one ever teach you how to do this?" Alex shouts over the music.

"Obviously not!" she roars back. "This is stupid." She makes a motion as if to step off the floor, but Alex grabs her arm gently.

"I'll teach you," he purrs in her ear. "Here, just... loosen up a bit." He sways with her in time to the music.

"Like this?"

"Better," says Alex, "but your hips are still stiff. You have to let go, let the music take you."

"You sound like you're on drugs," Lydia grumbles, but she tries to do as he says, letting her muscles relax and un-focusing her eyes so that the tables and chairs, even the other dancers around them become nothing but a blur. She concentrates on the music, feeling its urgency, its energy, its life as the orchestra steps up the pace.

"There you go," he says, as the two of them sway in sync. "Now, let's dance."

Lydia gasps as he whisks her practically off her feet, and hardly catches her breath for the next few minutes as they whoosh and swirl around the dance floor. She's on a wild ride, like a rollercoaster, and loving every moment. Finally, with a crashing crescendo of drums and cymbals, the song comes to an end and the sweaty musicians in their white suits take a break. Lydia collapses against Alex in fits of giddy laughter.

"Told you you'd enjoy it." He beams happily.

"Oh my god. I need to sit down…"

"Well it's that time of the night folks," announces a white-suited singer on the stage, "when I must ask every gentleman to accompany the lady he accompanied here tonight onto the floor for one last, precious waltz."

Alex and Lydia suddenly find their path back to their table blocked by other couples flooding towards them. "Well," says Alex with a shrug, "I guess we have no choice."

"I guess not," Lydia agrees, taking his hand as he slides his arm around her waist. Her other hand at his shoulder, her ruby ring sparkling like fire as it consumes the light of the fabulous chandelier overhead, as well as the dozens of candles dotted around the room. Once again, Lydia allows herself to be led, and Alex sweeps her around the room with a strong yet gentle confidence, their eyes locked together, breaths synchronised, heartbeats in perfect harmony. He is the lion; strong, confident, safe. She the raven, soaring effortlessly through the air, a blur of ebony and crimson, but for those soft, golden curls flowing like honey.

Here, in the arms of another, for the first time ever, Lydia feels free.

Twenty-Eight

Mother

The colours are too bright here. From the blue plastic chairs to orange and green swirls on the walls and shiny, garish magazines on the tables, all lit by an overwhelming fluorescence. It makes Lydia's brain throb behind her bleary eyes. A threadbare length of red tinsel is draped along the wall, and Lydia tries her best to ignore it lest she rip it down and strangle somebody with it.

A loud, metallic rattling makes her wince as a male nurse rolls a trolley full of instruments past the waiting area. The glimmer of a needle poking from a syringe catches her eye, which then wanders up to the nurse's face; tanned skin and tousled, dark brown hair, and pale blue eyes that hint at a bright yet melancholy soul. He has an alluring quality, Lydia thinks, power and beauty. Patients must be drawn to him all the time. As she allows herself to slip into a lazy fantasy about this oblivious stranger, a woman approaches. Mid-thirties maybe, dressed in a blue smock with a tight bun of faded blonde hair, the nurse tilts her head to catch Lydia's attention.

"Lydia Tune?"

"Yes?" Lydia replies absently, slipping out of her daydream. She instantly remembers Alex's words from the previous evening and feels a pang of some emotion she cannot place.

"You can see her now," says the nurse, whose nametag reads 'Maggie'. She turns away before waiting for acknowledgement. You must need an autopilot setting to work somewhere like this, Lydia thinks, rising from the uncomfortable chair and hurrying as best she can on her high heels to catch up.

"How well do you know Mrs Devere, Maggie?" Lydia asks, catching up with the nurse half-way down the sterile corridor.

"Not very well," replies Maggie. "She doesn't say much. Seems like a lovely lady though. Been here a few weeks."

"What happened to her?" asks Lydia.

"Fell down the stairs in her house, poor thing," says Maggie. "Lucky she managed to crawl to a telephone or she'd have been done for. Don't think she has any family. Least, none I've seen visiting."

"Will she be able to go home?"

"Not now," says Maggie, shaking her head sadly. "Once they lose their mobility, they need round the clock care. We're trying to find her a place at an assisted living facility, but she didn't have insurance so it's a waiting game, as usual." She makes a sharp right turn onto a large ward with maybe twelve beds and walks to the last one on the right, pulling back the emerald green curtain around it just enough to see its occupant. "Evelyn?" Lydia hears a soft, croaking sound. "You have a visitor." She steps aside, and Lydia gets her first glimpse of the small, white-haired old woman dwarfed by this big hospital bed. "I'll leave you alone," Maggie says to Lydia. "Call if you need anything."

"Thank you," Lydia replies, quietly.

"I can't see," says Evelyn Devere, her breath rattling, cloudy eyes twitching side to side.

"Hello, Mrs Devere," says Lydia, stepping close to the bed. "My name's Lydia."

"Lydia Tune?" Evelyn squeaks. Lydia notices that her nails are bitten to the quick, cheeks sunken in, loose folds around her eyes. What teeth she has left are broken and hollow.

"Yes," says Lydia.

"Come sit down," says Evelyn, raising a hand with some considerable effort and swinging it towards a bedside chair. Lydia sits as she's asked, smoothing her blue silk shirt and black skirt.

"I hope I'm not disturbing you," says Lydia.

"I am… disturbed," Evelyn says, every word an effort. "I am… haunted… by my son." She turns her shrunken head towards Lydia. "That's why you're here, isn't it?"

"Yes," Lydia replies, taking out her phone to begin the recording. She hates doing this. Feels like a vulture.

"What a… lovely ring," Evelyn breathes. Lydia looks down at her ruby, glinting as always, but particularly dark today.

"Thank you," she says, "it was my mother's."

"Mmm…" says Evelyn, thoughtfully. "Something to remember her by."

"Tell me about your son," says Lydia awkwardly, not wanting to drag this out any longer than necessary.

"Which one?" Evelyn shifts underneath her many sheets. Her attention is failing already.

"Jason." Lydia takes her notepad and pen from her bag.

"Ah yes," says Evelyn, "he was a good boy. Good as gold. Always looking out for his brother."

"Really?" Lydia asks, surprised.

"Oh yes," Evelyn nods. "Inseparable, those two. Went everywhere together."

"Were they alike?" Lydia asks.

Evelyn shakes her head very slowly. "Finn was a quiet boy. Shy. Jason was the loud one. Very... protective of his little brother."

"Do you think," Lydia pauses, hating herself more by the second, "do you think Jason feels responsible for what happened to Finley?"

"It wasn't... his fault," Evelyn croaks, "but... he changed after that. And after... Adam left."

"Adam was your husband?"

Evelyn nods, and her head wobbles so alarmingly that for a split second Lydia is afraid it might fall off. "He couldn't... cope."

"I'm sorry," says Lydia. Evelyn raises her hand again, but not as high this time. She doesn't have much left in her.

"Long time ago," she says. "Have to move on."

"So you noticed a change in Jason's behaviour?" Lydia asks.

"When?" Evelyn looks confused.

"When he was a child," Lydia says, gently.

"Oh... well he acted out... at school, but he was always

234

a good boy at home." She turns her head to look at a vase of white tulips on the bedside table.

"Was he involved in any other traumatic events?" Lydia asks. "Accidents, that sort of thing?"

"Accidents..." Evelyn thinks. "There was one time he got his finger caught in a garden chair. There was blood everywhere... drama. But he was fine." She chuckles.

"Okay," says Lydia, making a note. Suddenly Evelyn Devere's hand shoots out and grabs her wrist and Lydia lets out a startled gasp.

"He's a good boy, deep down," says Evelyn, staring straight at her. "Please understand that."

"I... Okay." Unsure quite how to react, Lydia places a comforting hand on top of Evelyn's, but the old lady withdraws hers slowly and closes her eyes.

"Are you okay?" Lydia asks, gently. "Should I fetch the nurse?"

"No need," Evelyn murmurs. "I'm fine."

"Mrs Devere, I have to ask you," Lydia says uncomfortably, "is there any history of mental illness in your family?"

"Not on my side, dear," Evelyn smiles. "Though, maybe we're all a little bit crazy by the time we get to the end."

"Maybe," Lydia agrees. "What about your husband's family?"

"Adam?" Evelyn thinks. "His mother was a loan shark. Mary, that was her name. Used to beat up grown men!"

"Really?" Lydia scribbles in her pad.

"She was a mad one, I reckon. She once..." Evelyn succumbs to a hacking cough. "She once stabbed Adam in the leg for having his feet on the table."

"She stabbed him?" Lydia raises an eyebrow.

"Said she just cleaned it!" Evelyn chuckles again.

"Did Jason take after his father at all?"

"In looks, maybe," says Evelyn, smiling. "Adam was a handsome man. But Jason was always his mother's son."

"Do you think he loves you?"

"Of course he does." Evelyn prickles at the question. "I'm his mother."

"I'm sorry," says Lydia, "it's just that sometimes people like Jason are incapable of love."

"My son..." Evelyn says with conviction, "has a good heart." She lays back in bed, looking away from Lydia. "A mother knows these things."

Lydia can hear the emotion in the old woman's voice. It would be cruel to press any further. "Thank you for talking to me, Evelyn," she says, packing up her things. "I hope it wasn't too difficult for you."

Evelyn doesn't respond. She's staring at those tulips again. Lydia takes the hint, and leaves quietly, pulling back the mint green curtain behind her. Already she is hatching a plan to break this story open based on what she has just heard. It will be risky, but Lydia Tune feels the time is right to take a few risks.

Twenty-Nine

No Good Deed

Lydia stretches out her arms, pale hands gripping the leather steering wheel, squinting to focus on the road ahead as the vein in her temple throbs like an electric current. Driving usually helps ease the pain, clear her mind and cleanse the pulp that clogs the cortex.

Either side of her people walk the streets, going about their daily routines, getting coffee, Christmas shopping. Ordinary people. Mediocre. She will never understand why people settle for lives like this when they have the potential to be so much more. How can they be happy with so little? In Lydia's mind they have succumbed to a vicious circle; they fail to care about themselves, and as a consequence the world stops caring about them. Would it really matter if the Krimson Killer knocked off a few more? They are just the extras in life's story. In her story.

Lydia knows she is a narcissist. When you know what you truly are, it is easier to make a mask that fits well, and Lydia wears many masks. One for the world, one for her family, one for her friends, at least when she had any. But she never shows anyone her true face. Few people do.

Her thoughts drift back to what Alex said about daydreaming, and she realises that she doesn't have a clear idea what happiness looks like to her. That she's never been able to picture it. Her goals were always linked to her career, to her success. She just assumed that by the time her story was over, it would all have been worthwhile because she had faith in her work. But seeing Alex again after all these years, spending time with him, enjoying his company, has made her question her approach to life.

As if summoned by her thoughts, a family crosses the road in front of her when she stops at a red light. Mother, father, two kids – a boy and a girl. The typical nuclear family, wrapped up in coats and scarves and carrying bags laden with gifts. The Christmas theme makes Lydia balk, but then she sees their faces. They are so happy, smiling, laughing, faces pink and creased with genuine joy. She realises with a pang that she has never known that feeling. Could it be that she never will? Would that mean that her life had been wasted? Perhaps she deliberately doesn't think about such things because she knows deep down that she will want them, as everyone else does. They all want to be loved. Is that what she wants?

Lydia's troubling train of thought is cut short as her phone rings. She pulls over into a space outside a quaint little shop to answer it.

"Hello?"

"Miss Tune?" asks a voice she recognises from earlier in the day.

"Nurse Maggie?" Lydia replies, confused. "Is something wrong?"

"It's Evelyn Devere," says the nurse, sounding shaken. "She passed away this afternoon."

"Oh my god. How?"

"That's the thing," Maggie whispers, "it's being written up as heart failure, but her eyes were bloodshot and she had skin under her nails."

"I don't understand."

"It looks like she was smothered," Maggie says urgently. She sounds scared.

"Surely you don't think that I—"

"Of course not," says Maggie quickly. "I saw her after you left, she was fine."

"What do the police say?"

"There are no police. She was an old lady with a broken leg. There's nothing to go on, besides anyone could have just walked in."

"That doesn't seem fair," says Lydia, surprised at her own genuine concern for a woman she barely knows. "Everyone deserves justice, no matter how old they are."

"Like I said, they have nothing to go on," says Maggie, a note of despair in her voice. "There's no working security cameras except the ones out front; budget cuts as usual, and we get thousands of people coming and going every day. Be like looking for a needle in a haystack. That's why I'm telling you. I know about your books, you know, how you get to the bottom of things. Maybe you can figure out who did this."

"Oh," Lydia sounds surprised. "This isn't the kind of thing I usually—"

"If you can. Like you say, it isn't fair. Look, I have to go."

"Okay. Listen, I'm sorry about all of—" There's a click. The line is dead.

Lydia sits quietly for a moment, in her car, in the snow, outside the little shop. She feels sad about Evelyn. She seemed like a kind old lady, and nobody deserves to die alone and afraid. But already Lydia's mind is moving past that, trying to figure out how she can use this situation to her advantage. Have the hospital called Mortem yet? Have they told Jason? Perhaps there is a window here to crack this beast's back and finally get to the dark heart of his story.

Thirty

Spider's Web

A rickety fan chopping through the cold evening air is the only sound to be heard as the wolf circles his cell in the cavernous room below, his restless gaze shifting between the fading rays of light spilling in through a high, small window, and a large, shimmering spider's web stretched across the corner of his room. In the centre of its silvery strands, a fat, unfortunate fly struggles to free itself as its doom creeps towards it cautiously, letting it tire itself out before moving in for the kill. The prisoner freezes as he watches the spider wait, and wait, and then lunge, sinking its fangs into its prey and rolling it up tight in a silken shroud.

His expression now becomes one of sadness as he licks his dry lips, hands twitching, when suddenly his senses are on high alert. He whips around; eyes trained upon the only door, expectant, predatory instincts stirred. Sure enough, the handle turns and the beast's mouth begins to water.

"I could smell you before you even parked your car," he growls, baring those yellowing teeth.

"Hello, Jason," Lydia replies calmly, approaching the cell. "How are you?" The wolf doesn't reply. His shoulders rise and fall slowly, and she can hear his deep breathing from twenty feet away. *He's upset. Does he know?*

"Oh I see…" Jason Devere turns his head slowly to look at her. "You want to play nice, after your boyfriend came after me?"

Lydia makes a show of looking him up and down. "You look fine to me," she says pleasantly. "Are you in pain?"

Jason steps towards her, pressing himself against the bars, but Lydia is a few feet out of reach. "Constantly," he breathes.

"I'm sorry to hear it."

"And how is your…" he touches the back of his own head, "little scratch?" His face works furiously as he fights to control his rage. He radiates power. Up close, it's quite terrifying.

"I'm quite recovered," Lydia replies, forcing a smile.

"Find out who did it yet?"

"Not yet. But I will."

"I'm sure."

"Jason," says Lydia, beginning to pace a small area in front of him, "I need to talk to you about something."

"Questions, questions," replies Jason, pacing alongside her, as though the bars of his cell are some kind of mirror. "Well go on then, I haven't got all night."

"Oh no," says Lydia innocently. "No questions. Not today." She watches Jason's face as he processes this remark, enjoying the confusion it betrays.

"Then why are you here?" he snarls.

"Well," Lydia begins, dragging out the tension as much as possible, "you see, I went to visit your mother this morning."

"You *what*?" Jason lunges towards her, his eyes daggers. "What did you say to her?"

"It was more what she said to me," Lydia replies, getting as close as possible in order to read his responses without getting grabbed.

"And what was that?" Jason breathes heavily.

"She wanted me to know that you're not a monster."

"She didn't use that word!" Jason roars. High above, a guard on the walkway stirs. "What did she tell you?"

"I assure you she did," says Lydia casually. "She said that you weren't a bad boy, that you'd just had bad things happen to you."

"Well that's life, isn't it?" he replies, spitting out every word as though it were poison. Lydia takes in his suffering, raw and genuine, and she feels a pang of guilt. *You couldn't tell him anyway*, a voice in her head says, soothingly, *you're not allowed. You shouldn't know. Maggie would get in trouble.*

"Not for most of us," says Lydia, peering into his feral eyes. "At least, not exclusively."

"What's that supposed to mean?"

"Jason," she slips on her kindest mask, "don't you want the world to know that you're not the monster they think you are?"

He glares back at her, his body shuddering as he fights to control his racing heart. "What if I am?" he growls softly.

"But you aren't," Lydia says gently. "Your mother knows it. I know it."

"You know nothing," he spits.

"She knows that you love her, Jason," Lydia presses on. "She knows that there's goodness still in you. Please, show me that kindness and your mother can be at peace."

"Stop talking about her!" Jason bangs on the bars of his cage with an open hand.

"She feels responsible," says Lydia, "and she can't bear it. Your redemption is all that she wants."

"Shut up!" he smacks the bars again, this time with a closed fist.

"Please, Jason, let me help you. Let me help your mother. I promise I won't let you down."

Jason turns away, his hands raised to his face, shoulders hunched. It's hard for Lydia to tell because of his long, filthy mane of hair, but she thinks he may even be... crying.

"Jason?" she prompts gently, after a moment.

"Alright," he says quietly.

"Alright... you'll help?" she asks, trying to cover her excitement.

"I'll tell you what you want to know," he says, turning around. If he has been crying, there's no trace of it now. "On one condition."

"What's that?"

"You let me tell it in my own words. Unedited. You publish them just as I write them." He leans up against the bars again, but softly this time. At peace.

"Done," says Lydia. "I will have them bring you a pen and paper."

"Come back tomorrow," he says. "I'll be done by then."

"Alright," says Lydia. "Thank you."

"I'm not doing it for you," Jason says. Lydia meets

his cold eyes, and for the first time she sees the truth behind them.

"I know," she says, then turns and walks back towards the door, trying her best to remain calm while her skin crawls with electricity. Finally, she has the beast caught in a trap.

Now all she has to do is spring it.

Thirty-One

Thank Goodness

The morning sun looming large over Decanten looks pale as the snow beneath it from Lydia's vantage, a window on the top floor of Mortem Asylum. Storm clouds roll in from the east, creeping towards the white-hot orb until they have completely engulfed it, throwing the world into milky shadow. The outskirts of the city, just a moment ago populated by red brick buildings, green trees and tiny, twinkling festive lights, are instantly drained of all colour. Muted. Sombre. Almost as if they have died.

Something like a gentle breeze passes along the corridor behind Lydia, and her heart quickens. Old buildings like this tend to be full of leaks and gaps, tiny pockets of decay that allow nature inside. But this feels different.

"Any luck?"

Lydia spins around to find Gretchen Engel standing no more than a foot from her, red hair spilling over her usual doctor's coat, patient file in hand.

"Oh, Gretchen!" Lydia replies, touching her chest and breathing a sigh of relief. "You startled me."

"I can have that effect," Gretchen replies, peering idly out of the window.

"I think I've made some progress," says Lydia. "Once I changed tactics."

"Oh?" Gretchen raises a curious eyebrow.

"A little guilt works wonders," says Lydia, folding her arms and feeling a little satisfied with herself. "And you'd be surprised how many serial killers have mummy issues."

"Very clever," Gretchen replies, looking Lydia up and down coolly.

"Is the warden around?" Lydia asks, her eyes flicking to the end of the corridor.

"Oh," Gretchen rolls her eyes, "he's preparing his speech for the Christmas party tomorrow night. It's kind of a tradition."

"Sounds nice," Lydia replies, her stomach churning at the thought of the monstrous Shade delivering a festive speech to people blissfully unaware of his true evil.

"It's thoroughly depressing actually," says Gretchen, a smile playing about the corners of her mouth. Lydia laughs. "You could come, if you like?"

"I'm not really a party girl." Lydia remembers brief flashes of her wonderful night dancing with Alex, and once again feels a pang of some emotion she can't place.

"Shame," says Gretchen. "Although to be honest I might not make it either."

"Why not?"

"Once I've fed the kids and put them to bed, I can't usually be bothered to do anything but collapse in front of the TV," Gretchen replies, yawning. "They're exhausting. But I wouldn't have it any other way." Her face lights up, and Lydia feels a pang of jealousy. Has she ever experienced anything that made her so happy? "Do you have kids? I never asked…"

"God, no." Lydia snorts with laughter. "Oh no, I wouldn't be any good at that. I'm not exactly mother material."

"You might surprise yourself," Gretchen offers with a smile Lydia finds a little too knowing. "I didn't think I was the motherly type either until I had mine."

"I guess…" says Lydia, doubtfully.

"Though I admit sometimes it feels like an uphill struggle."

"Why's that?" asks Lydia.

"Michael's autistic," says Gretchen, matter-of-factly. "Sometimes it takes a little more effort to do the simple things. And then you've got teachers calling for help because they've never met a kid like him and they don't know what to do." She laughs, a little hollow this time.

"I'm sure he'll be fine," says Lydia. "I was."

"You?" Gretchen asks, frowning. "Huh?"

"I have dyscalculia," says Lydia. "Couldn't put two and two together when I was ten years old. My teachers said I was stupid. Drove my parents mad. But did it hold me back? No."

"I suppose it can be hard to see the big picture while it's still being painted," says Gretchen, thoughtfully. "Kids are under so much stress these days."

"These days?"

"Sorry," says Gretchen quickly, "I didn't mean that you weren't, I was just thinking of my two. But you're right," she smiles, "you've certainly done very well for yourself."

"Miss Tune?" A surly guard pokes his head out of a nearby door. "He'll be ready in a few minutes."

"Thank you," Lydia replies.

"Seeing Jason again?" asks Gretchen. She's trying to sound casual, but Lydia picks up on the note of surprise in her voice.

"Yes," Lydia replies absently. "He has a promise to keep."

Gretchen eyes her warily. "Anything I should know about?"

"Oh," says Lydia, snapping back into the moment. "No, nothing important. I'll fill you in when I'm done. Does he know about his mother yet?"

"Yeah," Gretchen frowns, "the doctor called this morning. How did you know?"

"Hmm?" Lydia remembers that she's not supposed to know, and her mind races to find a cover.

"About Jason's mother."

"Oh," says Lydia, as airily as she can manage, "the hospital called me too, about an hour ago. I was supposed to go and visit her today, so, they just wanted to let me know not to bother I guess."

"Alright..." says Gretchen, now looking and sounding flat-out suspicious. "Well I'll let you go then."

"Thanks. And hey, don't forget to tell your little boy about me. Tell him he can be anything he wants to be."

"I will," Gretchen replies. "See you then." She turns and heads to the end of the corridor, before making a right turn and disappearing out of sight.

Lydia watches her go, and then turns back to the window. The large, pale disc behind the clouds hangs low in the sky now, and the scene seems to darken by the second. The shadows of the tall, spidery trees that line the road to Mortem race across the ground towards her. Again, Lydia feels a peculiar rush of cold and looks around. The corridor is empty, but significantly darker than it was a moment ago, shadows shifting in corners high and low.

"Gretchen?"

Her voice echoes into the empty darkness, which seems to creep towards her. Lydia takes a step back and bumps into the window. Turning her head to look out, she thinks she sees a figure racing from the trees towards the building, not fully formed, more like a dense, misty outline of a person moving quickly with awkward, jerky movements. She blinks, and it's gone.

"*Lydia…*"

Lydia feels a cold burst of air in her ear and spins around. There's something at the end of the corridor, but she can't see it clearly. A pale shape against the shadow.

"Miss Tune?" The guard appears in the doorway again.

"Yes?" Lydia jumps, her heart racing.

"Are you alright?" He looks her up and down with concern.

"Yes…" Lydia takes a deep breath. *Get a grip*, she scolds herself. *You're tired. It's all in your head.*

"He's ready."

But as she follows the guard to Jason's cell, she looks around again for the figure in the darkness, not knowing what might be looking back at her.

Thirty-Two

A Deal with the Devil

Fragile rays of evening sun spill through the bars high above, dust shimmering like gold in the pure light, particles of long-dead patients, doctors, visitors and victims. Amidst this ethereal cloud of memories, two towering figures, two juggernauts face off for one last time. The game has gone on long enough.

"You knew." Jason's voice sounds hollow.

"It wasn't my place to tell you, Jason," Lydia replies. She's standing a few feet away, out of reach.

"Bullshit!" he roars.

"There are procedures," Lydia says calmly. "Your doctor has to be the one to—"

"What else do you know?" Jason's fingers glow white, clutched around the thick steel bars of his cage. "What else aren't you telling me?"

"Nothing," Lydia replies, looking him right in the eye. "I promise."

"You promise..." Jason spits, bitterly.

"She seemed like a nice lady," says Lydia genuinely. "I'm… I'm sorry."

"You will be," he growls, wolf eyes boring into her.

"This doesn't change anything, Jason," she says, ignoring the threat. "The reasons why you want to tell your side of the story are just as valid today as they were yesterday." She takes a step towards him. "You can make this right."

"No," he says, looking away, voice heavy with grief. "It's too late for that."

"It's what she would have wanted…"

"*Don't you dare!*" Jason roars, wrenching the cell bars so hard that the whole thing trembles. "Don't tell me what my mother would have wanted. You didn't know her."

"You're right." Lydia says gently. *Ease off. Give him some space.* "So what do you want to do?"

Jason releases the bars and shambles to the back of his cage, half hidden in shadow. "I'll do it," he says finally.

"That's…" Lydia begins.

"If you do something for me," he says over the top of her.

"What is it that you want?" Lydia asks, opening her palms towards him.

"Come back tomorrow," he says in a soft growl, idling towards her. "I'll tell you then. And I'll tell you the truth. Everything."

"Why not now?" Lydia asks, unable to conceal her impatience.

"I need time to prepare," Jason replies. Lydia thinks she can see the flicker of a smile playing around the corners of his lips, but it might be the fading light playing tricks on her.

"Prepare what, exactly?"

"You'll see." He walks to his bed and sinks down onto the edge.

"I thought we weren't playing games anymore, Jason?" Lydia chides, sounding like a disappointed teacher.

"Oh? Then perhaps you can tell me how my mother died?"

"They said it was heart failure."

"Okay," he says in an artificially bright voice. "See you tomorrow."

Lydia feels a wave of panic rising within her. *He knows. How? What else does he know? Why won't he tell? Is the person who killed Evelyn the same person who attacked me? Will they try again? Is that why he needs more time?* "Jason, I—"

"Tomorrow," says Jason, firmly.

Lydia blinks. Suddenly she feels alone, and small, and powerless. "Alright," she concedes. "Tomorrow." She turns to go.

"Oh and Lydia," Jason calls out after her.

"Yes?"

"No guards. No cameras. Just you and me."

"That might be difficult," says Lydia. She knows this isn't true, but doesn't want to give any more ground. The balance of power is shifting, and not to her advantage.

"You'll find a way," says Jason, reclining on his bed, his back towards her. "If you want the truth."

"Why should I trust you?" Lydia asks.

"What choice do you have?"

Lydia can't see Jason's face. She can't read the emotion in his voice. He knows something she doesn't, and it's causing her more than just frustration. She's uncertain, and afraid.

Ice grips her heart, and without another word she turns and heads for the door. Far from being over, the game is suddenly spiralling out of control, and she is losing.

Thirty-Three

Transference

The skunk-like miasma of Mortem fills Lydia's nostrils, seeps through her skin, eyes, ears, clings to her clothes and suffocates her as she navigates its dark corridors. She needs to get out, to get air, to reach safety and reassess her options. Figure out a new plan. When she walked in here, a flame of confidence deep in her heart had shielded her from the lingering evil of the place. Kept it at bay. Now the flame is flickering, fading, dying, and the shifting figures at the corner of her vision stalk her every step, waiting for their opportunity to pounce.

"Did he bite?"

Lydia jumps as Gretchen's voice drifts out from her office. "What?" she asks, stepping into the doorway.

"Jason," says Gretchen, looking up from a pile of work. "How did it go?"

"Oh, fine," Lydia lies.

Gretchen peers at her over the top of her thick, black spectacles, red hair spilling off her shoulder and onto the desk. She sweeps it back and tucks it behind her ear with a practised motion. "I bet," she replies, coolly.

Lydia frowns. "Is something wrong, Gretchen?"

"Of course not," says Gretchen. "I just…"

Suddenly a terrible, blood-curdling scream pierces the air from somewhere below, causing both women to jump, eyes wide.

"What was that?" Lydia asks, voice trembling.

"The intensive patients…" Gretchen whispers, her face frozen. She bolts out of her chair and almost knocks Lydia to the ground as she sprints out into the corridor.

"Wait!" Lydia calls after her, but Gretchen isn't stopping. Lydia hesitates, torn between the desire to find out what's going on, and the desire to get the hell out of there. Curiosity gets the better of her, and she chases after Gretchen.

A maze of dark, haunted corridors leads finally to a small, enclosed outdoor area, and then the cold, grey concrete of the intensive patient block. Lydia feels her stomach churn as they enter. This place wasn't part of the tour when she first arrived, and now she sees why. Cramped and freezing, tiny windowless cells with concrete beds, no toilets, no nothing. Lamps that emit a mocking orange glow but no heat.

In the midst of this desperate setting, overall-clad guards are stabbing prisoners with tranquilizer-filled syringes and strapping them to stretchers. Four prisoners, two men, two women, all grotesque and evil in their own special ways. Like the four horsemen of the apocalypse. Lydia recognises their faces from the stack of case files she reviewed when she first arrived at the asylum. Henry, short and stocky. Waylon, large and muscular. Holly, slim, busy, beautiful. Hillary with her wild mane of hair. Murderers all.

"Take them away!" barks a voice as its owner emerges from one of the now-empty cells.

"Warden!" Gretchen exclaims, running up to him. "What's going on?!"

"Progress, Doctor Engel," barks Shade, thumbs tucked into his waistband, looking very pleased with himself.

"What do you mean?" Lydia asks.

"We've helped these patients as much as we are able," the warden replies, "now they're moving on to receive more…" a nasty smile creeps across his face, "specialist care."

"These are my patients." Gretchen protests. "You can't just take them away without my consent."

"On the contrary, doctor," Shade's black eyes glint with malice, "their transfer has been approved by the highest authority. I couldn't prevent it if I wanted to." He eyes the four limp, drooling figures with disgust. "Not that I do want to."

"Who?" Gretchen asks, desperately. "Who ordered this?"

"Government officials," Shade growls, "that's all you need to know, and all I am going to disclose. Now, why don't you be a good girl and get back to work?"

"You can't speak to her like that," Lydia bursts out, horrified. Warden Shade rounds on her.

"I hardly think you are in a position to be giving orders, Miss Tune," he glowers, menacingly. "Perhaps you have already forgotten our little chat, hmm?" He leans towards her and whispers darkly. "Perhaps you need a little reminder?"

Lydia takes a step back and looks to Gretchen, who is frowning at her with confusion and fear.

"Good," Shade booms, interpreting her silence as

submission. "I already have quite enough on my plate to deal with. Although," he grins nastily, "it will certainly be easier managing the reputation of this place without these four degenerates." He looks at Lydia again. "Wouldn't you agree, Miss Tune?"

"Where are they being taken to?" Gretchen interjects as the burly guards start carrying the loaded stretchers out of the cell block.

"Classified," replies the warden, pointedly.

"That's not right," Gretchen protests. "I need to speak to their new doctor, pass on my notes at least."

"I'm afraid that won't be possible," says Shade, smoothly. "But don't worry, doctor, you won't get in trouble. Everything has been taken care of."

He turns and follows the last patient carried out, leaving Lydia and Gretchen alone in the empty prison, staring at each other in fearful, disbelieving silence.

Thirty-Four

Only You

"**H**ello?" A chirpy, cheerful voice answers on the thin, crackling phone line and Lydia seizes upon it like a comfort blanket.

"Donna?"

"Lydia! Darling!" The agent's voice is dripping in honey. "How is it going down there? Are you almost done?"

"Yes," Lydia replies, smiling with relief like she genuinely believes it. "I've made a deal with the killer to reveal all of his secrets to me tomorrow."

"Oh, well done, darling," says Donna enthusiastically, like a parent praising their precocious toddler. "Well, get it wrapped up and you can be back in New York in time for the holidays."

"Yes…" Lydia sinks onto her soft bed, enjoying the thought of being home so much that she is even prepared to forget her hatred of all things Christmas for the sake of enjoying the moment.

"Is something wrong, dear?" Donna asks, picking up on the uncertainty in Lydia's voice.

"No, no," Lydia replies quickly. Donna doesn't need to know about the teacher. She doesn't need to know that her most valuable client is caught up in a deadly game she does not yet fully understand. Lydia peers out of the window, where heavy snow is falling gently through the black night. "It's just... him—"

"Him?" asks Donna, confused. "Him who, dear?"

"Jason," Lydia replies. Just saying his name causes her to feel an incongruous uncertainty, as though something is wrong with the world, as though a colder, darker alternate reality is grinding violently against the warm, comforting one she inhabits in this moment.

"Who's Jason?"

"The Krimson Killer," says Lydia in disbelief. "The guy I'm writing this book about."

"Of course," Donna replies, "serial killer, crazy, I knew that."

"Honestly, Donna," says Lydia, exasperated, "do you care about my books at all? Or just the royalties?"

"Oh, darling," Donna replies, sounding grievously wounded. "How could you? Of course I care." There is a brief silence. "So, do you have plans for the holidays?"

"I plan to do nothing," says Lydia.

"Nothing?" asks Donna, dramatically.

"I'm not really the Christmassy type," says Lydia. "I'll probably do what I do every year. A warm fire, a good book and a dry martini."

"Sounds good to me," Donna laughs. "Well listen, I

have a meeting, but let me know how it goes tomorrow, okay?"

"Will do," says Lydia. "Thanks."

"See you soon, darling!"

The phone rings off, and Lydia lets it drop out of her hand as she falls back onto the bed. What now? She turns her head and catches sight of a hotel brochure propped up on the bedside table. *Oooh*, she thinks, they have a spa. *That sounds good...*

An hour later Lydia finds herself in heaven, lying face-down amidst a sea of warm, flickering candles releasing their soothing fragrance. Strong yet soft hands massaging slippery oil into her back, gently easing her worries away. *Maybe upgrading hotels wasn't such a bad thing after all.* She lets go, surrenders to the hormones triggering in her brain, delicious explosions of pleasure breaking down the dams of stress and tension. She smiles a wide, satisfied, genuine smile, and her thoughts begin to drift to later in the evening. She has arranged to see Alex again, and wonders what he might have in store for her. Dinner? Dancing? Their last night out had awakened something within her that she had not felt in a long time. Ever since she was a teenager, she had viewed men as threats and/or useful resources. That's what Alex was too, at first. She liked him, but she didn't feel for him. Now the thumping in her chest and warmth in her skin as she thinks about him tells a different story. She wonders if the masseuse can feel it, and her cheeks glow pink with mingled shame and pleasure.

Is this feeling what she thinks it is? Could she really, truly be capable of something as selfless as... love?

Thirty-Five

'Tis the Season

The eyes of passers-by in the hotel lobby linger on Lydia as she waits for Alex to arrive. She doesn't wonder why, or even begrudge them a peek as she smooths the skin-tight scarlet dress underneath her luxurious black fur coat. Her hair is pinned loosely up tonight, giving the impression of effortless elegance.

Lydia's eyes flick to the glass front door, through which she can see heavy snow still falling, then to the phone in her hand. He's late, and she has no messages. In the back of her mind the image of Alex lying on the ground somewhere, bloody and butchered like poor Dorothy Eagle, tugs at her fidgeting consciousness. Whoever assaulted her and murdered the two old women was still out there, and Jason had stalled for more time. Had he sent his accomplice to take care of them once and for all?

A small girl enters through the lobby with her parents; she has blonde curls and a confident, almost arrogant gait, and Lydia is reminded forcefully of herself. Except that the girl is wearing a broad, genuine smile. She and her parents all look happy, not superficially happy but the kind of happy you know comes from somewhere deep inside. They are chatting and laughing, their energies bouncing off each other and mingling together perfectly like a beautiful, invisible dance. It takes Lydia a moment to realise that she is just enjoying the spectacle of them rather than trying to analyse their minds and behaviours as she does with every other human being she comes across. Even the sprig of festive holly pinned to the little girl's dress isn't conjuring forth Lydia's usual resentment. A smile creeps across her lips too. Is she rediscovering an aspect of herself that has been so long buried?

The family leaves through the front doors and the little girl holds the door for a man in a black leather jacket. He thanks her with a courteous bow before spotting Lydia watching them.

"You're late!" Lydia chides, playfully.

"Traffic," he grins back.

"You're such a liar."

"Look who's talking!" He raises both eyebrows. "Are you ready?"

Lydia licks her lips and takes a deep breath. "Ready," she whispers.

Twenty minutes later, Lydia finds herself blindfolded, being led up several flights of stairs.

"I'm beginning to regret asking you to surprise me," she giggles, squeezing Alex's arm.

"Just another couple of steps," he replies. "Aaaand…"

here we are!" Lydia hears the click of a door opening, and feels a sudden blast of chilly air as Alex's fingers move to gently untie the silk scarf covering her eyes. They are looking out onto a snow-covered roof terrace where a table has been made up in the luxurious fashion of a fine restaurant on Valentine's Day. Giant silver cloches cover the place settings, fairy lights strung elegantly from surrounding foliage twinkle magically, and a delicious smell of food fills the air.

"You did all this for me?" Lydia breathes, stunned, stepping out onto the terrace. The snow has stopped falling, and she gazes up, open-mouthed at the clear, black sky filled with stars.

"It's nothing really," says Alex, with blatantly false modesty.

"Alex," she whispers as he leads her to her seat, "it's amazing. How did you do it?"

"Called in a few favours," he replies cryptically. "But never mind that now. Here." He produces a thin, square, perfectly-wrapped gift from his jacket pocket and offers it to her.

"What's this?" Lydia asks, accepting it.

"Open it and find out."

Lydia turns the gift over in her fingers, then holds it up to her ear and shakes it gently like a squirrel testing a nut.

"Open it!" Alex urges gently. Lydia carefully slits the papers with a nail and out slides a compact disc case with a handwritten cover. The letters elegant and decorative, the design detailed and thoughtful. A labour of love.

"This is…" she scans the writing, "all my favourite songs. How did you…?"

"I thought you could listen to it in the car, you know, save you from all the dreadful Christmas music." He eyes her warily, trying to read her shocked expression. "Do you like it?"

"Oh, Alex!" She looks up and throws her arms around him. "I love it! Thank you."

"You're welcome." His cheeks glow even pinker than before in the biting winter air.

"I mean," Lydia says, pulling back but keeping her hands on his arms, "thank you for everything. You've turned a miserable trip into a wonderful one." She gazes into his eyes and digs her nails gently into his arm. One of them is shaking, but Lydia can't tell if it's her or Alex, if it's the cold or...

In a heartbeat his lips are upon hers, warm and soft and tender, and her fingertips are stroking his rough cheek. A surge of electricity rushes through Lydia, spreading from her centre to the tips of her frozen fingers and toes in a split second, warming them through.

Then just as quickly they are breaking apart again, looking at each other like awkward teenagers, hands lingering awkwardly in mid-air as they fumble for a comfortable place to settle. Alex settles for his pockets, while Lydia's fall limply at her sides.

"Drink?" Alex asks after an awkward pause, stepping up to the table.

"Please," Lydia replies. While he pours, she takes a few idle steps towards the edge of the roof terrace. "Good grief," she says, noticing for the first time an enormous Christmas tree in the square below, the top ten feet or so of which reach up past the terrace, "that's quite a tree."

"They're turning on the lights tonight," says Alex, offering her a mug of some steaming brown liquid. "Here."

"What's this?" she asks, lifting it to her nose.

"Hot chocolate," Alex replies, producing a paper bag from behind his back. "Marshmallow?"

Lydia grins and fishes in the bag without breaking eye contact, producing a giant, fluffy white marshmallow and dropping it into her drink. Immediately it begins to melt, a thick, white covering spreading over the brown liquid like snow over earth. She takes a big, greedy sip and beams at Alex, her bright eyes twinkling over the top of the mug. For a few moments they just stand there, drinking their chocolate and glancing from each other, to the sky, to the giant tree.

"So…" Lydia says finally. "Here we are."

"Here we are."

"You know," she begins to laugh, "if someone had told me that I would be spending Christmas in Decanten with Alex Gilbey from school, drinking hot chocolate on the roof of… what is this building anyway?"

"The police station." Alex grins.

"Oh my god…" Lydia covers her mouth.

"Well," says Alex, stepping close to her again, "I'm glad you're here."

"Me too…" she whispers. Their lips meet again briefly for a kiss that tastes like chocolate and marshmallows.

"Listen," says Alex seriously, looking down at the mug in his hands as though embarrassed about what he's about to say, "I know we haven't known each other very long, as adults I mean, but this past week has been…" he hesitates, searching for a fitting description.

"I know," Lydia rescues him. "For me too."

"I hope," Alex seems to be steeling himself to say this, "I hope that when you've finished your work here, you'll consider staying for a while."

"I…" Lydia stammers, taken aback.

"It's just that if you go back to New York," Alex presses on, "I know that'll be it. We'll promise to keep in touch, but that's a promise people always break. And it would be a shame to let this just fizzle out because I think we have something…" he looks up into her stunned face, "… special."

"Oh, Alex…" It's Lydia's turn to look away. "I don't want to leave, but—"

"Then don't!"

"But my whole life is in New York. I can't just pick up and move on the off-chance this works out." She takes a step back, peering at him with sad eyes. "If I can even do this."

"Do what?" Alex frowns.

"This!" Lydia gestures between the two of them. "Whatever this is, or could be between us, I don't even know if I'm capable of doing it properly."

"Have you ever tried?" he asks, a hint of aggression in his voice now.

"What?" Lydia looks hurt.

"Have you ever tried to do this thing you're not sure you're capable of?" He takes a step towards her. "Lydia, you know I would never hurt you."

"I know…" She looks down again.

"Then why don't you trust me?"

"It's not about that!" Lydia protests, clearly frustrated.

"Then what is it about?" Alex demands, his eyes blazing.

"I..." Lydia turns away quickly to hide her watery eyes from him. "I can't do this right now, Alex, I'm sorry. It's too much."

Alex doesn't answer, and Lydia can't bring herself to turn around and see the look she imagines on his face. Instead she walks to the edge of the terrace again and stares at the giant Christmas tree. A week ago, it would have stirred feelings of hatred in her, but now it symbolises something different. A glimmer of something undefined, something that could be joy or tragedy depending on whether or not she can be brave and face up to her fears.

"I'm sorry," says a soft voice in her ear as she feels Alex's strong hands on her arms. "I didn't mean to put you on the spot like that."

"It's okay..." she replies, turning to the side.

"I'm not asking you to give up your whole life or anything like that," says Alex, "just... think about staying a while, that's all."

Lydia looks into his eyes, big and brown and full of hope, and her icy heart melts. "Okay," she says gently, "I'll think about it."

"Promise?" Alex cracks a grin.

"I promise!" Lydia can't help but laugh at him. "Just give me a little time, okay?"

"Okay."

Suddenly an explosion of colour fills the air around them as the hundreds of lights wound around the tree burst into life. Reds, greens, blues, pinks, and a giant golden angel shining bright at the very top. The cheers of the crowd in the square below drift up to the terrace, followed a moment later by the singing of carollers.

"What do you think?" asks Alex, sliding his arm around Lydia as she turns to face the scene.

"I love it," she says quietly, entranced by the display, rainbow lights glittering in her eyes.

"But I thought you hated Christmas," he teases.

"People can change," Lydia replies, turning to grin at him. He beams happily at her, then looks back to the tree.

"You know," he says, "I'm not really a religious guy. But Christmas... I mean it just has a way of lifting people's spirits, you know? Like when the snow falls just right, when the lights glow bright, when the bells are ringing and people are singing, it's just..."

"Magic," Lydia finishes for him.

"Exactly."

Lydia pauses. "You planned that little speech, didn't you?"

"No!"

She peers at him accusingly.

"Okay fine," Alex admits. "But you have to admit, it was a good speech."

"It was," she replies, holding back a smirk.

"So..." he says, "did you think about it yet?"

"Think about what?"

"Staying."

"Oh god!" Lydia cringes.

"I'm just saying," says Alex, "this can't be our last night together. It just can't be."

"Well," Lydia replies thoughtfully, wandering over to

the table. "Just in case it is, I guess I should give you your Christmas present now."

"You got me a present?" asks Alex, following her. Lydia snaps a twig of mistletoe from the centrepiece and holds it above her head, a wicked glint in her eye. "Damn, Lyd..." Alex breathes. "You are a tease."

"I know," she whispers, leaning in for the kiss. This time it feels more comfortable, like slipping into a warm bed. And when it ends, they remain locked in a tight embrace, two hearts beating together as one, as the fairy lights twinkle, and the carols drift from far below up into a starry sky.

Thirty-Six

No Rest for the Wicked

The mattress welcomes Lydia like a delicious, giant marshmallow as she flops onto it, utterly exhausted. Running through her head, the last song playing in the car on the way back to the hotel, 'Mr Sandman' by Nan Vernon, one of her favourites from Alex's Christmas gift. Lydia loved this version because of its darker and edgier tones compared to the original. More elegant. More beautiful. She mumbles along with the words as she rolls over and kicks off her high heels, clumsily.

She wonders if Alex is lying on his bed right now thinking about her. Will she be the last thing on his mind before he goes to sleep tonight? The thought makes her giddy, but also scared. She wasn't kidding up on the roof of the police station; she really isn't sure whether this is something she can do. Something she's even capable of.

Outside the window, snow has begun to fall again. Beyond the drifting snowflakes, Lydia thinks she catches sight of something flitting by in the darkness. A bird maybe, or a bat. Some creature whose nature would never be subject to the uncertainty hers now was. Predators don't go soft.

Her thoughts turn to Gretchen. Did she make it to the staff Christmas party? Probably not, especially after the drama with Shade today. Lydia imagines the doctor looking in on her sleeping children, her pale face vivid in the glow of a night light. She imagines the warden too, starched pyjamas and a stiff nightcap, celebrating his little victory. Would he really follow through on his threat to torture her? It's just one of the many reasons why her doubts about staying in Decanten a moment longer than necessary, are still eating away at her.

Her heart feels heavy with the weight of the biggest decision she has ever made, maybe will ever make. Alex's face appears in her mind's eye, that cheeky grin playing about his lips, those big, brown eyes gazing back at her adoringly, and she feels sleep begin to overtake her.

As it does, in the shadowy corners of her imagination, another figure lurks. A feral creature, a wicked thing with sinister intentions. It is watching her, but she cannot see it clearly. Not yet. Soon.

Just a few miles away, Jason Devere lies on his bed, in his cell, staring up at the window high above. Crisp winter air whistles through the old building and he can taste it on the tip of his tongue, something at once fresh and ancient, light and dark, good and evil. Tomorrow is the day. The final chapter is about to begin.

Thirty-Seven

A Change in Plans

An ethereal presence creeps slowly over Lydia's sleeping face, gently warming her pale skin, coaxing her consciousness back from the depths of a dream. Sunlight. Eyes still closed, she stretches her arms and legs, muscles groaning and joints cracking. Then she lies still again, an unfamiliar satisfaction flowing through her body from head to toe. It is pleasant. Peaceful. She savours it for a few long, lazy minutes.

Finally, she turns her head to look at the clock. Nine thirty-three. Earlier than her alarm, yet she feels completely rested and full of energy. What witchcraft is this? She reaches for her phone and the screen lights up. A message from Alex, timestamped exactly seven o'clock. He must have work this morning. She swipes to read it.

TURN ON THE NEWS. URGENT.

Lydia sits up sharply, her heart racing. What on earth could be so important to her at seven in the morning? She jumps out of bed, crosses to the television and turns it on. The local news station shows a reporter speaking to the camera outside of a familiar-looking building. The police station from last night, she realises with a start. It looks different in the daytime. 'BREAKING' says the ticker scrolling across the bottom of the screen. 'BODIES OF KRIMSON KILLER'S FINAL VICTIMS FOUND.'

"... names not being released at this time," says the reporter. "But police confirm that the bodies bear the identifying hallmarks of serial killer Jason Devere, who is behind bars at Mortem Asylum. All eight bodies were discovered in a storage facility in the warehouse district of Decanten."

Lydia stares at the screen. Can this be a coincidence? These poor people have been missing for years; now she shows up sniffing around the case and suddenly the bodies are found?

"My locker's the next one down," says a short, round man wearing camouflage pants and a white T-shirt. "I was just grabbing my gear to go fishing when I smelt something real nasty that definitely wasn't me. So I called the manager and he called the police, and here we are."

Lydia frowns as the stranger's pale blue eyes stare at her from the television screen. Many things about this turn of events are troubling her, yet none of them explain the peculiar feeling of panic now causing her heart to race. She picks up her phone again. But who will she call first? Alex? Gretchen? What will she say? She drops the phone onto the bed. Think, she commands herself. This changes things, but how?

The answer comes to her in a flash. There's only

one person who can tell her for sure what happened to those people, and he has promised her the truth. Lydia knows something is wrong about this situation. She knows that she is playing her opponent's game now. But there is nothing else for it at this point.

She needs to see Jason Devere again, and find out once and for all the secrets of the Krimson Killer.

Thirty-Eight

Crying Wolf

The door of the Mortem Asylum lobby bursts open and icy winds roar inside, swirling around the force of nature that is Lydia Tune. She strides purposefully past the front desk, thoughts focused like a laser on one thing and one thing only.

The woman behind the desk, phone clamped between ear and shoulder, makes a half-hearted attempt with her free hand to get Lydia's attention, but to no avail. She wrenches back the elevator grate and hits the button with a closed fist, tapping her foot impatiently as she waits for the ancient mechanism to grind into life.

Once on the second floor, Lydia heads down the now-familiar corridor towards the cavernous east wing where Jason's cell is housed. The twisted shapes on the walls seem to feed off her energy, writhing and squirming at the very edge of her vision. She grits her teeth and ignores them. *They're not really there*, she tells herself. *It's all in your mind.*

"Lydia?"

Lydia is so busy ignoring her surroundings that it takes her a few seconds to register that the voice is real.

"Lydia!"

She stops, turns and walks back to the open door from where the voice came. Gretchen is standing in the middle of her office, surrounded by other doctors and looking quite exhausted.

"Gretchen?" says Lydia, alarmed. "What's going on?"

"It's okay," Gretchen replies in a deliberately calm voice.

"I'll be the judge of that," Lydia snaps. "Have you spoken to Jason? What did he say?" She eyes the other doctors in the room warily. "And who are all these people?"

"Please," Gretchen pleads, "take a breath."

Lydia opens her mouth to protest, but meets Gretchen's gaze and thinks better of it. Instead she does as she's told, takes a long, deep breath and collects her thoughts. The doctor is right, she needs to be clear-headed and in control. The dank, moist air inside the asylum leaves a wooden taste in her mouth and makes her feel ill.

"Alright," she says finally, "I'm calm. Tell me what's happening."

"Well," says Gretchen, taking Lydia's arm as the other doctors file out of the room, chattering amongst themselves in low, conspiratorial voices, "you recall from Jason's case notes that he was sentenced to death, but his lawyer argued insanity and he was transferred here instead?"

"Yes," Lydia replies, "so what?"

"The governor filed a petition this morning to enforce the original sentence," says Gretchen.

"What do you mean?" Lydia frowns at her, panic rising from within.

"Jason's being executed. Today."

"Today?!" Lydia grabs hold of Gretchen's desk to steady herself.

"We were all meeting in here to discuss options, since…" Gretchen scratches her head and sighs, "well, we haven't done this here in a while. Not in my time, anyway."

"Can't he appeal?" Lydia asks, her mind working through all the different ways she might be able to help, without stopping to wonder why she wants to.

"No," says Gretchen. "His guilt was determined already. There's nothing we can do."

"But—"

"Lydia," Gretchen says, firmly. "Listen to me. We still have procedures to go through and the warden won't be here for another half an hour." She looks meaningfully at Lydia. "So if there's anything you need to talk to Jason about, you best do it right now."

Lydia throws her arms around Gretchen, burying her face in the doctor's mane of copper hair. "Thank you," she gasps.

"Don't thank me," says Gretchen, pushing her away gently. "Just hurry."

Lydia glances up at the ticking clock on the wall as she dashes from the office. Time is not her friend. Apparently, it never has been.

Giant ceiling fans spin slowly overhead as a uniformed guard escorts Lydia to the cell in the middle of the room. There are more guards than usual today.

"Is this really necessary?" she asks, uncomfortable in the man's hulking presence.

"Afraid so," grunts the guard. "Warden's orders."

Jason Devere sits on a metal chair facing the bars of his own personal prison. He looks up as Lydia approaches, and she sees that his eyes are pink, and his cheeks raw. He's been crying. In his hand, something catches the light and glints silver and blue. His mother's locket, the heart-shaped one Lydia had given to him when she first arrived.

"Time to talk, Jason," she says coldly. There is no time for sentiment. Theirs is a business relationship now, and she is running out of time to close the deal. "Last chance."

"What do you want to know?" he asks, in a hollow voice.

"Why did you do it?" asks Lydia.

"Christ," Jason mutters, "you can't let anything go, can you?"

"Tick-tock, Jason." Lydia taps her watch.

"You know," he says, shoulders slumped in a melancholy fashion, "I never thought it would end like this."

"How did you imagine it would end?" asks Lydia, impatiently.

"I always imagined that I would die peacefully in my sleep," Jason replies. He looks up at her and the wolf smile plays around his lips. "Or else go out in a blaze of glory." He wets his lips. "How about it, Lyd? Wanna help me make it one for the road?"

"You're disgusting," Lydia replies.

"And you're not?" He raises an eyebrow. "We're all the same sort of animal."

"If you don't tell the truth now," says Lydia, sternly,

"then the world will think the worst of you until the end of time. Is that what you want?"

"Does it matter?" Jason shrugs.

"You made a promise," Lydia reminds him.

"I did," Jason concedes, nodding his head gently. "You're right." He gets slowly to his feet and faces her. "I'll keep my promise to you, Lydia Tune."

"Tell me why you killed all those people."

Jason leans forward, looks her dead in the eye and whispers, "*I didn't.*"

"You're lying," Lydia snaps. The nearby guard takes a step towards them.

"I'm not," Jason whispers. "I didn't do it."

"Fine," says Lydia flatly. "Have it your way. Die just another mad serial killer." She turns to go. "Your mother will be rolling in her grave."

"You know," says Jason loudly, "you've been far meaner to me than I ever have to you." Lydia turns and sees the look of hurt and anger on his face. "What do you think that says about you?"

"That you bring out the worst in me." Lydia glares at him. Jason smiles a sad, hopeless smile.

"You promised me something too," he says.

"Excuse me?"

"You promised to do something for me."

"Alright," says Lydia, folding her arms. "Not that you've held up your end of the bargain, but what would you have had me do for you?"

"Listen."

"I am listening."

"No." Jason shakes his head. "I want you to really listen to me, like you haven't since you first got here."

"I don't understand a word you're saying," says Lydia with a wave of her hand. "Maybe you really are just mad."

"You will understand soon," says Jason, calmly. He has an odd look about him now that Lydia finds unsettling. He seems at peace. Serene. "My death will trigger events that nobody will be able to stop," he says. A chill creeps up Lydia's spine. "And only you will be able to make sense of them."

"Me?" Lydia stares at him in disbelief. "Why me?"

"You wouldn't believe me if I told you. You will have to see the truth with your own eyes."

"Why don't you try me?"

"I will give you the answers I promised," says Jason, leaning against his bars and peering at her through strands of lank, greasy hair. "But only in death."

"Stop speaking in riddles."

"They're only riddles if you're not really listening," Jason shoots back. "You're a smart woman, Lydia Tune," he smirks, "but you're going to need to learn to think like a monster if you want your answers." He tilts his head to the side. "If you want to live."

"Then help me," demands Lydia. "You're the monster, aren't you? Tell me how I'm supposed to figure this out!"

The heavy jangling of keys makes her look around to see a pair of guards approaching from the door.

"Looks like our time is up," says Jason, calmly. Lydia stands and stares, dumbfounded, as the guards unlock Jason's cage and step inside, shock batons raised. "No need, gentlemen," he says, turning around and crossing his hands behind his back ready to be cuffed. "I'll come quietly, Just bring pen and paper wherever it is that you're taking me. I have a promise to keep." They bind him tight, then half lead, half drag him from the cage. Jason keeps smiling the whole time, as if the whole thing is a joke and only he has been let in on it.

"Wait. Wait!" Lydia calls out as the guards heave him past her. "Tell me, please. Tell me what I need to know." For a fleeting second, she is close enough to smell the wolf's pelt, and it's only now she notices that Jason is wearing his mother's locket around his neck, tucked into his dirty vest. Her eyes flick from it to his face, and some unspoken message passes between them. Though she doesn't yet know what it means.

"Stay back, miss," grunts one of the guards, easing her away with his massive forearm.

Jason's voice carries back to her as he's carried away towards the door. "Good luck, Lydia Tune."

A moment later he is gone, the heavy steel door crashing shut behind him. In fact, all of the guards have gone. Nothing left for them to do here, Lydia realises. She turns and stares at the empty cell as the fan spins slowly high above.

Thirty-Nine

Broken

Sitting alone in the Mortem reception, head bowed dejectedly, time leaches the hope from Lydia like a sandcastle gradually blowing away in the wind. She feels her very essence draining away, power fading, the warmth that had been rekindled in her heart over the past week cooling and dying.

She looks at her phone. No messages. No calls. It has been less than twelve hours since she was with Alex, yet it feels like a lifetime. She needs him now. She can't do this alone, struggling silently to arrest the onslaught of cynicism that generates from within herself. Judgement from which she can neither run nor hide.

Footsteps on the polished floor make Lydia's stomach turn over. She has come to like Gretchen Engel, even feel some uncharacteristic affection for her, but the doctor is the last person she wants to see when she looks up.

"Is he...?" Lydia can't bring herself to finish the question.

Gretchen nods slowly, pink patches around her eyes betraying recent tears.

"Yes," she replies, weakly.

Lydia feels a sickness growing deep within her, and realises with surprise that it is grief. She doesn't know Jason Devere very well. She certainly doesn't like him. He may very well have been complicit in her assault, as well of course in the murders of over a dozen people. But the thought of him being taken to a premeditated death, the idea that she is complicit in it not only as a member of society but as an active player in the events that led to this point, makes her feel sad, and guilty, and bereaved. She remembers the kindly old woman she spoke to in the hospital just a few days ago. Lydia had promised to help. Instead here she sits, completely powerless.

"Can I see him?" asks Lydia.

"I'm sorry," Gretchen replies. "Nobody can. Warden's orders. His body's to be kept under guard until they can get the incinerator lit. There's some sort of problem. Maintenance are working on it now." Lydia's hate for Shade grows. "Here," Gretchen offers her a small box; the same one Lydia had given to Jason, containing his personal effects. "He wanted you to have this back."

"Thank you," says Lydia, surprised, clutching the box tightly. Gretchen sits down next to her.

"Did you get what you wanted?"

Lydia shakes her head, biting her lip hard to keep the tears at bay.

"What will you do now?"

"Nothing," Lydia replies, in a hollow voice.

"Nothing?" Gretchen asks, a note of surprise in her soft voice.

"I'm done," Lydia says. "It's hopeless."

"Nothing is hopeless," says Gretchen, laying a hand on Lydia's arm and smiling. It would have been easy, Lydia thinks, for all of the terrible people in this godforsaken building to drain Gretchen of her empathy, her compassion. But her bedside manner is as kind and genuine as it is possible for a person to be.

"You know that's not true," says Lydia, forlornly. "Soon Jason is going to be gone. And what about the four patients you lost the other night? They're gone too."

"I haven't given up on them," says Gretchen, a tiny twinkle in her eye. "And you haven't given up on Jason. I know you haven't. Listen, I… I've heard your conversations with Jason, all of them." Lydia looks up at the doctor. "And in doing so, I think, I'm starting to realise that there is more going on with his story than I initially thought. And you know there's more to this story, don't you? You can still help him."

Lydia looks into Gretchen's eyes, wanting so badly to believe what she says, but the positive words bounce off the ice core now re-crystallising around her heart. She hangs her head. "I don't even know where to start," she says quietly. "I have no leads, no ideas. Even Alex won't call me back." She sighs. "This book is dead. There's nothing more I can do here."

Gretchen listens patiently, considers Lydia's words, then pats her gently on the leg and stands up. "I don't believe that." She starts to walk away.

"You don't know me," says Lydia, suddenly flaring up, her temper boiling over. Gretchen turns around, a shocked expression on her face. "I didn't get where I am today by looking out for other people," Lydia says, eyes blazing. "I did it by looking after myself. That's how you make it in this world. It's the only way to survive. Nobody wants to admit it, but that's the brutal truth."

Gretchen stares at her coolly, all trace of bedside manner vanished. "And how is that working out for you?" she asks. "Are you happy?"

Lydia glares at her furiously, then looks away without answering.

"I hope you find what you're looking for, Lydia," Gretchen says. "I hope you find that happiness." She turns and walks to the elevator, and when Lydia looks up again Gretchen is gone. Probably from her life forever. After all, there's no reason for her ever to return to this place now.

Just another person who hates me, Lydia thinks bitterly. But that doesn't quite sit right. The words fester in her mind like an infection. Gretchen doesn't hate her. Lydia is too adept a student of humanity to so lazily misread what just transpired. It wasn't hate, she realises with a pang of embarrassment. It was pity. Gretchen feels sorry for her. Sorry for her selfishness, her loneliness, her arrogance, her ego. Sorry that a man is dead and all Lydia seems to care about is her book. Sorry because Gretchen knows, just as Lydia does, that her fling with Alex is destined to crash and burn because of what Lydia is. What she has allowed herself to become.

She looks down at the box in her lap. When she packed it

originally, it was as a tactic. Just another piece on the game board, to try to outmanoeuvre a man she hadn't yet met. A gift of poor intent. Lydia opens it now with trembling fingers. Inside is a photograph, creased and torn around the edges, of two young boys, Jason and Finley, with their mother and father, Evelyn and Adam. All wearing genuine smiles, happy, peaceful, content, like the family from the hotel lobby last night. Like a family should be. Lydia stares at their faces, and realises with a pang of sickness that they are all dead now. The Devere family is gone, taking their secrets with them to the grave.

Underneath the photograph, a comb and mirror, and the silver, heart-shaped locket she had seen in Jason's hands just yesterday. Lydia reaches for it, but can't bring herself to touch the thing. A voice in her head is screaming that she isn't allowed. That it isn't right. That she has let down both mother and son, and to touch the locket would violate their memory. She snaps the box shut and jumps to her feet. She has to get out of here.

Lydia strides across the lobby in as composed a fashion as she can muster, aware of the receptionist's eyes on her, aware of the cameras. Then as soon as she is out the door she breaks into a run, high heels skimming across the snow towards her car. The winter sky is pale blue, peaceful, completely at odds with the dark storm raging inside of her. She unlocks the car door and throws herself into the driver's seat, slamming the keys into the ignition and stirring the engine to life with a roar. The radio blares loudly, and Lydia smashes the power button with her palm to silence it. She doesn't want to hear her favourite songs right now. Doesn't want to be reminded of the man who still hasn't called her back.

Just as she feels her anger towards him boiling up, a chime rings out. It's her phone. A message from Alex.

Forty

Heart of Darkness

*H*i *Lydia, meet me at Harkem House, the Devere's old place. I have a surprise for you.*

Underneath the text, a tiny marker blinks on a map square. Lydia stares at it for a moment, then re-reads the words. What was Alex doing there? Had the police found some new evidence? More bodies? Why would he invite her? Would she even be allowed on site, if it's a crime scene? Her fingertips glide across the glass as she composes her reply.

What is it?

She doesn't have to wait long.

You'll see. Come quickly.

The little monster called anxiety gnaws at the already-chewed corners of her mind. Something about this seems wrong. Alex knows she doesn't like surprises. He knows what she's been through. He's sworn to protect her for crying out loud. But Gretchen's cold rebuke still rings in her ears. If Lydia wants to change, she knows, there are two things that she must do. First, honour her promises to Evelyn and Jason to unearth the truth. And second, give Alex the chance he deserves. At Harkem House, there may be a way to do both. Two birds, one stone.

Okay, on my way.

She is about to set her phone down on the passenger seat, when the screen lights up again.

See you soon.

Lydia keeps an eye on her satnav as she traverses the treacherous, snow-covered country roads to Harkem House, way out past the north edge of Decanten. The stereo is playing her Christmas gift, an attempt to keep nerves at bay and stay positive about the twin tasks at hand.

A pothole jerks the vehicle with a sharp shudder, and Lydia's slender fingers grip the wheel tightly as she fights to keep control. The snow is starting to fall heavily again, heavy clouds gathering and blocking out the sun's rays. She flicks on her headlights, and in their yellow-orange glow a sign looms up ahead. 'CAUTION: DEEP WATERS'.

Lydia scans her surroundings, confused. There's no water here. The James River is miles to the south and the Chesapeake Bay to the east. Then she comes upon another sign. 'TRAVELLER'S BRIDGE'.

"Traveller's Bridge…" Lydia says out loud, a flicker of recognition in her voice. This is where Jason's brother Finley fell to his death. The hairs covering every inch of Lydia's skin prickle as though charged by an electric current. Another coincidence? She doesn't like this at all. Jason's words float into her head. "My death will trigger a chain of events that nobody will be able to stop."

Lydia considers turning back, or pulling over and calling Alex, but before she can make up her mind, she is on the bridge itself. Dark grey concrete, slick with ice that makes her wheels slip as she peers over a low wall to the fast-flowing river below, chunks of snow and ice swirling in its powerful currents. No child could survive that. She feels sick.

Over the bridge and into the woods. Densely packed trees seem to close in, shuffling towards the winding road, reaching their twisting branches overhead to block out the sun. High above in their branches, dozens of pairs of eyes peer down, resident ravens taking note of everything that happens in their domain.

Suddenly they are gone. Lydia's little red car bursts free of the claustrophobic woods and into a clearing of flat fields that stretch on for miles. At their centre, a single red-brick building bathed in the eerie blue glow of the rising moon. As she gets closer, Lydia can make out the sharp, pointed roofs above large windows that peer at her like giant, haunted eyes. The house looks old, but not in any noticeable state of disrepair. Pulling up in the driveway, Lydia sees Alex's car parked right by the door. It is the only one here. Where are the other police? Where are the investigators? What is going on?

She parks her car next to his, and flinches when the porch light flicks on as she approaches the front door. Just a sensor, she tells herself. The wooden slats on the porch creak like grinding teeth. She raises her hand to knock, and then hesitates. Nobody lives here. Why are you knocking? Instead she reaches for the handle and pushes gently. The door swings open.

"Alex?" she says uncertainly as she steps inside. The entrance hall is dark, the only light coming from somewhere up the stairs straight ahead. Lydia reaches for the light switch, but its soft clunk is accompanied by no illumination. Lydia takes out her phone and calls Alex. No answer. She tries again, listening hard this time for a ringing somewhere in the building. But there is none. *This isn't right*; the voice chews her mind ever more frantically. Every fibre of her being is telling her to get out of there, to run, to drive back to town, go straight to the police station and tell them everything. But Alex's car is here. What will he think if she abandons him now?

Using her phone as a torch, Lydia presses on into the front room. The air in here is thick, and still, and suffocating. The décor a nightmarish corruption of homely. A grand piano takes up around a third of the room, opposite a majestic fireplace scattered with twee ornaments. Perched on an ornate, upholstered wooden chair, a handmade doll stares straight ahead with button eyes. Lydia's eyes travel over the many stitches crisscrossing its face like scar tissue. Without taking her eyes off it, she crosses to the piano and sits down on the stool. A framed photograph atop the giant instrument features the entire Devere family. They're not all smiling in this one. Adam looks stern, Lydia thinks. Serious. Evelyn is so young and vibrant, full of life. Young Jason is unmistakable; Lydia would know that sneer anywhere. Then there is Finley. The same pale blue eyes as his brother, lighter hair maybe, and a wicked smile that is like Jason's but not like it at the same time. There is something... unsettling about it. Lydia stares at the picture, trying to put her finger on it.

She sets the photograph down and lifts the piano lid, laying her slender fingers on the cool, ivory keys. She hasn't played since she was a little girl, but some things just stick in your memory. Softly, gently, Lydia begins to play a simple lullaby, one that her mother had played for her when she was just a little girl. At first the melody is comforting, almost warming the room as snow falls outside the window. The house begins to feel like a home. But then the notes begin to slip out of tune and the sound becomes chaotic, menacing, like nails on a chalkboard.

Lydia snatches her fingers from the keys just as the creak of a floorboard overhead almost makes her topple backwards off the stool.

"Alex?" she calls out, warily. No answer. She reaches out to close the piano lid, when a thin ray of moonlight spilling in through the window hits her ruby ring, causing it to blaze blood red in the darkness. A memory comes flooding back to her, of Jason in Mortem Asylum, a similar effect flaring about his hands only pale blue like his eyes. The locket. On a curious hunch, Lydia reaches into her bag, pulls out the box and flips it open. Sure enough, the diamonds and sapphires sparkle obligingly up at her. She fishes it out, turns it over in her hands, then digs a nail into the groove and prizes it open.

Inside she finds a tightly-folded scrap of paper. Fingers trembling, she unfolds it and begins to read by the eerie blue light of her phone.

Dear Lydia,

I'm sorry I couldn't tell you this before, but events must unfold as they are meant to do. In a few moments I will be dead, so now is the time to call in that favour you promised.

Firstly, and please believe that I am truly sorry about this, but your life is in danger. I had hoped to avoid this, but unfortunately we have both run out of time. I am not a good man, it is true. I am a drug addict, a thief and a liar. But I am not a murderer. The man the world knows as the Krimson Killer is still alive.

You have heard that my brother fell from a bridge where we played as children. This is not true. I was the one who fell. Finley pushed me. He knew what he was doing. He had always been a troubled child, pulling the wings off insects and hurting other children when they played with him. But that day was when we realised that he was truly broken.

Miraculously, I survived my fall with a few small broken bones. My mother nursed me at home so as not to arouse any suspicion at a hospital. My father yelled at us both for being so stupid – I had never seen him so furious before. Days later he committed suicide by drinking bleach. It was made to look like suicide, but my mother and I knew the truth. Finley murdered him. I wanted to tell the police, but mom was terrified of losing her son on top of losing her husband, so we buried my father in the yard and never spoke of it again. We had to protect Finley and his 'disappearance' from being found in any investigations that may have taken place around the house.

'Family is family' my mother used to say. She became paranoid that the world would discover what my brother was and take him away from her, so she faked his death, forcing me to lie to the police about him falling off the bridge. They searched for months, but Finley was locked in our attic the whole time. Mom hoped that he would grow out of his madness, that it was just a phase, but I knew that wasn't the case. Nevertheless, I still loved him as a brother and would keep him company when I could, telling him stories about my adventures at school, smoking and drinking with him in the attic.

But Finley resented being locked up. He started breaking out during the night and going hunting in the woods, bringing back dead animals and leaving them in the kitchen. He never said why. My mother began to lose her mind worrying about him.

Soon enough, I got myself that girlfriend I told you about, Anna, when I was eighteen. I was so happy, happier than I ever had been, but then Finley threatened to 'get rid of her' if I spent any more time with her. I don't know if he was jealous or bored, but I couldn't let that happen. So, I did what I had to do and broke it off with Anna, for her own sake. I let her go and live her life. Doing that broke me I must admit, and, it was a shame; I did genuinely like her.

As time went on, we saw the stories on the news about the Krimson Killer, and I knew at once who it was. I searched the attic while he was out one night and found the crude calling cards he made, marked with a K just like on TV. I didn't know what the letter meant to him. I still don't.

Again I wanted to tell the police, but my mother's tears prevented it. I wasn't strong enough to break her heart, even though it would have been the right thing to do. For a while we pretended it wasn't real, but then Finn got caught on a security camera, and the police pinned it on me. We did look alike. My mother made me promise not to tell, not to let them take him away, she told me he wouldn't be strong enough, mentally, to survive imprisonment. What I never told her is that Finn threatened to harm our mother if I didn't take the fall. So I kept quiet and let them pin all of his crimes on me. I became the Krimson Killer. Doomed to die for my brother's sins. I could at least do this one thing for my mother: protect her.

But now she is dead, I have no more promises to keep. I am certain that Finley killed her when he realised that you were on to him. Being locked up in the attic all those years has made him terrified of jail beyond all rational thought. He will come after you, and anyone else he sees as a threat, in order to prevent that from happening. You must be ready when he makes his move.

Finley is sadistic and cruel. You saw the crime scenes. He will play with you for his amusement. He will want you to run. He needs the chase. He needs to smell your fear. That is his nature. Do not give him what he wants. Do not show him what or who you care about. Use his nature, his desperation against him. I'm sure you will figure out how.

I wish I could have righted these wrongs while I was alive, but now that burden falls to you. You must stop my brother before he kills again.

One last thing Lydia. I know that you made a promise to my mother to clear my name. As hard as I know this will be, I am asking you to break it. The stain on her character if people found out that she hid a murderer in her house all that time would be unbearable. I don't want that. Please let that secret die with us. I have already died a murderer. Let me remain that way. It is no less than I deserve. I could have stopped this, but didn't. Their blood is on my hands.

Good luck, Lydia Tune. I really did like you.

Your friend,

Jason Devere

Lydia stares down at the piece of paper, her mouth open. Every word scrawled upon it has drained another ounce of strength, and now every inch of her body feels numb. She has been fooled. They all have.

With a stab of horror, Lydia remembers the creak of the

floorboard directly above her. Very slowly, she raises her head and looks up.

"Alex..." she whispers.

Suddenly everything in the room feels like a threat. Every shadow, every dark corner could be harbouring danger. Lydia catches sight of the doll staring right at her with its sewn-on eyes and her skin crawls. She is shaking so hard that she drops her phone, causing it to cast light chaotically around the room, making inanimate objects shift and glint. She cries out, crouching and fumbling to pick it up again. She needs to get out of there, but even though her car is just outside, right now it feels a million miles away.

Another thump on the floor above makes Lydia jump to her feet. Heart pounding so hard and fast she feels like she might pass out any second, bitter adrenaline in the back of her throat making her mouth water. She lunges for an iron poker propped up near the fireplace and spins around, waving it towards the door. Silence. She hesitates, options racing through her mind. Stay here and wait for whoever it is to come to her, or make a dash for the car.

Courage overcomes fear and Lydia bolts into the hall, practically falling upon the front door and wrenching at its brass handle with trembling fingers. But the door doesn't open. It's locked. Lydia pulls with all of her might, fumbling desperately for a key, or a bolt, or something. But there is nothing.

Behind her, a stair creaks. With a cry of fear, head down and without looking in the direction of the noise, Lydia sprints back into the living room, scanning its dark walls frantically for a door she knows is not there. The raggedy doll grins evilly at her. *No escape*, she hears its high, gleeful voice in her head.

A gap in the thick cloud drifting lazily in front of the full moon causes the windows to glow eerily, and suddenly another escape route presents itself. Lydia snatches up the poker again, smashing the creepy doll and sending it flying across the room. Then she grabs the chair and hurls it at the nearest pane of glass which shatters with a loud crash, and a cascade of fragile tinkling as the broken shards tumble to the floor. A blast of cold air rushes into the room, and Lydia throws herself towards the source of it, bending her knees ready to launch herself through the hole still surrounded by jagged glass. But as she does so, a strong arm around her waist holds her back, lifting her effortlessly off the ground. Lydia screams, kicking her legs and flailing her arms wildly as a hand presses a soft rag over her nose and mouth. The sting of chemicals is harsh, and sickening. The room spins, everything a blur, and she feels herself falling. As her ragdoll body hits the ground, the last thing she sees is a wild figure looming over her. Then the darkness takes her.

Forty-One

The Perfect Crime

Lydia's dreams have been coming thick and fast lately. Dreams about the past, about choices she has made to disown her abusive father, to pursue the career that has made her so famous. Different situations, but a common theme. In every dream, she chooses loneliness over heartbreak. Every night she must make the decisions all over again, and every night she struggles to understand how things could have gone any other way. She was right, wasn't she? But then, why was she always so sad?

With great effort, she forces her heavy eyes open. They feel dry and sore, as if she hasn't used them in days, and for several long moments everything is a blur. She tries to rub them, but her hand refuses to move. Her feet, too. Then there is pain, heat, friction. She is bound with rope, upright, tied to a chair that creaks as she shifts and squirms. Her skin is burning up white hot, and she now sees herself dressed in a red sequin dress that sparkles in the dim lighting. Adjusting herself slightly, she can feel that her underwear is loose, unfastened. And there is pain inside too, stomach burning, womb screaming, waves of violation breaking over her again and again as her consciousness grows.

She blinks again and squints as her surroundings begin to come into focus. Bare, dusty floorboards strewn with crimson blankets. Wooden beams supporting a sharp, angled roof. Red and green fairy lights twisted around them, dangling like nooses, keeping the dark whispers lurking outside at bay. Paintings both hung and propped up against exposed brick walls. One in particular catches her attention: an image of two young boys with cheery smiles. The painting is exquisite, but their faces are eerie, haunted.

An eclectic selection of furniture dotted around the room. A baroque chair here, a Victorian lamp there, mismatched companions hoarded over many years. And a desk. A large, heavy oak desk covered in photographs. Lydia cranes her neck to try to see them; twisted limbs, vacant faces, and blood. So much blood. Lydia starts to cry as she realises where she is.

"How do you like my work?" asks a chilling voice behind her. Lydia's blood runs cold. How stupid she has been. How arrogant. How blind. She had wanted so badly to find the evil in Jason Devere that she had failed to see his humanity. Now evil had found her, its presence clear and unmistakable in just six words. She tries to turn to face her captor, but her binds are too tight, her chair bolted to the floor. "Don't bother," says the voice. "You're mine now."

Just hours ago, Lydia had given Gretchen a lecture about hopelessness. Now, too late, she truly understands what it means. She will die here. Nothing can save her now. She hears footsteps on the wooden floor, and sees movement out of the corner of her eye, then Finley Devere steps around in front of her. The happy little boy from the photographs, now stretched and twisted. An embodiment of pure wickedness.

"I hear you're something of a connoisseur," says Finley, his hollow voice completely devoid of emotion, of humanity. "I've read all of your books. Tell me," he bends down, his voice quieting, "how do you think I measure up?"

"Please..." Lydia whimpers, refusing to meet his chilling gaze, "let me go."

"Really?" Finley sounds disappointed. "That's the best you can do? The famous Lydia Tune, mistress of the mind?" He snorts. "You disappoint me."

"I'm n-not going to insult you with... with m-mind games," Lydia stammers, her body shivering as though fevered. "I know what you've done. What you're capable of."

Finley swoops down on her, his mouth barely an inch from Lydia's ear, icy breath making the hairs on the back of her neck prickle violently. "You don't know *anything*."

Lydia closes her eyes. This is it. No point fighting. Be brave.

"I know that you're a monster," she says, her voice hard, forcing herself to turn and face him.

Finley's eyes burn into her for a second, then his sharp face cracks, and he starts to laugh. Lydia sees Jason in his features; the strong jaw, the blue eyes like lagoons that could drown a person in their clear water. The same long, dark hair, only in Finley's case it is slicked back, oily and shining, baring his sharp features to the world and making him look more snake than person. His clothes are tight, too tight, black trousers and an intricately-woven waistcoat over a crisp, white shirt. "We are all of us monsters," he smirks. "You included."

"I'm nothing like you," Lydia spits back.

"We both know that's not true," Finley hisses, circling around the other side of her. "I've been watching you, Lydia Tune." He leans in again and whispers. "I've seen your darkness."

"I'm not a murderer," Lydia replies. "I'm not insane like you."

"That's where you're wrong." Finley's voice rises sharply. "I'm not crazy. I'm just ahead of my time."

"You're crazy," Lydia snaps, "*and* deluded."

"History will remember otherwise," says Finley, crossing the room to his desk and lifting a glass jar from one of the drawers. It is filled with insects. "My work, my life, my mind." He shakes the jar, and the tiny creatures inside skitter about desperately. They are prisoners just like Lydia. Victims with no voice. "My philosophy," Finley continues, "my torment," he sets the jar down and gestures around the room. "My art."

"Your *art*?" Lydia spits. "You *killed* innocent people."

"Nobody whose life was worth living." Finley shrugs. "They were insignificant, like insects." He wanders over to an ornate mirror on the wall, adjusts his collar and smooths his hair, before springing back around to point toward her. "Do you like the dress by the way?"

"Where's Alex?" Lydia demands in the glittery blood-soaked number.

"I was worried it wouldn't fit you, it being mother's old dress and all, but what would you know, it's a perfect fit!" he merrily remarked.

"What have you done with Alex?" Lydia grits her teeth.

"Ah yes." Finley's grinning face reflected in the mirror makes Lydia's stomach lurch. "Poor Detective Gilbey. You should have seen his face when he realised he'd been wrong about everything." He turns to look at Lydia directly. "A memory I shall cherish forever."

"Where is he?!"

"Perhaps you should reflect," says Finley coldly, his smile fading in an instant, "on the fact that your pathetic emotional connection to that fool is the reason you're in this dire situation." The reptilian smile creeps back over his face. "And it is, I'm afraid, a very dire situation."

"You let your own brother take the blame for your crimes," says Lydia. If she was going to die, she may as well try to get some answers first. "You let the world think of him as a murderer. How could you do that?"

"Oh, poor Jason," says Finley, donning a mocking mask of sadness. "What a shame. He was such a clever boy." He takes the jewelled locket from his pocket and holds it up to the light. "Using this to send you a message. Inspired, really." He sighs. "Such a waste. I was genuinely upset to have to engineer his death."

"How could you possibly...?" Lydia stops, staring up into Finley's pale blue eyes. "You... you were on the news. You were the one who 'found' the bodies."

"Clever girl!" Finley beams, gleefully. "I knew those lazy police would chalk them up to Jason without a second's hesitation, and then they'd have to execute him." His face falls in mock sadness. "It's a shame, but I do so dislike loose ends."

"He was protecting your mother," Lydia growls, contemptuously.

"Then he wasn't doing a very good job, was he?" Finley raises an eyebrow. "I mean, he was nowhere to be seen when I pressed that pillow down over her weeping face."

"How could you...?" Lydia grits her teeth.

"It was a mercy." Finley glares at her. "They can be together now, wherever they are." He glances upwards. "I do hope they're watching."

"If they're in heaven," says Lydia, "they don't care about you anymore. They'll never have to see you again."

Finley grins maniacally. "I'd rather go to hell. That's where all the fun people are."

"Well go on then." Lydia sits up straight. "Get on with it. Or are you all talk?"

"Oh no, no, no," says Finley, wagging a finger. "No need to rush. Besides," he stands before her, one hand behind his back, like a servant ready to please, "I know you want to know all of my dirty little secrets."

"Like what?" Lydia spits. "Your stupid card?"

"My what?" Finley looks genuinely confused. "Oh, those!" He laughs. "They didn't mean anything. Just a little bit of mystery, a bit of theatre to keep the baying hordes interested."

"I couldn't care less." Lydia looks away haughtily.

"You're a poor liar," says Finley, that cold bite back in his voice. "I'm the reason you came to this god-awful city. I'm the one you wanted to write a book about. *You* pursued *me*." He jabs his finger at her, and then himself. "So don't tell me you don't care, Lydia Tune."

All I care about is Alex, Lydia thinks, realising as she processes the words that they are genuinely true. She mustn't let Finley know. If he's still alive...

"Patience, my dear," Finley says, as if in reply, admiring one of his own paintings on the wall, a hunter spearing a great, black bird with a jagged arrow. "All in good time. By the way," he turns back to face her, "what do you think of my Christmas tree?"

Lydia blinks at him. "Your... what?" She looks around. There's no tree. Then Finley, grinning gleefully, lifts his eyes just above her and jerks his head. Almost paralysed with fear of what she is about to see, Lydia forces herself, shaking uncontrollably, to turn around.

A huge, bushy pine tree towers over her barely a few feet away. Like the rest of the room, it's strung with blinking lights, but no baubles or candy canes. In place of ornaments, human organs and severed limbs hang from the branches. A finger here, a rib there, feet, flesh, heart... and at the top, where a star or fairy might sit, the severed head of Cecil Sprinkler staring down at her with accusing eyes.

Lydia looks away, her own eyes screwed tightly shut, whimpering softly.

"I knew you'd love it," Finley says, gleefully. "Oh, you should have been there, Lydia. I made him sing Christmas carols to me while I sawed off his hands and feet. Promised him that I wouldn't hurt you if he did as he was told."

"Me?"

"Oh, yes." Finley swoops down upon her, his horrible smile inches from her face. "Rather fond of you, he was. Funny how people get attached so soon, isn't it?"

No. Alex. No. Where are you?

Finley pulls up a chair and sits, one leg draped lazily over the other, poised like a dandy in front of her. "Don't you want to know how I did it?"

"Did what?" Lydia mutters.

"Got into here, of course." Finley leans forward and taps the side of Lydia's head with a bony finger. She recoils with disgust. "You see, I've been with you since the moment you arrived."

"What are you talking about?"

"Well," says Finley, with the manner of someone beginning a story, "as you know, my mother was a talented costume designer. The house is full of wonderful clothes, and wigs, and makeup. I've found them extremely useful over the years."

Lydia turns her head to look at him, squinting her eyes. She had thought him familiar because he looked like Jason. Was there something she'd missed?

"Oh yes," says Finley happily. "Let's see, on your first date with lovely Alex I was a bearded man enjoying a hamburger." He starts counting off on his fingers. "When you got terribly drunk in that awful bar, I was an army vet covered in tattoos. The dog walker in the park, the guest in the hotel lobby. At the asylum of course I had to be extra careful, so I went with a simple suit and moustache to blend in with the official types." He leans in and touches her arm in an exaggerated, mocking manner. "That was the time I clubbed you around the back of the head with a pipe. Do you remember?"

"Why didn't you kill me?" Lydia asks in a hollow voice.

"And give those stupid police reason to doubt that my dear brother was really the Krimson Killer?" Finley looks comically alarmed. "Oh no, that wouldn't have done at all. They would have come looking for me. Such an inconvenience. No, to tell you the truth, my dear, I just wanted you to go home." He smiles, sweetly. "I bet you wish you had now."

"You're lying." Lydia glares at him. "You love the attention. You wanted me to stay and figure this out. To find you. You wanted to gloat to someone about what you've done."

Finley peers at her, then his face cracks into a sly smile. "You've got me," he says, generously. "Bravo, Lydia, you've figured me out." He leaps to his feet and strikes a dramatic pose. "I'm a performer, you see. A natural. And a performer is nothing without an audience." He leans down towards her. "Are you sitting comfortably?" Lydia looks away, disgusted. "I'll take that as a yes," says Finley, gleefully. "Then let's begin the main portion of tonight's show."

He bounds past Lydia, who squirms in her chair to try to see what's happening but to no avail. She hears a door opening, then a low rumble that shakes the floorboards, growing louder until out of the corner of her eye she sees a seated figure approaching in a wheelchair.

When she sees the figure slumped in it, bound to the chair with thick electrical tape, face slick with blood and sweat, eyes wide with terror, Lydia's heart stops.

Forty-Two

Cruel Timing

"**A**lex!" she cries out, struggling against her bonds with all of her might.

"Well done!" says Finley, gleefully. "You really are the expert sleuth from your books. Found this big lug at the final scene of my masterpiece of a crime, disguised myself as a cop, chloroformed him when no one was looking, put him in his trunk and here we are!"

"Let him go!"

"How likely do you think that is to happen, really?" asks Finley, sarcastically. Alex's eyes flicker. When he sees Lydia, they open wide and he starts to struggle madly, screaming into the tape sealing his mouth.

"Please," Lydia begs, looking back at him with tears in her eyes. "Don't hurt him."

"I'll do as I please," says Finley. "He's mine now. I've won. Haven't you realised yet?" He rips the tape from Alex's mouth and punches him hard, causing blood to gush from his broken nose.

"Don't!" Lydia screams. "Alex!"

Alex looks up at her from the ground with desperate, pleading eyes. "Lydia…"

"I'm sorry…" Lydia whispers, gazing into the helpless, stricken face of the man she has only now realised she loves.

"Aww," says Finley, mockingly. "Did you hear that, Al? Your girl's sorry." Lydia closes her eyes and turns her face away defiantly. "And it looks like she doesn't want to watch me torture you," he goes on, as Lydia's whole body shakes with sobs. "But, oh dear, Lydia," says Finley, stepping close to her, "I'm afraid you've got it wrong again. You see, he's not the entertainment." He leans in close and whispers. "*You are.*"

"No, please…"

"I've always been curious about love." Finley pulls up his chair again, resting a foot on Alex's head. "Other people are just so… revolting, don't you think?" He looks down at Alex with pantomime disgust. "Why on earth would you want to spend more time with one than is absolutely necessary?"

"Please don't." Lydia shakes her head helplessly, her fragile sanity hanging by the finest of threads.

"You can't rely on other people, Lydia. No one really cares about anybody but themselves. Oh, they all pretend, some well, some badly, but all for their own selfish good." He snatches a clock from the wall and holds it next to Alex's head. "Time ticks away, tick-tock, tick-tock, and those we thought we loved become crutches for us to bear. Burdens we resent. Vacuous, animated lumps of flesh with no redeeming features at all." He hurls the clock away and it smashes into pieces. "It's all just a grim façade, Lydia. All of it. What matters is us," he taps his own chest, "ourselves," he taps Lydia's the same way, "what *we* want. Don't you see? When all the pretence is dropped and the mask slips, that's who we really are. Selfish. Greedy. Lustful. Hurtful." He breathes the words as though savouring each one on the tip of his tongue. "*Wicked.*"

Lydia tries to tell Alex with her eyes that everything will be okay, that she will get them out of this. *How?!* The voice in her head screams at her. *How?!* She whimpers involuntarily.

"Do pull yourself together, Lydia," Finley chides her. "This isn't the real you. I know the real you. You're dark, and lonely, and fascinating, and untroubled by such mundane emotions. This is some temporary madness you've been afflicted with, and I am going to cure you."

"I'll do anything you want, please…"

"Excellent. So tell me then, what is it exactly that you love about this… pathetic creature?" He removes his foot from Alex's head and gives it a swift kick. Lydia screams.

"Don't hurt him!"

"Then tell me."

"I can't!"

"You *will.*" Finley rises in a passionate temper and hurls the chair away. It crashes against the wall and falls to the floor in pieces.

"I love…" Lydia stammers, gazing into Alex's desperate face. "*Everything.*"

In that moment, time freezes for all in the dank room. Alex's retinas widen upon being hit by the open declaration from his lady love. Lydia feels her chest open like a butterfly's wings, leaving her heart bare. Suddenly, in this grim situation, she feels free in a strange way; even if this is the end, she knows now that she can finally breathe. The couple take each other in for all they can, as the world around them melts away into a haze, just as Finley rolls his eyes.

"What a cop out."

Finley, without hesitation pulls a pistol from behind his back, and before Lydia knows what's happening, he shoots Alex straight through the heart.

BANG!

"NO!" Lydia's heart cracks. Her lungs freeze. Her brain swims. This is a bad dream. It has to be. She stares, mouth wide open, saliva dripping onto the dusty floorboards, as blood spills from her lover's chest and spreads slowly over the floor towards her. Alex's eyes are glassy and then lifeless. He's gone.

"Grief is terrible, isn't it?" Finley whispers, watching Lydia's face greedily. "And beautiful." He takes a slow, deep breath. "Intoxicating…"

Lydia is paralysed with grief. She wants to look away, to scream, to cry, but every inch of her is frozen by the pure horror of the moment. Finley reaches out and slaps her face hard.

"Oh come now," he says, bracingly. "Don't get all mopey over a wet bag like that. He isn't worth it."

"*Why?!*" Lydia manages a strangled cry.

"Why what?" asks Finley, confused.

"Why did you kill him?!"

"Oh." Finley looks down at Alex's body. "Why not?" He shrugs. "Like you said, I *am* a monster."

Lydia slumps in the chair, head bowed. She is still

breathing, but for all intents and purposes she may as well be dead.

"That's it," says Finley, sinking to his knees in front of Lydia, bony fingers clutching at her. "Feel the pain. Understand it. Embrace it. Die and be reborn with me, and together we will do such beautiful things."

Lydia lifts her head slowly, eyes burning with cold hatred. "Go to hell," she hisses.

"That's the plan." Finley gives her a gentle shake. "But I don't want to go alone, Lydia. These past years have been so empty. There was something missing from my life." He gazes up at her meaningfully. "I know you know how that feels."

Lydia grimaces, blocking out the tiny voice in her head telling her that he is right.

"We must have a purpose, Lydia," Finley says earnestly. "We must each find our own meaning in this sick, broken world. Ours will be to fix it. To cleanse it of the hypocrisy, and the waste, and replace it with a pure, chaotic beauty. It can be our art of darkness."

Lydia swallows hard as the nausea swells deep inside her. She visualises the block of ice encasing her shattered heart, closes her eyes and plays the game through to the end in her mind. She only has one chance.

"Why me?" she croaks, hoarsely.

"You know why." He's circling her now, like a predator sensing an imminent kill. She hasn't long left. "We are as one, you and I. You must have felt it when you saw my beautiful works. When you read about my great deeds. You may not have known my name, but you knew *me*, and you understood the truth of my nature."

"What truth?" She forces herself to look him in the eye. She has to let him read her. *Let him believe.*

"That I, like you, am drawn to darkness. Pulled by its invisible gravity. I am both its servant, and its master. Creator and destroyer. I have the power to take life," he kneels again next to Alex and touches his bleeding heart reverently, "and to give it back." He takes his finger, covered with Alex's blood, and anoints Lydia's forehead like a priest at a baptism. She shudders as the warm liquid trickles down her face and into the corner of her mouth. "Yes," Finley breathes, intoxicated by the scene, "taste the power." He licks his own lips hungrily as though the blood were on them instead.

Fighting the impulse to wretch with all of her strength, Lydia closes her eyes, extends her tongue and tastes the blood. She can't see the look of ecstasy on Finley's face, but she knows it's there. Keep going. It's working.

"Oh, bravo my dear, bravo!" Finley claps his hands together and Lydia opens her eyes, startled by the sudden noise. "I knew you felt it. You poor thing. You've been in hiding your whole life, like I was in this wretched attic. But now you are free. I have set you free, and together we will make such beautiful things." He slips a knife from his pocket and cuts her bonds.

Lydia shakes her head. "The police will come," she whispers, massaging her wrists, getting to her feet, which she can now see are encased within sequinned shoes. "There's no way out," she adds.

"Oh, Lydia," Finley coos, like a smitten lover, "you forget who you're talking to. I am the master of evading detection.

Even you wouldn't have found me if I hadn't lured you here, hmm?"

Lydia looks up at him, her eyes wide. Impressed. No, *awed. Sell it. Make him believe.* "How…"

"By the time they arrive, we will be long gone. And this house, full of… bitter memories, will be nothing but ash."

"And then?" Lydia sounds desperate, as though she really wants to believe.

"I will make you a master of disguise," Finley purrs, "like me. You can be whoever you want to be, wherever, whenever. You can kill whoever you want to kill, any way that you can dream of. I will help you fulfil your potential, and," he cradles her cheek in his hand, "in time you will become beautiful and terrible. The *angel of death*."

Lydia's heart swells. Her breath catches as she gazes into his wild eyes. Is she still pretending? The desire, the hunger, it feels so real. And before she knows what she's doing, she is kissing him passionately, their arms around each other, hearts pressed tightly together, beating as one.

Then they break apart, and Finley doesn't notice that she is holding his gun until the first shot rings out. The euphoria on his face turns to surprise as the bullet rips through his chest and he staggers backwards. Lydia fires again; once, twice, three times. Finley's body hangs momentarily in the air, suspended in time, then crumples to the floor with a sickening thud.

Lydia drops the gun and dashes to Alex, kneeling down and touching his face gently with her fingertips. "I'm so sorry, my love," she whispers, a single tear rolling down her cheek and falling onto his bloodstained chest. "This was all my fault." She strokes his hair tenderly.

The thumping and thrashing of Finley's death throes fades to silence, as Lydia leans down and kisses Alex on the lips for the last time in the cold midnight glow.

Forty-Three

Blood Lust

Lydia rises slowly, the weight of her grief like a great stone inside of her, and returns to the body of Finley Devere. She gives him a kick just to make sure, then retrieves the knife from his trouser pocket.

She cuts Alex free of the chair and lays him down flat on the floor, covering his bloodied chest with his own leather jacket. The softness of it beneath her fingers reminds her of their kiss on the rooftop, and she has to fight to hold back more tears. There will be a time to grieve, but she needs to draw a line under this saga first.

Lydia looks around for her clothes and phone. Both are gone. Finley must have hidden them somewhere she realises. Her clothes were not essential, not right now, she could manage the draping dress, at least until she found a phone. Maybe the one in the hallway works. She turns around to find the way out of the attic and freezes, her blood running cold. Where Finley's body was a moment ago, now there is nothing but a pool of blood, and footprints leading to an open hatch in the floor.

"You have got to be kidding me," she whispers. She could wait up here for help to arrive, or... "No," she says out loud with a shake of the head. "Enough." Picking up the gun from the floor near Alex's feet, she follows the footprints to the hatch and begins to climb carefully down the wooden ladder attached to it. As she begins to take her first steps down below, she feels a slight tug pulling her back. It's the damn dress, caught on a nail from the ladder. Still pointing the gun with steely determination and on high alert, Lydia proceeds to pull and tear the bottom of the dress, allowing her to hunt with absolute free mobility.

The first floor corridor is straight, and narrow, with doors on either side. Lydia looks down at the carpet for signs of blood, but the trail ends at the bottom of the ladder. "How did he manage that?" she mutters, irritated. No matter. She will be methodical, as she always is. Lydia reaches for the first door handle and grips it, the cold metal sending a shiver from her fingers right the way up her arm. "One," she counts in her head, "two, three." She turns the handle and pushes the door open. Beyond is a bedroom; neat, pale, dusty. Unused for many years by the looks of it. Jason's parents' room, maybe? She is about to move on, when a thin, rattling voice carries through the air.

"I will break you, Tune..." it hisses. "I will make you quiver with fear. I will show you exquisite pain. I will cut that mask from your face and show the world what you really are. Only then will you be allowed to die."

"You blew it," Lydia calls out, scanning the room for the source of the voice. "It's over."

"Your arrogance is the most predictable thing about you," Finley whispers. It's coming from the bed. Lydia shoots the duvet twice. Silence, then hoarse laughter fills the air.

"Come out, you coward!"

"Come and find me…"

Lydia edges to the bed and rips off the covers. Underneath, a two-way radio. She clips it to her thin shoulder strap, then checks the en-suite cautiously. Nothing. She moves to the next room, takes a deep breath, then bursts in, gun first. This looks like a boy's room; small bed, blue curtains, baseball pictures on the wall. Random items dotted over surfaces. It doesn't know whether it wants to be cluttered or tidy. Jason's room?

"I have big plans for you," hisses the radio.

"I've got plans for you too," Lydia murmurs, hefting the pistol and moving to the next room.

Three doors later, the first floor is cleared. Lydia creeps to the staircase and begins to descend, eyes wide and alert.

"We could have been something beautiful," Finley breathes through muffled static. "We could have had a future, but you ruined it."

Lydia edges along the wall, peering into the living room opposite. It looks just as she remembers; window smashed, chair broken beneath it, creepy doll staring accusingly at her from the floor. "You asked for it," Lydia mutters at the doll, creeping carefully through to the kitchen. It's a large room, traditional, wood and tile. Everything clean and orderly. Everything in its place, from gleaming pans to wooden chopping blocks. Atop the central island sits a vase of fresh flowers… and a telephone. Lydia glances around, pistol held high, as she inches towards it. She picks up the receiver. The line is dead.

"Are you really just going to leave your boyfriend up there?" asks the rattling voice. Finley sounds breathless. Maybe if she just leaves, he will die. *No*, Lydia thinks. She doesn't want to take that chance. This has to end tonight. She retraces her steps back to the hall. There's only one room left to check. She takes a deep breath, turns the handle and pushes the door gently. Beyond is a large dining room table bearing a single bowl of fruit. Wooden cabinets either side loaded with fine china and cutlery, but nowhere a grown man could hide.

"Where the hell are you?" Lydia mutters. The soft thump of foot on carpet behind her makes Lydia flinch and spin around, firing off a round in the process. Finley lunges towards her, eyes wild, a mixture of blood and saliva foaming between his lips. In his hand is a large kitchen knife, and he swings it in her direction, stabbing and flailing frantically. His waistcoat is undone, his shirt torn and bloody, a single strand of lank, greasy hair stuck to his face. Lydia backs up, firing off two more rounds and then two hollow clicks. "Shit!"

Finley seizes his opportunity, hurling himself forwards and knocking Lydia to the ground. She kicks out at his face and crawls desperately through the nearest door, finding herself awkwardly positioned on her stomach at the top of a set of hard, stone steps leading down to the basement. In the second Lydia hesitates, wondering whether to crawl down or try to stand up, Finley seizes her by the bare ankle and raises his knife, grinning and exposing a bloodied set of teeth. Lydia thrashes around frantically as Finley tries to slide on top of her, pinning her down. With a sickening crunch, her knee connects with his jaw, and as she scrabbles to get away, they both go tumbling down the stairs, landing at the bottom with a painful thump.

Lydia recovers her senses first and scrambles to her feet. The lights are working down here, bright bulbs hanging loosely from the ceiling, illuminating the sheer, brutal horror of what she now sees. Seven bodies, intertwined in sick, unnatural ways, eyes gouged out, faces torn away, bones protruding from their rotting skin. A wave of nausea surges through Lydia and she gags hard, while on the ground nearby Finley stirs.

Lydia dashes to the stairs, but as she reaches the top, she feels that bony hand around her ankle again. She kicks out hard, connecting sharply with Finley's face and his neck snaps back with a sickening crunch. Lydia stares for a second. Is he dead? Then slowly, horrifyingly, he turns his face back towards her with a broad grin, eyes bulging. Lydia kicks out again and wrenches herself free, reaching the top of the stairs and slamming the door behind her. It traps Finley's groping fingers with a crack, then begins to swing back again. Lydia sprints straight ahead towards the broken window at the far end of the living room, but half way there a huge weight collides with her, knocking her to the floor.

The carpet burns her flesh as Lydia squirms and fights, desperately trying to break free of Finley's grasp. But he has the advantage now. Using his sheer weight and strength he straddles her and pins her down, grinning maniacally as his good hand slides up her body and tightens around her throat, bony fingers slowly choking the life out of her. Lydia's nails sink into his flesh, but to no avail. Her face glows pink, then red hot, her lungs burning, brain swimming. She knows she is about to die.

As Lydia's weakening hands claw desperately at her attacker's face, something crimson ignites in the moonlight streaming through the window. Her mother's ring. Summoning her last remaining strength, Lydia clenches her fist and slashes at Finley's face, opening a gushing wound over his cheek and eye. Finley screams and releases her. Gasping and fighting for breath, Lydia rolls onto her side and spots the iron poker on the floor just a few feet away. Stretching out with her fingertips, she grasps hold of it and swings it around hard, connecting with Finley's head and sending a spray of blood cascading through the air. He collapses like a sack of potatoes, and Lydia raises the pointed iron implement high in the air to deliver the fatal blow. But something makes her hesitate. If she kills Finley, she will never know the whole truth. The world will never know. She won't be able to finish her book.

She stares down at him, the monster that killed her true love, and the deadly weapon trembles in her hands as she fights every impulse she has to smash his brains into pulp. Is that who she really is? What she really wants? Finley believed so. If she kills him, does she not prove him right? Where would she go from there?

Lydia grits her teeth and screams as the darkness within swells and churns, and threatens to overcome her. She fights it so hard she feels like she will black out. But then it subsides, and she feels as calm as she has ever felt in her life.

Hating herself even as she does so, Lydia drops the poker. She reaches down and takes hold of his wrist. His skin is cold and clammy and the touch of it makes her shudder, but he still has a pulse. He's alive. Then she notices the handcuffs, dangling now from his trouser pocket. Lydia snatches them up and rolls him over with her foot, pinning his arms behind his back and cuffing his wrists together. She drops the key into her bra, grabs him by the collar and hauls his limp body to the front door.

Outside the snow is still falling. Lydia heaves Finley through it and, with a huge effort, packs him into the trunk of her car. Then she stands, still in that awful dress and stares at what she's done. This is a terrible idea. What if he comes around before she gets to the police station?

What are your options? asks the voice in her head. You need him. You need this.

"Right," she mutters to herself. "Screw it."

Lydia slams the trunk shut and throws herself into the driver's seat. The roar of the car's engine is the sweetest sound she has ever heard. She drives furiously through the open fields, wheels spinning and brakes screeching, through the twisted woods towards Traveller's Bridge. Only when she sees its low, grey walls ahead does she allow herself to slow down, to take a breath and think. *Don't slip on that ice now and go sailing into the river*, she thinks to herself. *Don't you dare mess this up now.*

She flicks the heater and a blast of warm, welcome air begins to return her to life. The horror of what she has just experienced already starts to feel like a bad dream. She relaxes a little, hands loose on the wheel, gets comfortable in the seat, and reaches for the radio dial.

In the split second that she is distracted, a huge grey wolf looms out of the darkness on the bridge ahead. Lydia screams and wrenches the wheel hard to one side. A violent crash sends the car tumbling over and over, landing each time with a sickening crunch. Her head thuds, and spins, and cracks... and finally comes to rest inside the battered metal coffin. And all is silent again, as the gentle snow continues to fall in the peaceful winter night.

Forty-Four

The Price

Searing pain shoots through Lydia's head, her brain drowning in thick, white fog. The coppery taste of blood fills her mouth and spills out, warm and sickly, over her cheek and ear. Her body throbs like an electric current, every rhythmic pulse threatening to burst her apart at the seams. She's dizzy. Disoriented.

As her consciousness gradually returns, she realises that she is upside down. She tries to move, but everything hurts. It feels like every bone in her body is broken, every inch of flesh bruised.

You'll die if you stay here.

Lydia opens her eyes and sees her hand twisted against the steering wheel in front of her. Some of her nails are broken, but her ruby ring looks undamaged. She peers into its black depths for a moment, thinks of her mother, and with an almighty scream manages to push herself out through the shattered window onto icy stone covered with inch-deep snow where she lays for a while, staring up into the black night as the blizzard continues all around her.

Get up. Get up. GET UP!

With a roar of pain, Lydia hauls herself to her feet and staggers, clutching her aching stomach, falling onto the side of the car and fighting to keep her feet. The car has crashed into one low wall at the side of Traveller's Bridge, overturned and spun across to hit the other, knocking holes in both.

"No..." Lydia stares at the popped-open trunk and an icy fear grips her heart. "No, no, no..." Holding on to the car for support, she edges around to get a clearer look inside. "NO!"

Finley is gone. Lydia looks around frantically, blazing pain wracking her stiff neck every time she turns it. The trees all around are silent. The freezing water far below a distant whisper. *Where are you?*

Suddenly a tormented scream pierces the frigid air behind her, and before she can turn around something heavy falls on her back, knocking her down. Icy fingers scrabbling at her neck, gradually squeezing it shut as Finley's mangled, bloodied face looms into view. Lydia grabs his wrists tightly and he screams, yanking one hand clean away and loosening his grip with the other. Lydia seizes the opportunity, raising her feet underneath Finley's body and kicking out hard, flipping him up and over her head. He lands with a crack on the ice but rolls over and springs unsteadily to his feet, blood pouring from his mouth full of broken teeth. He's cradling his right hand in his left, which still has the handcuffs hanging from it, and Lydia can tell from the angle at which it's bent that his wrist is broken. He broke his own wrist to free himself from the cuffs. Finley's breathing is heavy, his movements tired, laboured. But he has a wild animal's will to survive at any cost, eyes glowing with a hunger that Lydia recognises only too well. The hunger for blood. For death.

"You've ruined everything!" Finley hisses. "All I wanted was for you to understand. To see the world as I do." Lydia tries to reply, but it hurts even to breathe. Her lungs are empty. Her throat dry. "You've wasted my precious time," Finley growls, "and for that I will paint this bridge with your blood!"

He lunges for her. Lydia tries to run, but slips on the ice and lands hard on her face. Her insides feel like they've been through a blender. She has nothing more to give. With a triumphant yell, Finley yanks her to her feet by her hair and slaps her hard across the face twice, each strike like a bullet to the cheek. Lydia kicks out wildly towards Finley's bleeding gut and connects. He screams and releases her, and she falls to the ground again, scrambling to get away. She reaches the broken wall on the far side of the bridge and peers over to the river below. How had Jason survived that drop? It must be a hundred feet high.

"You think you can beat me?" Finley screams, staggering towards her. "I'm the Krimson Killer! I've snuffed out more meaningful lives than yours in my sleep! I tricked the whole world, and gave it some of the most beautiful art it will ever see. And I will *never, ever, stop*." Lydia braces herself, but Finley does not go for her. He's just staring at her with those deranged eyes, grinning his malevolent grin. She follows his gaze to her leg, fresh blood trickling down it. Is she cut? Her back hurts, low down, like she's been punched. Her legs are giving way beneath her. Right before they buckle, Finley lunges drunkenly forward and grabs her, spinning her around and throwing her through the car's windscreen which shatters with a deafening crash. Lydia gasps for air. She is in so much pain. Unable to move. Unable to breathe. Hot, wet tears form in her eyes and trickle down her frozen cheeks. This is it. She is going to die.

Finley reaches for the car door to wrench it open, but something stops him. A reflection in the glass. A person. He roars and spins around, but there's nobody there. He looks back to the window and squints through fast-fading eyes. A handsome young man smiles serenely back at him. His brother, Jason. Not the Jason Lydia knows, but the healthy, clean-shaven Jason from before he went to Mortem.

"B... brother?" Finley whispers, his misty breath disappearing into the night like a ghost. The reflection nods serenely. Finley's broken face cracks into a twisted smile, then something heavy slams him full in the face, sending him flying backwards to land with a sickening crack on the edge of the bridge. He wriggles frantically like an upside down spider to get to his feet, clutching his torn gut, eyes searching desperately for the source of the blow.

The car's heavy chrome bumper is in Lydia's hands, her eyes burning with hatred, and a flicker of doubt crosses Finley's face for the first time. Doubt... and fear. He was death incarnate, but in his bloodlust he had created something even worse. Far worse.

Lydia grips the makeshift weapon tightly, blood thundering through her veins, heart about to burst through her chest. The whole world turns red. A whole lifetime of pain boiling over. Alex, gone. *He did this.* She knows what she is going to do, and in this moment, finally, she understands, and hates what the darkness has done to her.

Finley's shoulders drop. He is beaten. He knows it. Betrayed by his own ego. The irony stings more than any wound. His eyes move again to Lydia's waist and he smiles a strange smile with open arms, welcoming her. "Alright," he growls. "I'm ready."

With a roar, Lydia lunges forward and smashes him hard in the face with the cold metal. For a moment he just stands there, frozen in space and time, eyes rolling up in his head as his spirit begins to leave his body. But Lydia is taking no chances. Summoning every ounce of her remaining strength, she hurls herself at him and wrestles his spasming, heavy body over the edge of the bridge. Finley screams, arms spread wide, a look of what seems like euphoria on his smashed-in face as he plummets to the darkness. Lydia listens for the horrible, cold, distant splash as the body finds its watery grave, then sinks to her knees and sobs. She is a killer now, and always will be. That is a mark she can never wash off.

Still gasping for air and wracked with pain that seems to get worse by the second, she crawls back to the car and fumbles in the glove compartment for a flask she keeps hidden there. Then she pushes the power button on the radio. The rich, dulcet tones of Frank Sinatra spill out across the snow, *Under my Skin*, echoing off the trees all around and down to the frozen river below as Lydia unscrews the flask and takes a long, greedy drink. The liquor burns her throat, but warms her heart. She looks at her watch. Ten-thirty. Jason must be gone. She thinks of his body burning right now in the dark depths of Mortem, and more tears roll down her frozen, clammy cheeks.

She thinks of Gretchen, beautiful Gretchen, the good doctor she had treated so meanly, but who had shown her nothing but kindness and been right about her all along. She would be at home now, kids in bed, perhaps snuggling with her husband on the couch.

Lydia looks down at her own blood staining the pure, white snow, and remembers the wicked voice of the warden, Winston Shade, threatening her with a fate worse than death. *Too late you bastard. You can't get me now.*

She starts to laugh, then splutters and chokes, wincing in pain. Her eye catches her ruby ring, caked in blood. She licks her fingers and rubs it clean until it glints brightly in the moonlight.

Finally, the thought she has been keeping at bay rises to the surface of her consciousness. The thought of Alex lying dead in the attic of that horrible house. The thought that she will never again see his cheeky smile, or hear his soft, kind voice, gaze into his pretty brown eyes, feel his heartbeat with hers. She was a fool; she never could win.

And at last she realises what is causing the escalating dull pain as she lies down in the snow, a cold shaking broken ruby glittering amongst an ocean of white, staring up into the black sky, bleeding steadily from the cuts etched across her body as well as the knife wound in her back. This is the life that she chose, and it has been both a gift and a curse. Finally, Lydia knows. Everything comes with a price. The true question now: was it a price worth paying?

Epilogue

Eight months later...

Tiny people rush around like ants on a warm, summer night, watched from the penthouse overlooking Central Park. Cars drift idly between lanes, slotting into gaps like tiles on a puzzle. In the park itself, the early evening moon reflects off rippling water and makes the trees and bushes glow with life.

Lydia sips peppermint tea and turns her attention back to the photograph pinched between her fingertips, the one that always soothed her to her core. Her nails are shorter than they used to be, smooth, rounded, painted soothing cream rather than her trademark scarlet. She lifts her other hand and runs it softly over her swollen belly.

A knock at the door interrupts this peaceful moment. Lydia places the photograph face down on the table, hauls her considerable self to her feet and waddles to answer it.

"Lydia, darling!" Lydia's agent Donna, perfectly coiffed curly hair and a blue silk power suit, grasps Lydia's arms and pulls her into the most superficial of embraces. "You've done it again!"

"Come in, Donna." Lydia laughs, holding the door open.

"Pre-orders are through the roof," Donna gushes,

shuffling inside. "I'd wager this one will stay at the top of the bestseller lists even longer than the last!" She pauses to look Lydia up and down. "Goodness, you've gotten big, haven't you?!"

"Thanks." Lydia grins and rolls her eyes.

"In a good way, of course, darling, you know I'm over the moon for you. When is the little angel due?"

Sudden flashes of both Alex and Finley flash through her mind as she clutches her stomach. "Next month," says Lydia, sinking down into her chair again.

"Oh, how thrilling," Donna gushes.

"Yes, if only Alex was here to actually help raise his child," Lydia coldly states, feeling a stabbing coming from down below as Donna awkwardly tiptoes around the comment.

"Not taking too much time off, are you?" She glances at Lydia anxiously.

"I haven't decided yet," Lydia replies, smiling. "I'll let you know."

"Oh." Donna looks disappointed. "Well, in your own time, dear, of course. Anyway," she checks a gaudy gold watch, "I can't stay. Just wanted to drop by in person and let you know how wonderful you are!"

"Right..." Lydia's face falls, her gaze drifting out of the window.

"Something wrong, dear?" Donna asks, carefully.

"It's nothing."

"Well it's obviously something!" the agent replies, her chin wobbling slightly. "Come on, you can tell me."

"I said it's nothing," Lydia says sharply. She picks up her tea and stirs it with a petite silver spoon.

"You've been thinking about him again, haven't you?" Donna gestures to Lydia's bump.

Lydia forces a fake smile. "I just need some time."

"I'm going to say it one more time," says Donna stubbornly, "are you sure you don't need counselling? It's very good these days you know. Not just for crazies anymore."

"I'm sure," Lydia replies, stiffening a little, "but I can take care of myself."

"Well if you're sure…" Donna looks doubtful. "Darling, this isn't about those idiots, is it? You know, the ones who…"

"Think I'm a liar who staged the whole thing?" Lydia finishes the question for her. "No, those people are idiots. I couldn't care less."

"Well, quite right," says Donna primly. "I mean the police found his DNA didn't they, all over those… poor people."

"Yes," says Lydia flatly, keen to get away from the subject.

"Did they… ever find the body?" Donna asks, hesitantly.

"No…" Lydia sighs. "I don't know why. Like I said, he was definitely dead. I smashed his face in with a piece of metal and then he fell a hundred feet into a frozen river."

"Goodness me, darling!" Donna fans her own face. "How you can say it so casually I just cannot fathom."

Lydia shrugs. "That's what happened." Her stomach lurches as she remembers the promise that she made to Jason, to keep the truth about him and Finley a secret. A promise that she had made in good faith. But the world had a right to know, she'd decided.

"Of course," says Donna. "Of course." She pauses. "You don't think, you know, he might have had an accomplice?"

"No," says Lydia flatly. "There was nobody else there."

"Alright!" says Donna, holding her hands up. "I'm just looking out for you, darling. Don't want some lunatic slaying my best client!"

"I'm touched." Lydia smiles.

"And what about the copycats?"

"Donna…" Lydia closes her eyes and sighs.

"I'm just asking!" says Donna, defensively. "I heard that there's a whole cult of them using your book like a kind of Bible!"

"That's just a crazy story," says Lydia, wearily.

"Alright then, if you say so." Donna checks her watch a second time. "I'd best be off then. No rest for the wicked!"

"I wouldn't be so sure about that," Lydia mutters under her breath, hauling herself to her feet again to show Donna out.

"Maybe you could write a book about becoming a mother?" suggests the agent.

"One step at a time," Lydia replies. "Let me have the thing first."

"Of course, of course. Well, goodbye, darling!" Donna embraces Lydia again and gives her a gentle squeeze.

"Goodbye," says Lydia, smiling. "Thanks for stopping by."

She closes the door and waddles back to her chair, flicking her long, golden locks back over her shoulder. She settles herself and picks up the photograph again, turning it over and touching the smiling face of Alex Gilbey with a soft fingertip, willing herself to feel something. But she feels nothing. No love, no guilt, no sadness. Just a great, gaping void where those emotions should be. Emptiness.

Lydia sits back and strokes her belly again, her ruby ring glinting softly in the fading evening light as she ponders what sort of child it will be? Boy? Girl? Blonde? Brunette? Brown eyes? Blue eyes? Good? Evil? Lydia hesitates at the thought, the dread, but then realises it does not matter, for she plans to love the child, no matter its origin. Whether Alex or... otherwise. "It's just you and me now," she whispers. "Just the two of us, alone in this terrible world. But don't worry, I'll protect you. I'll keep you safe. Always."

She reaches for the stereo remote, points and clicks, and The Ronettes burst into life. 'Be My Baby'. How beautifully ironic.

Lydia takes one last look at the photograph, then drops it back onto the table. Flat. Now looking outward. She won't forget about Alex, she knows, but life goes on. Even if she hasn't found happiness in love, the world still has plenty to offer. It's time to turn the page. Time to write a new chapter. She has a future, she knows that now. In many ways, her life is just beginning...

The Facility

Waylon Warrington, former inmate at Mortem Asylum, has been strapped to a creaky gurney on this plane for hours. This had not been a part of his plans, nevertheless, here he was. His temple racked with pain, mind tumbling from turbulence that makes him sick, engines roaring in his ears and salty sweat trickling into his tired eyes. The tranquiliser they administered before take-off has all but worn off and Waylon is, regrettably, awake. And he wants off this ride.

Half a dozen of Uncle Sam's finest soldiers, lips sealed and triggers poised, guard Waylon and his three fellow inmates, all strapped up tight and muzzled as he is. That they think him so dangerous makes Waylon smile. They're right, of course, but it's still nice to be appreciated.

Is the plane descending now? Hard to tell when you're lying horizontal until the wheels touch down with a bump. Then the gurneys are rolling again, jolting bones, boiling blood, across concrete and then something softer, through the cold night and then...

WORMWOOD FACILITY

Tall, white letters on a dark, grey wall. Waylon's heart thumps a little faster. Through endless, lifeless corridors, over metal grates, past barred windows through which the occasional glimpse of monsters in glass tubes makes Waylon's adrenaline spike. Finally, they reach a kind of holding area, and one by one are wheeled through the doors ahead. First Hillary, then Henry, then Holly... and now it's Waylon's turn for judgement. Is this the afterlife? A purgatory state? Is it too late for redemption?

The guards roll him inside. Blinding bright light directly above but shadows all around. Silhouettes of people. One woman with spiky shoulders hovers nearby, flanked by two more holding some sort of utensils.

"Patient number forty-three," says a voice so sterile as to be terrifying, "Waylon Warrington." The spiky woman steps forward, but not close enough yet to reveal herself.

"Begin the procedure," she barks. Masked doctors step into the light wielding the most gruesome instruments of torture Waylon has ever seen. He yelps helplessly into his muzzle as they begin to slice, probe, jab, saw. The last thing Waylon Warrington ever sees is that strange woman turn away, as a silver syringe pierces his right eye.

Hell has come at last.

About the Author

GEORGE MORRIS DE'ATH is an Essex-based author, actor and model with a flair for exploring the dark and twisted aspects of human nature. With his thrillers, George intends to leave his readers with shocks, questions and most of all, wanting more.

Hello from Aria

We hope you enjoyed this book! If you did let us know, we'd love to hear from you.

We are Aria, a dynamic digital-first fiction imprint from award-winning independent publishers Head of Zeus. At heart, we're committed to publishing fantastic commercial fiction – from romance and sagas to crime, thrillers and historical fiction. Visit us online and discover a community of like-minded fiction fans!

We're also on the look out for tomorrow's superstar authors. So, if you're a budding writer looking for a publisher, we'd love to hear from you. You can submit your book online at ariafiction.com/we-want-read-your-book

You can find us at:
Email: aria@headofzeus.com
Website: www.ariafiction.com
Submissions: www.ariafiction.com/we-want-read-your-book

f @ariafiction
𝕏 @Aria_Fiction
◎ @ariafiction